Denis

I love your spirit!

You lift the
atmosphere wherever
you are doing
your excellent work!

I love you,

Ann

Somewhere Else, Something Different

The Story of Francis Brayton, an Early American

by Ann Jewett

TABLE OF CONTENTS

ACKNOWLEDGMENTS

I gratefully acknowledge those who helped me in countless ways to write the story of Francis Brayton (1612-1692). It has been a new experience to be on the writing side of eighty-some years of reading the writing of others. The transition has been an illuminating experience—learning to transfer ideas into words and endeavoring to mold those words into good literature has been humbling. I had much help, and there are a few people who I want to recognize for getting me to the end of this project—of writing a book.

Portsmouth Rhode Island Historians
For over four hundred years, the people of Portsmouth, Rhode Island, have safeguarded records of the unique founding of their community. I have benefited from these records, and my enthusiasm was heightened by archivist, Bob Pimental, of the Portsmouth Public Library. Bob made copies of the land grant maps of 1638, and soon we became lost in the seventeenth century, egging each another on from one document to another. In the Afterword, I expand on how I became familiar with Portsmouth's history.

National Society of the Daughters of the American Revolution
For many years, the NSDAR has been an organization that offers information on ancestors. It benefits the individual researcher and also the organization that maintains an archive

in Washington D.C. It is an American historic treasure. I am a lifetime member of the DAR, and it is because of the NSDAR that our family has so many historic documents.

Kevin Brennan—my editor, sponsor, consultant
Getting to know Kevin professionally came about by a loose connection that, in time, tightened into a good consulting relationship. Kevin gave me sound advice and guidance with caring optimism. What more could a neophyte writer desire? As we worked together, I came to appreciate his prompt replies, careful consideration, and succinct advice that has advanced my learning curve. About the loose connection … how fortunate I am that Kevin and my daughter-in-law, Lucy Beard, have been friends for over forty years, and that Lucy reached out to him on my behalf. But then, Lucy, as the President of the Alice Paul Institute, is used to making connections that help others.

Dick Jewett—my husband of sixty-two years
Dick has been typing and retyping my writing, with careful attention to detail for most of this year, without complaint. In our past we have traveled many roads together, and this new partnership is proof that a new horizon is before each of us with every sunrise.

Judith Hebenstreit—master grammarian, writer, and sister
Judy, despite challenging health issues, has eagerly reviewed my manuscript at various intervals. Her praise is coveted—after all, I have been following in her footsteps all my life. We have a long intimate history as sisters and we know that family is central to a good life.

Carol Farley—friend and writer
Carol and I were quick friends when we met in Kansas in 1967. I eagerly read each of Carol's books as they were available and was proud of her when she was awarded The Golden Kite Award Book in 1975 by the Society of Children's Books Writers. *The Garden is Doing Fine* is still doing fine for children who desire to understand life issues that are painful and perplexing. A few years later Carol dedicated one of her books to me, and she has always been an encouraging and loving friend.

Denise Farley—writer, producer and friend
Denise shares the same apple branch with her mother, Carol, and she urged me to send my writing along her way. She responded to my Francis stories with cheerful messages, which helped me when I was doubting myself. I have watched Denise's career expand and spiral, and I'm proud to know her.

Anna Margaret Dible (1908-1999)—my mother
My mother wrote on topics of interest as well as poetry until her ninetieth year. She was passionate about all things historical and became an expert on antiques, ancient Indian tribes, nature, and local historic events. She was involved in local museums and researched assiduously whenever she wrote articles or gave oral presentations. Mother was a marvel, and I could never walk in her footsteps—her stride was much too far-reaching.

Laurell Frazier (1933-2017)—sister, writer, historian
Laurell learned by doing, and what she did always was greatly admired. She gathered and researched material that resulted in a family history from 1612 to 2008, covering the lineage of

seven families, the Braytons first. She put together pictures and vignettes of hundreds of present and past family members. Her large album was assembled and copies given to her siblings. I have referred to her book as a source time and again. I wish I had her views on my Francis Brayton story, but I do have wonderful memories of our childhood. A side note: Our father, Joe Dible, had special names for us three daughters—Judy Pudy, Relly Pelly, and Annie Panny. Our brothers, Joe and Dan, were not nicknamed, possibly because being male was considered serious business.

I acknowledge that I am not a historian, and I do not intend to mislead anyone to the belief that the events of this story are historic fact. On the other hand, I do hope the people who preserved the historical records of the founding of Portsmouth do believe that this book has been a sincere effort to honor them.

DEDICATION

This book is dedicated to our family.

Dick—I can't imagine what my life would have been without you. Together we have had many exciting adventures. This has been my favorite.

Tim, Eric & Meg—You are special each in your own way and together we have had delightful experiences all over the United States and Europe.

Lucy & Midge—You both are creative, bright, fun and now part of our family as well.

Stefan, Carrie, Ben and your significant others, Kristin, Aaron, and Anna—You are projecting our family into the third generation, helping your grandparents with the gadgets of the cyberworld. Family fun just gets better.

Part One

SOMEWHERE ELSE

Chapter 1: French Emigrant

New beginnings are often disguised as painful endings. —
Lau Tau

1 ~ 1568

Jean Brejon walked beside the wagon loaded with makeshift coffins, one of which carried the pox-riddled body of his mother, the last of his family to make this dismal journey to St. Martin's Cemetery. The early April air was misting as the warm rays of sunlight mixed with the cool air of the ground. It was a scene of peace and beauty, as if nature were determined to triumph over the travails of man. The familiar sounds of horses' hooves and the groaning of the overloaded wagon belied the wagon's intended purpose in the fields—fields that were awakening after a dormant winter, waiting to be planted.

The plague had taken decent, healthy lives and left behind fear, grief, and despair. All normal living had been disrupted—farm animals neglected, ordinary services discontinued, and, most disturbing of all, the dead being buried without ceremony. The seventeen-year-old son had made a promise to his mother to leave the desolate land and to save himself from the pox. Jean could not tarnish the memory of his mother with his disobedience, so he had given his promise. Somehow, some way, he would emigrate from France to live in England.

The wagon arrived at the cemetery where men, too weary to stand alone, leaned on their shovels amid the mounds of dirt. They did not notice the boy by the wagon; they saw only the coffins to be buried.

Jean was remembering how his parents had argued before their family had been ravaged by the pox. Elaine had begged Paul to take them to England to escape the dreadful disease, but Paul had scoffed, saying, "Leave for England? Why? We're all healthy, and we're safe here in the country. The pox will not reach us, Elaine."

Still it had come, and people suffered and died, as did the Brejons. The first of the family to die were his sisters, Clara and Molly. Paul begged Elaine to forgive him and she did, but he too got the pox, as if God were meting out retribution. Paul died, and the pox spread to Elaine. Jean stood by unable to help. There was not even a priest to offer her comfort. It had been rumored that the last rites were suspended because priests feared for their lives.

Elaine, forgetting herself, had begged Jean to leave, to go to England. He refused because by then the pox had infected her as well. Just before she died, she grasped his blouse and said, "Go, Jean. Promise me you will go to England." He had promised, and she had died that same day, the fifth of April. He was filled with grief, asking himself, "How could this have happened?" Retracing his steps, he returned to his silent, empty house with only memories of his family to cling to.

His father was a good farmer, and he patiently taught Jean to respect the soil, to keep it nourished and moist; he taught him to plant seeds that burst miraculously through the soil, shooting up on slender stems by some mysterious power. Jean wanted to see his father hoeing and raking with his strong arms, and then to see him tenderly hold his mother with the same arms, as if two men possessed the same body. Jean wondered if he would be like Paul—strong when necessary and tender when desiring to be.

Elaine had cared for her family continually. She kept a garden and was an expert with herbs, adding them when cooking her savory meals for the family. All the members of the family would seek her for a need of their own and would find her somewhere in the house doing one duty or another. She guided her three children with firmness but mostly with love.

Jean thought of Clara, who for most of her fourteen years had gone faithfully every Sunday to kneel and pray even though the rest of the family were indifferent to the spiritual life. He had a picture instilled in his mind of Molly and her sweet smile, flittering, spreading cheer around the house, her beautiful curls bouncing as she ran. The pox had forever stopped this twelve-year old lively child.

Walking the countryside, now too quiet, and the fields empty of workers, Jean thought of his best friend Henri Lucas, who lived on a farm close to his own. They used to meet other friends in the square in Ardeau, just to laugh, boast, and act like boys do when they are not quite men. He and Henri had talked of going to Paris, but now only Henri would see that wondrous city. Henri, along with his brothers, sisters, and mother, had gone there to escape the pox.

Jean also remembered the neighbor girls gathering in the square on Sunday—none came alone—giggling and flirting with the boys. They had given Jean the name "The Swede" because he was tall and slender and had light blue eyes. Gone, gone—all of this was over and gone. He was going to England alone.

He neared the Lucas house and he saw Pierre, Henri's father, feeding his swine behind the house. "Belle," Jean said aloud with concern in his voice "I forgot about Belle. She's probably mooing now, closed up in the shed."

It was at this moment that Pierre saw Jean and came around the house to meet him.

"Hello, Jean. I know where you've been this morning and I'm grieving for you. These are terrible times." Pierre paused, shaking his head before continuing. "I'll be leaving for Paris soon. I want you to know you're welcome to come with me."

"I promised my mother I would go to England, but there is one thing you could do for me. Would you take Belle?"

"Yes, of course," Pierre said at once, then added, "Would you wait here a moment?"

Jean nodded and watched as Pierre went into his house. When he returned, he handed Jean some coins and said, "These aren't enough to pay for what your cow is worth, but it might help you get to England."

Jean was moved, and, thanking Pierre, said, "I'll miss your family, especially Henri. Tell him I will always remember him." To keep away the tears, he busied himself putting the coins in a pouch in his trousers, making sure there were no holes.

"I'll bring Belle over before dark if that's all right."

"Yes, Jean, that will do."

Then Jean remembered something important. "You probably know that our landlord died. The state has given me notice to vacate the house in two weeks. I can't take anything with me, but you're welcome to take whatever you want from our farm. I'll leave the house unlocked."

"I'm sure there are things we can use. Thank you."

Jean turned to go, and they both waved as was the custom.

At his home, the first thing Jean did was to check on Belle.

He was exhausted, but the cow needed to be cared for. Her bag was full, so he put hay in front of her, put the milking stool and bucket in place, and began pulling on the teats, watching the milk flow. He rested his face on Belle's belly, and the smooth, warm hide began lulling him to sleep, so he sat up and finished the milking. Once the milk had been put in a cool place, he untied Belle and led her to the Lucas farm.

He told Pierre, "I had to milk her, so I hope it's all right to bring her now."

"She'll be fine," Pierre said. "I'll take good care of her."

Jean leaned over the cow, put his arms around her thick neck, and said, "You be a good girl now, Belle."

Pierre watched, moved by all that the goodbye had meant—a young man without family, leaving the only home he knew and going to a foreign country.

"Be cautious, Jean. People are acting from fear all around us. Don't assume you can trust anyone. My family will miss the Brejons."

Jean nodded and said, "Thank you, Pierre."

Back in his own home, Jean prepared for bed even though it was not quite dark. His stomach churned, and he realized he had eaten nothing all day. He went to the shed and got the milk. He drank his fill and left some to drink in the morning. Then he went to bed.

He woke at first light and for breakfast he drank the remainder of the milk. He would get food in the first village on his way to Calais. It was time to pack his cloth valise with the few items he would take along. He got the idea to use his father's leather belt as a shoulder strap so he could have his arms free as he walked. He packed a clean blouse and jerkin, his father's shaving set, soap, a towel, a clothes brush, and a knife and spoon.

In the pouch with the coins, he had the gold ring his mother had given him when she knew she was dying. She'd said, "This was your grandmother Cora Brejon's wedding ring. I hope you find a good woman to marry, Jean, and I hope she will treasure it as I have."

2 ~ 1568

The sun was well above the horizon as Jean headed northwest to Calais. He didn't look back. There was nothing for him now in the place of his birth, and he walked with a confident stride. It wasn't until he stopped in the village of Ardeau for bread and cheese that he had a disturbing thought. "I'm going to England and I don't know how to speak English."

He sat against a chestnut tree and thought about his dilemma. He would not succeed in England if he couldn't communicate with anyone. He was faced with a problem and tried to stay calm as he considered his options. He couldn't afford a tutor to teach him English. It would hold him back to try to work for the English if he didn't understand their language. Then he remembered hearing it was ten years ago that Henry II had taken Calais away from the English who had been in control for over two hundred years. Surely English was still being spoken there after all those years.

Encouraged, he ate his bread and cheese and decided he would work in Calais until his understanding and speaking of English was good enough to get by in England. His mind was in a whirl as he thought about Calais. He had heard that on the docks rough men worked loading and unloading ships. He thought, "At least I'm told I look older than seventeen." There was no other choice. He had to learn English.

It was early afternoon when he arrived at the docks and he was weak with hunger. He went to a tavern nearest to the docks named the Wooley Way Inn. He ordered roast beef and vegetables and ate with gusto. The inn had rooms for rent, and he chose to pay for a single room, turning down the cheaper offer of a bed shared with strangers. He was exhausted from grief and the heightened emotional state he had been in for such a long time. Once in bed, he was soon asleep.

In the morning, the inn provided ale and buns, and he ate more than his share. He talked with the concierge, Giles Raynol, who was pleasant enough, and he asked if he would lock up his valise for him. Giles looked dubious until Jean told him he planned to stay at the inn and would pay each week in advance.

It was a short walk to the docks. There he saw sheep being urged down the ramp of a ship and onto a wagon. He was curious, so he followed the horse and wagon about half a mile to an area that was obviously in the wool business. The bleating of the sheep was a dreadful sound, but the workmen seemed oblivious to it. In the first of many pens, men were expertly shearing the animals. It was fascinating to watch the precision of the clipping, but he knew this was not for him.

He walked to the next area, which had no sheep—just wool—and several men were bundling wool into bales. There were more men than work, so he walked on to another area where the bales were being loaded into a wagon. Two men were busy loading the bales, one on the ground and one in the wagon. Jean observed how awkwardly the process was going because the bales were heavy to lift. The man in the wagon was obviously supposed to be taking the bale from the man on the ground who lifted it up, but the bale wobbled so much that neither had a good hold of it.

Jean was startled by a man who had come up beside him. "You're a tall fellow," the man said. "Do you think you could put bales in the wagon on your own?"

Jean was quick with an answer. "I'd like to try."

"Another wagon will be here in a few minutes. I'll watch you load it on your own to see if you can handle it better than two. My name is Rene Millet, and I'm in charge of getting wool to the mills."

"I'm Jean Brejon, and I'm looking for work."

The wagon and donkey arrived, and the driver maneuvered it close to the bales. Jean picked up a bale, steadied it with a raised knee, and put it on the wagon. He loaded several and accomplished it in less time than the two men on the previous wagon. Rene was quick to hire him for the rest of the day. Jean asked, "Where are the wagons going with the bales?"

"There are woolen mills up the road about a mile. Wool is the major business in Calais and has been for many years. The market for wool is up and down, so it isn't stable work for laborers. What are your plans?"

"I need money and I need to learn English so I can go to England. I want to farm, and I've heard that some estates hire men to farm and offer leases. I won't succeed if I can't understand the language."

"You might try the markets on Saturday. The merchants set up stalls on Market Street, and many of them are Englishmen. It's an idea for you. I can offer some work on Monday—another ship is arriving then. Just be here early in the morning if you want the work."

"Yes, I'll be here, and I'm grateful."

During the next two days, Jean explored Calais, and on Saturday he located Market Street. There were many stalls and people were going from stall to stall as Jean watched the trading. He stood by those where English was spoken, and it wasn't helpful. All day he hung around listening and picked up words often repeated, like "what will you take for." Jean could see this was not going to be easy.

He had an idea. Since the English had ruled Calais for a long time, he thought there might still be an English church. He walked the streets and did find a church with an English sign in front. He asked people going by to help him with the words on it until a man who understood French and could read English came along. He told Jean, "It's an Anglican Church and there's a service on Sunday at nine o'clock."

The next day he came to the church and was greeted by the priest, Father Philip Cobert. He welcomed Jean and introduced him to his son Clair, who Jean thought was probably ten or twelve years old. Clair spoke French and English and he ushered him to a pew. He introduced him to a family, explaining to them that Jean only knew French. The service began shortly after that, and the women helped him with the prayer book and the hymn book.

He listened to the sermon and picked up words that were similar to French and others that were often repeated. Father Cobert also said many things in both languages. After the service, Father Cobert introduced his wife Deidre and daughter Cloe, who was probably five. They didn't ask questions, instead inviting him to activities and other services at the church. Jean said he would be coming again and admitted he was needing to learn English.

The Coberts were bilingual and eager to help him. He was honest about his past relationship with the Catholic Church and his sporadic attendance. They were not ruffled by his admission and urged him to return for Wednesday evening communion.

The next day he loaded three wagons for Rene, who said he would not have a need for him until Thursday, when another ship was due to deliver sheep. Jean went exploring and found a café that had an outdoor section serving food. He ate and had conversations with a few people. He met a young man named Leonard, probably his own age. The affable Leonard was also looking for work, since he had quit his job at a forge because it was boring. His parents were English and had remained in Calais when King Henry II had reclaimed the port city in 1558. His father worked in an office at the port, but Leonard didn't want office work.

The two young men spent a while talking in the sunshine, then they decided to go to a nearby tavern that served English ale. They didn't have much in common except spare time, youth, and curiosity. Leonard was interested in what life on a farm was like (Jean was good at reinventing his former life—leaving out his family tragedy), and Jean was interested in English manners. They arranged to meet the same time the next day.

They walked in the country, and Leonard helped Jean with common English words and how to pronounce them. Leonard talked about his parents and their concern with his lackadaisical attitude about getting and keeping a job. Jean had not shared his promise to his mother, the real reason for going to England. Somehow the grave circumstances of his family seemed out of place in Leonard's world.

The leaves had fallen, snow now covered the ground, and Jean's activities continued with Giles at the Wooley Way, Rene at the Wool Works, Leonard and himself on the prowl, and the Cobert family—a reminder of his mother and his vow to her. He tried speaking English with Leonard, who resisted until he sensed how seriously Jean took his effort to learn it. Leonard's mission was now to help his friend, and he began enjoying the teaching.

What occurred was surprising. Leonard decided his parents were right about his education, and he decided to apply to the University in Caen. He would become a teacher of English. Jean was supportive of this, assuring his friend he would become a great teacher. Leonard was accepted for the next session, which left time for helping Jean. They enjoyed their last weeks together and promised to keep in touch by writing letters.

By mid-April, Jean was ready to leave France for England on the Dover ferry. It was difficult saying farewell to the people who had made the past year bearable for him, but his promise was too important to delay any longer. And another thing: He had changed his name to John Brayton. If he was going to live in England, he would have an English name.

3 ~ 1569

John Brayton felt a surge of excitement as he set foot on English soil on April 28, 1569. He exchanged his sous for shillings and began walking out of Dover, a town that did not appeal to him. He walked northwest toward Middlesex, intending to learn more about the leasing of land. John was impressed by the orderliness of the landscape—with its village houses clumped together, some shops nearby, and always a tavern. Rock and wood fences and hedgerows encased the fields and meadows, and he watched yoked oxen being guided by men steering plows through the soil.

The weather was clear and warm, and whenever there came a spring rain it moved on in a few minutes' time. The first night he stayed in a village named Milton and spent an evening in a local tavern listening to the men talking of spring planting—what had already been done and what had yet to be done. They were curious about this French man with an English name, but his well-practiced story satisfied them and soon they were again talking of seed, oxen, and sharpening plows. When anyone asked John about France and the current political climate there, he changed the subject with a timely question about England.

For several more days, he continued walking northwest, enjoying the undulating hillsides and visiting the taverns in the evening with the friendly English men. On May third, he arrived in Middlesex and was directed to the town of Hounslow, situated on the edge of the vast estate of Lord Henry Fulham. A local person, hearing that John was interested in leasing land, directed him to go to the estate office of the overseer. Instinctively he decided instead to go to the tavern and hear what the locals had to say about the lease contract.

The Houndstooth Tavern was larger than most taverns he had seen on his walk, and there were rooms to let as well. He booked into one, paying a week in advance. It was good since it was pouring rain and staying in the cozy tavern was inviting. Many men stood about, enjoying a day off from spring planting. John got a mug of ale and idled at the bar listening to the men until someone asked, "You're a new fellow, aren't you?"

John nodded. "I've been hearing so much about Hounslow," he said, "I came to see for myself. My name is John Brayton, and I'm a farmer."

"A planter, are you? Well, you've come on a bad day for that." The men around him laughed, causing more men to gather around.

"Yes, but then I figured you'd be enjoying a day at the tavern, and I see I was right about that!" The men laughed again. John Brayton had made a good start in the place he would call home the rest of his life.

During the first week in Hounslow, he met many of the planters and heard the history of the town and all about the leasehold agreement. It seemed the men enjoyed talking about this unusual place. When John asked what "leasehold" meant, a man answered, "It means the lord has the lease and he's got hold of ya!" The men standing by laughed but another man was quick to add, "It's a new idea that has been doing good for us since 1560, nine years now. We're much better off here than we would be anywhere else. Almost one hundred families live here, and there are only twenty houses left for newcomers."

John inquired, "May I ask your names?"

"I'm Alec Hutchinson," the man said, "and the jester here is Evan Warner. That's Caleb Springer, and that's Gideon Heck. Next to him are Hiram Sizemore and Gabriel White. All of us, except Gideon, were with the original group who signed a leasehold agreement with the Fulham estate. We all know we're part of something that's different. Lord Fulham is the only investor, and he had all these houses built, this tavern, the emporium, a forge, a granary, and a chapel. We pay rent each month for our houses, and we can either buy or rent an ox. We all have a line of credit at the emporium. We pay for the seed we plant, and at harvest we share the income with the estate."

"We all have a debt with the estate too," said Evan Warner.

"That's true," Caleb said, "but Lord Fulham hasn't demanded payment, now, has he?"

"We have good years and lean ones," said Alec, "but I don't know of anyone who's chosen to leave. A few were told by the estate they *had* to leave, but it was always for good reasons."

John felt he had good testimony about the leasing and that it would be a good time to offer to do piecemeal work in the community. Soon he was helping to repair fences, build sheds, work gardens, and clean out manure. He felt that he was trusted now. The whole community seemed to accept this Frenchman among them.

John had walked around Hounslow and observed that most of the homes had gardens and chicken coops, even a shed in back. He visited the fields, which were located away from the houses but close enough to walk to. He had a look at the ox barn (called simply "the barn") situated closer to the fields and noticed that the tracts of land were more uniform than fields in France. Each was ten acres, and only the leased fields were part of the Fulham estate. Lawson Woods was on the opposite side of the fields, and there were pathways in the woods as well as two security guards who made sure nothing was taken from there. Still it was a lovely place for residents to walk.

John went to the emporium almost every day for bread and cheese, dried nuts, and specialty items, like Harriet Quinlen's preserves. In June, he went to see Maud Crump about moving into the boarding house situated between the emporium and the tavern. It had been built by the estate, and the widow Crump had been chosen to operate the "temporary" housing for those who were investigating the lease program. John took a nice room and was pleased with it. Maud was also an excellent cook.

That summer, John went here and there to work in Hounslow and met many of the residents. He got attention from the maidens as well, but he was cautious since he was not in a position to court. After all, he had nothing to offer a woman, at least not until he had a field and home of his own.

Life got very interesting in November when John was invited to a social event held Saturday the fifteenth in the back room of Houndstooth Tavern. It was the community's place for special events and recreation, and it was here that an annual celebration was held after harvesting, whether it had been a successful one or not. When he arrived, the room was buzzing with activity. Three musicians were setting up their instruments, and women were arranging their prized dishes of food on the tables.

John noticed that people had brought their own plates and utensils, so he hurried back to ask Maud for an old plate and a spoon.

"I should have thought," Maud said. "I'll tell you what I'll do. I'll bring yours with my own as soon as I set my kitchen to rights. It won't be long, so off with you."

The great room was almost full of people when he arrived this time, and the musicians were playing a lively tune. It pleased John to see people so happy together. He talked with those he knew and watched people mingling. When some started dancing to the music, everyone moved to make room, as if it were a well-known ritual. John got some food, and as he ate he watched the dancing. A woman, about his age he figured, caught his eye because her curly hair was bouncing just as Molly's had. His eyes followed her bouncing curls as she circled the dancing space.

He was pulled to the dance floor by Eliza Hutchinson, with John protesting all the time, "I don't dance, I never have, please ..." She ignored him and showed him a step, back and forth, then side to side. He tried it and, something gave way inside, a reticence being overcome by the jovial atmosphere, and he moved with Eliza, enjoying himself dancing among these good people, feeling more at home, belonging here.

John instinctively made a move, leaning back, his tall body having surprising grace, and he began moving his head to the beat of the music. He knew he was doing all right. His body relaxed and, he followed Eliza and the music until it stopped. Another song followed, but he was unsure of the beat and was heading for the side when another woman grabbed his arm and said, "Follow me, John." It was the woman with the bouncing curls who had favorably caught his eye. She smiled and added, "This is your first Hounslow gathering, isn't it? I'm Isobel Dunston, daughter of Adam and Anne Dunston."

"Hello, Isobel," he said, and, following the others, he put his arms up. She moved close, and his arms closed around her waist. They whirled around, bending side to side and going up and then back, peeking looks at each other as they moved. When the music stopped, he wanted to keep holding her, but she smiled and moved away as another woman took her place. The dancing went on until the musicians were too tired to continue. The food dishes were cleared away, the keg of ale was empty, and the people drifted away. John found himself looking for Isobel, but she had gone.

That following Wednesday, he went to the office of the overseer on the Fulham estate. He was allowed a meeting with George Wilkins, and after a brief wait he told Wilkins why he had come.

"I'm interested in making an agreement to lease land. I've farmed with my father since I was ten years old, but now I'm on my own."

George asked, "Why did you leave your father?"

"He died, and I had no other relatives to turn to. I've come to Hounslow because I heard of your leasehold plan. I've talked with many of your tenants, and I'm certain it's the place for me."

Wilkins said nothing. Looking at John, he said at last, "You need two men to vouch for you and an address in Hounslow where you live. Are you married?"

"No, I've had family business to attend to, but now I can finally think of other matters. Family is very important to me."

Wilkins stood and said, "When you have those requirements, come back and we'll set a date for a meeting with our attorney."

John went to talk with Alec Hutchinson, who agreed to vouch for John, and he suggested Caleb Springer for the other person. He went back to the overseer's office the next day, and his appointment was set for December 5, 1569. John thought it was a good way to begin his nineteenth year, since his birth date was December 30, 1550.

4 ~ 1569

Alec and Caleb were with him when he met with George Wilkins and the attorney, Ephram Walker. The attorney read the agreement, and John didn't hear anything that did not seem equitable, so signatures were made all around and the business was completed, except for his assignment of land. They went to a large map of the fields of Hounslow, and Alec and Caleb helped John pick his allotment, since they were familiar with the terrain. Then they went to the

Houndstooth for toasting John's new future as a tenant of Hounslow.

The next Monday, John was at the emporium to buy some items, including a piece of canvas to patch his trousers at the knee. He didn't want to pay for an inch more than needed, and then Isobel Dunston came along and asked if he needed help.

"Hello," he said with eagerness, remembering her from the dance. "Yes, I could use a little help." He told her what he was needing, and she asked, "Do you have a needle and thread?"

"No, I don't," he said with some embarrassment.

"Well, John, I can sew the patches for you if I could have your trousers." They laughed, and John said, "I only have this pair at the moment. Maybe I could borrow your needle and thread?"

"All right. Let's get the proper amount of canvas, and then you can come to my house on Salisbury Lane, number seven, where I'll give you your needle and thread. Or you can find another way to patch your pants." She smiled with playfulness in her eyes.

"Thank you, Isobel, but I think my landlady will patch them. Discreetly I must add." He saw her disappointment. "Isobel, would you walk with me this Sunday to Lawton Woods?" he asked suddenly.

"I would enjoy that, John Brayton."

That Sunday, December fifteenth, he went to Salisbury Lane, where he met Adam and Anne, who had become familiar with this routine, having already "moved off" two other daughters. They had been hearing of John Brayton, who had made a good reputation as a hard-working trustworthy young man, and they did not hesitate to welcome him into their home.

John said to Isobel, “Are you ready?”

The conversation flowed easily with Isobel, who was cheerful and obviously in love with life. She noticed scurrying animals, called out the names of birds, walked with energy through layers of leaves. John put his arm around her back when a chilling wind picked up and she cuddled close to him, fitting perfectly under his arm. There was no artifice between them, or flirtation. They were happy to be together.

The next week they went to the bakery, which was small and cozy, and they overstayed their welcome in the little shop. The next week was the beginning of the Christmas season, and John was invited to dinner on Wednesday, Christmas Day. The Dunstons’ two married daughters and their families joined them: Harriet, her husband Everett Ainsley and baby Eleanor, and her sister Beatrice, along with her husband, Horace Vernon, and little Helen. It was a cheerful gathering with laughter, good food, and conversation all around, but Isobel was joy enough for John. He had fallen in love with this vivacious young woman. He felt blessed to be part of a family, and to be sure of that he proposed to her that evening. The announcement was made in the new year. Congratulations came from all their acquaintances in Hounslow, and the wedding was set for Sunday, January 15, 1670. John planned to give Isobel Elaine’s gold ring but first he felt he must tell her the story of his family’s tragic end.

They were alone in the Dunstons' parlor. He took her hands, saying "Isobel, I want to tell you of my life in France, a story I have not told anyone in England."

Isobel stiffened, thinking of some hidden, terrible secret—another woman, an illegitimate child? He continued, "I was raised on a small farm in an area southeast of Calais. I had two younger sisters, and my parents. Late in the year 1566, a pox plague came to our area, bringing death all around us. My mother wanted to move to England, but my father didn't believe it was necessary. It didn't take long for the plague to reach Ardeau, and then my sisters developed the pox and died in agony. My father was contrite, but he too was stricken and died. My mother begged me to leave, but I wouldn't because she had pox marks then and we both knew she was doomed.

"I have not told others of this tragedy because there is so much fear of the pox. People have strange ideas about its cause. It was hard to leave France, but as I promised my mother I would, I learned English, worked to save money, and came to England. I want you to know that I wasn't running away. I was only keeping my promise to my mother. I don't want any mysteries in our marriage, Isobel. I come from a good family. I have fond memories of my childhood. I want to have children and to live in the same harmony and happiness I did as a child."

"Thank you for telling me," Isobel said. "I have wondered and was willing to believe you were coming to England, not leaving France. Knowing that you fulfilled your promise to your mother just improves my good opinion of you. Don't you think that our coming together has an ultimate purpose? We will honor the lives of your family with our own."

He pulled her close, filled with relief from the fear of being harshly judged for not telling her of his past. He had come to this village and was accepted for who he was, not as the "Frenchman who escaped the plague in France."

Now Isobel held his past within her and that was as it should be.

5 ~ 1570

John and Isobel were assigned 10 Farley Lane as their rental home in Hounslow. They bought all their household furnishings on credit at the emporium. While John worked, Isobel and her mother Anne prepared the house for the couple to move into on the wedding night. John was upset by the large debt with which they had to start their marriage, but Isobel assured him it would be fine.

They were married in the chapel, and after the ceremony all the guests were in a merry mood from celebrating at the tavern. Later the bride and groom were taken by a carriage to their house on Farley Lane, where they climbed the stairs to their room under the eaves. The early evening moon hovered in the sky in line with the small window, giving the perfect light for undressing and coming together in the joy and happiness of their own marriage bed—snug under the eaves.

In the spring of 1570, John planted his first crop in the English soil, and, in honor of his French heritage, he planted an herb garden. He taught Isobel which herbs were best with certain foods, and soon recipes were being shared with friends and neighbors. They were working hard every day, but they were having fun together, which Isobel did as a matter of course. They enjoyed the young couple who lived next door, Silas and Ida Bame, and also the couple on the other side, Robert and Charlotte Comstock. The Dunstons were only a few streets away, as were the Springers, Hutchinsons, and Warners.

A good harvest arrived that year, which was a relief for John to be able to pay a substantial amount toward the debt at the emporium. The year was almost over, and Isobel was concerned that there was no sign of a pregnancy. Christmas came, the New Year came, and even Easter in March. And then, at last, she was expecting, to the relief of everyone who knew how Isobel yearned for a baby.

Thomas Paul was born December 30, 1571, and was healthy from the beginning. Isobel delighted in having a child and seemed to take everything with a natural ease. When Thomas started to walk, he ran on his tippy toes, and when he stumbled and fell, he didn't cry—he just got up and started running again. He had Isobel's nature and her joy of life. John adored him, and when Isobel expected another child, he rejoiced.

When Anne Elaine was born in November 1572, she was also healthy. Year-old Thomas had black curly hair, light blue eyes, and a ready smile. Anne seemed less like the Dunstons and more a Brayton, but time would tell. Anne was certainly more reticent in all childhood endeavors, very much the lady. Elaine Brejon had been that way, except she had so much energy. Anne loved to be carried and attended upon. Isobel and John took care of their children with joy, and people were fond of this happy family. Isobel was counted on to lift spirits and dispel gloom.

On September 11, 1573, Brett Adam was born. He had long limbs, and everyone predicted another tall Brayton. He had blue eyes and an eagerness to be doing like his brother Thomas. Thomas was three and chatting away at his sister and brother. John was pleased that Isobel was such a good mother. He tended his herb garden behind the house and enlarged the chicken coop too. He worked hard at his many tasks: going to the barn for his ox, Thor—which he had just purchased; plowing the soil, planting, cultivating, or harvesting, as the seasons required; and attending the infrequent meetings of the tenants to discuss matters of safety and security in the village.

The next pregnancy in 1574 was difficult for Isobel. She was very ill, lost weight, and grew so tired she even lost her perkiness. Mary Jane was born October 10 and was smaller than the other three, but perfect—a relief after such a difficult delivery. Dr. Sibley told Isobel this would be her last child. Mary Jane was loved as were all the Brayton children. Each was going about the business of childhood in a normal way, delighting parents and grandparents.

In the next half dozen years, the harvests were good, then not so good, then excellent, and then, in 1581, came a failure. John worried, but Isobel convinced him that nature had its own way of meting out its treasures. The years had a rhythm with debts up, debts down, and events continued, cheerfully attended, neighbors helping others in need, children attending school from November to May, and chapel held every Sunday for the faithful and unfaithful.

Isobel played with the children, making life seem like a game. John worried they wouldn't be prepared for the rough life that was the reality of farming. But he need not have worried because Isobel had a way of making work seem like an adventure.

6 ~ 1590

By 1590, the village was fully populated and already the next generation was marrying. The first wedding for the Braytons was Anne Elaine, who married Peter Jamison on March 24, 1589. Peter was the only child of Claude and Jeanette, so Anne became like their own daughter. The next year Brett joined the navy, leaving November 25—a sad departure for the Braytons. They had a calendar posted on the wall to mark the dates he would be in port.

Mary Jane was courted by Ham Porter from Layton, whom she had met when he visited a cousin in Hounslow. His coming on horseback created a stir, since horses were rare in Hounslow. When Ham and Mary Jane married on June 1, 1592, they galloped off on his horse, Trotter, her dress billowing around the animal. "Isn't that a beautiful sight?" asked Isobel. "I hope she stays happy."

With all the children moved out except Thomas, Isobel turned her cheery nature to the care of John and Thomas. These two were opposites in appearance, but not so much in personality. Thomas was very like the Dunstons: average height, sturdy and animated, using many extra movements in everything he did. John was over six feet in height, trim, and always keeping his back straight whether standing or sitting. He had blue eyes set in an almost square face, with a rounded forehead. He was stingy with his movements or, one might say, conservative, and when John and Thomas were working together it was like watching a whirligig beside a flag pole. They got the job done but, by the end of the day Thomas was the more worn out of the two.

Isobel was concerned that Thomas was unattached at the age of twenty-one, and she noted that many women had given a "try" to interest him, yet he seemed unaware. Isobel would talk up prospective women and John and Thomas always made light of it. It could never be explained why he showed an interest in the daughter of Jeb and Sarah Joyner, newcomers to Hounslow. Martha was their only child, and the family had moved around for years, Jeb working odd jobs in country villages. They rented a vacant row house in Hounslow, and he got work in the livery.

Martha had a pretty fragility about her. She was sober, quiet, and mostly unresponsive to friendly overtures. Thomas saw something in her, maybe helplessness, that appealed to him, and they married on November 30, 1592, at the Hounslow chapel. There were many at the reception, and Martha's demeanor was mistaken for shyness. John and Isobel welcomed her into their home. The older couple moved into the bedroom on the first level, leaving the room under the eaves for Thomas and Martha, though she never was "at home" at Farley Lane. Isobel thought it was because she had moved about so much in her life.

For whatever reason, Martha went from table to rocking chair to matins at the chapel back to the table, rocking chair, and finally to the bedroom under the eaves. If Isobel suggested she do something, Martha complied, and then returned to the rocking chair. Isobel taught her to knit, and soon friends and family members were donating yarn and needles to her. She was content to knit, do the washing, and go to the chapel. Isobel finally gave up trying to draw her out. The men were out of the house during the day, so it had fallen on Isobel to "do" with Martha.

Martha seemed to accept the idea of being pregnant, and when Charles was born on August 13, 1593, she cared for him, being coached by Isobel. Jeb and Sarah had already moved away, since Hounslow was such a close-knit community and they never made headway in it, or so they claimed. Charles had plenty of people to fuss over him: parents, grandparents, aunts, and uncles. Thomas believed that Martha didn't know how to love, so he was extra attentive toward her. She showed no feelings and seemed more comfortable in the chapel than any place else. Two more children were born, Gwen in 1594 and Byron the next year, October 21, 1595, and everything continued as before except for a slight shift in sleeping spaces. Gwen stayed in the lower bedroom with John and Isobel, and Charles slept on a mat in the alcove behind the fireplace and was eventually joined by Byron when he was two.

Thomas, John, and Isobel were playful with the children, and life was filled with work, family affairs, celebrations, and mourning of the dead. In 1598 Charles started school, which was held in the chapel, and the next year Gwen began, followed by Byron in 1600—the new century. People in England were taking note of the new century, but for the most part, it was much the same life as before for the laboring class. For some inexplicable reason, Martha began doting on Byron when the other two had started school. She pestered him, lured him with candies, and smothered him with hugs until he ran away from her in tears. Martha would pout, and the next day it all began again.

Everyone was relieved when Byron started school. The relief was short-lived, since he caused problems that vexed the teacher and turned the children away. Everyone had a try with Byron, and it was rough going that first year. The second year Byron behaved, began enjoying school and made friends with classmates. The tensions in the house let up, but with Martha it was much the same as before the children were born. Hounslow was still a happy community, even though there were a few failed harvests. The men were able to pay the rent on their houses, and neighbors helped the neighbor who was worse off than they were.

Three years into the seventeenth century, the Braytons suffered a tragic event. John awoke one morning to discover that Isobel had died in her sleep. The family and many villagers mourned the loss of this cheerful soul. There had been no warnings, and it took some time to ease the shock for John, Thomas, and the children. Martha did not mourn but went on as usual, completely absorbed in the world she had made for herself.

Two years later, on a beautiful day in September, Thomas was working in his squash patch while John was in his herb garden. Since the loss of Isobel, Thomas kept a closer watch on his father throughout the day. That day Thomas looked up from his work to check on John but could not see him. He shielded his eyes to get a better look, but John was nowhere to be seen. Thomas' heart began thumping, and he threw his hoe down and ran toward the herb garden. There lay John amid the sage and thyme. Thomas felt for a pulse and he knew his father was gone. He knelt, then sat down and pulled John onto his legs, cradling his head in his arms. The enormity of the loss overwhelmed him, and he wailed, startling the neighbors, who came running. Silas Bame was the first to arrive. He knelt next to Thomas, put his arms around his shoulders, and said, "I'm so sorry for your loss, Thomas—a great loss for all of us, to be sure." He rose and said he would go and fetch Doctor Sibley.

Other neighbors and their children came, as well as Martha, who tried to pull Thomas away from John. Doctor Sibley arrived then and said gently to Thomas, "May I have a look, Thomas?" The young man looked at him in his grief and slowly nodded, letting the doctor tend to his father.

John was laid to rest next to his dear Isobel. Thomas comforted himself by being convinced their souls were united in heaven.

The adjustment in the Brayton house was most difficult for Thomas, who farmed alone. Charles was ten, Gwen nine, and Byron eight, so Thomas gave them more responsibility in the house and field. It was a lot for children but not unusual. Martha spent much of her day at the chapel, having taken on custodial duties there. It was better when she was not at home, dampening the atmosphere with her doleful attitude.

In 1610, Charles left to marry Jane Bristol, who was carrying his child. They moved to Isley, where Charles got a job in the foundry. Gwen met John Weston at a separatist meeting. They married the next year in December and soon after moved to Limon, where John became an apprentice to a weaver. Martha was feeling poorly, and it wasn't until February of 1612 that it was diagnosed as a late pregnancy. Martha was beside herself with anger and dread. Resentment settled in and stayed with her until grief was added to her resentment.

Byron left one summer evening to go to the Houndstooth as usual, but he did not go there. Instead he left Hounslow and was never seen again.

Chapter 2: Late Child

Good, better, best; Never let it rest; 'til your good is better and your better best. — Saint Jerome

7 ~ 1612

Thomas and Martha were alone at 10 Farley Lane only a few months before a "late child" was born on September 5, 1612. He had the light-blue eyes of John Brayton's as well as long legs and a steady gaze. Thomas was immediately convinced they had an unusual child, and Martha was convinced that she had a burden. She comforted herself by naming him Francis for St. Francis of Assisi, and she took him along to the chapel.

That arrangement was satisfactory until her milk dried up and Francis became fussy, interrupting the quiet of the chapel. She insisted that Thomas take over his care so she could attend to her prayers. He took Francis to the field or garden where he was working and laid him on a piece of canvas in the warm April sun. The baby crawled off the canvas to explore the more interesting landscape that surrounded his tiny island of white. Thomas would rush to him, talk to him, but never use "baby talk," which did not somehow suit Francis.

"Frankie, you must not go so far that I can't see you. If I can see you, you'll be safe. See my hoe?" Francis looked at the stick Thomas held before his face, then looked at Thomas and smiled. But of course he crawled out of sight again, over and over. However, this difficulty for the father, who was attempting to do his annual planting, did not create animosity in Thomas. He and Francis played and laughed like companions. When Francis began toddling, he would trick Thomas and laugh as his father ran to bring him back in sight of his hoe. The scolding did not have the threat of punishment, and Francis felt free to explore his child-world without anxiety or fear.

When Francis started talking, he spoke complete sentences, as if he had been practicing them in his head. By the time he was three, he asked questions that challenged Thomas.

"Dada, why is the sky blue sometimes and gray other times?" or "How can worms breathe when they're stuck in the ground?" and "Why am I little and you're so big?"

Thomas decided that Francis needed to go to school at age four rather than five, the usual age. He visited Matthew Brooks, the teacher at the Hounslow School, to ask him to consider allowing Francis to begin school earlier. Once Matthew had met Francis, he agreed, and since Francis was tall for his age, he could hold his own with the other children. Francis began attending school in September of 1616.

Matthew was intrigued with Francis, who was curious about how things worked, and then why they always did so. Matthew was challenged to keep this eager child occupied during school time. Frankie had already learned to read, and by the end of the next school year he had read all the children's books Matthew had available.

Publishing companies had recently been producing a phenomenal number of volumes every year. People were able to buy books and were learning to read, even those who had no such opportunity before the printing press. It had taken time for the presses to be perfected; few could have imagined how it would bring the world to the fingertips of the ordinary person. However, very few books were printed for children. When Matthew left Hounslow for a teaching position in London in 1622, he gave Francis his copy of Miguel de Cervantes' *Don Quixote.* (He could picture his prized pupil laughing at the antics of the Don and his servant, Sancho Panza.)

The good teacher and the father kept the child's life in balance; Matthew challenged his mind, and Thomas taught him to appreciate the out of doors and the benefits of physical labor. Francis did not dwell on Martha's rejection; instead, he simply turned to Thomas, who welcomed his needs. The young boy had no companions his own age, but he was content.

When Francis was twelve and his father fifty-five, he noticed a subtle change in their relationship. The son was beginning to take the role of the father, the protector, and provider, and the father was doing the less arduous tasks.

Francis would say, "Here, Dada, let me get down there and do that," or "Dada, there's no need for you to be out in this nasty cold weather. You go inside and keep Mum company." Eventually, Thomas took over the chickens, the garden, stoking the fireplace, and helping Martha with the cooking and cleaning, and Francis did the farming.

It was during this time that Martha began having pain in her chest. Breathing was often labored, and she had violent coughing spells. It was difficult for Thomas and Francis to see her like this. Thomas administered poultices to her chest, which sometimes helped. He prepared various types of teas for her to drink, and it seemed that his fussing over her gave her more relief than anything else. Dr, Sibley could not be encouraging, however, and believed the symptoms were of the dreaded lung disease, for which there was no cure. Father Morton made visits to his faithful parishioner, which pleased her, and Thomas observed that the prayers had a calming effect on Martha. She read her King James Bible or Thomas read her favorite verses and she would recite the verses as he read. And in these ways, the days went by for Martha and Thomas.

Often Thomas would say, "Well Francis, where do you want me today?"

Francis would connect Thomas with work that would keep him close to the house. "Well Dada, what do you think? Is it time to prepare the soil for planting? I thought I might do that, if you would fill the seed bag for me."

The seasons went along always different and yet always the same, too. Francis did the marketing at the emporium, and he enjoyed it when Clive Steadman got new items. Francis read the pamphlets with the latest advice on farming. They offered information such as how to improve the yield of crops, how to nurse a sick animal, or what new items were on the market. Clive knew that Francis was doing the farming instead of Thomas, and he respected the boy, who did not complain about the long hours of work he had each day.

Francis had asked him questions about the leasehold agreement. Clive told him that Edward Childs, the overseer for the estate, would be the right man to answer his questions. Clive said, "It seems you enjoy farming. I'm sure your father is pleased about that."

"Oh, but I don't intend to be a tenant, Clive. I want to get an education and explore the world beyond Hounslow."

"Well," Clive said, "I wish you well."

8 ~ 1628

In March of 1628, when Francis was sixteen, he overheard a conversation between Carl Sanborn and Wilbur Owens. He didn't know what had given rise to the serious discussion of the tenants, but he listened intently.

"Wilbur, you have to admit the arrangement we have here with Lord Fulham is beginning to be a problem with the debts we all have on our accounts at the emporium. Does it not bother you to see the amount go up instead of down every year?"

"Why do you say that?" Wilbur responded. "Lord Fulham hasn't once in all these years demanded payment. I think we'll be able to pay it off with a few really good harvests."

"A few good harvests in our lifetime won't be enough," Carl said. "Our children will inherit our debt. It says so in the agreement. The lease can't be cancelled if any debt is owed to either party. You and I both know Lord Fulham will never owe *us* anything. When we started, we expected we could at least keep the account even, but we can't get ahead. We pay every month for the rent on our house, and some families pay for an ox and stall in the barn. We buy all our provisions and seed at the emporium, plus all our household necessities. We all work from sunup to sundown, yet we fall further behind. That's a bad thing for us to leave to our sons."

Wilbur was quick to respond. "Look at how we live here in Hounslow. We have better homes than we could have hoped to provide for our families before. Our children are getting schooled and we have medical care available. The emporium purchases and our rent money are a good return to Lord Fulham on his investment. When there's a poor crop he loses too—a great deal, since he's responsible for the whole estate. We're living much better than before, and we have more say in what we do. I wouldn't want to go back to the way I was living before, would you?"

"Maybe I'm seeing things differently now, I admit, but something's not right in all of it. We shouldn't work all our lives only to pass debts onto our sons."

"I guess we'll just have to think our own way and do what we must," said Wilbur.

"I'm going to make the most of every day," Carl added, "because I don't think this is going to last."

Francis knew he had heard something very important just then. Foremost in his mind was to ask Clive Steadman how much the Brayton debt amounted to. Was he going to inherit a debt he could not pay off? Would he be facing debtor's prison if he just walked away from it? He had to know what he was facing. With his parents already in their late fifties, he felt the urge to talk to Clive that very day.

Clive was not too surprised when Francis asked for the amount of the debt on the Brayton account. The records going back to 1568, when John and Isobel had started the open line of credit, showed a growing amount every year for sixty years. The debt was now eighty-two shillings and a few pence. Francis was overwhelmed. As Clive looked at Francis, it was the first time he was sorry that he was the manager of the emporium.

His mother's lung condition was getting worse and Thomas needed to be with her. Francis tried to assure him. "Of course, Papa, you must be with her," he said. "She needs you by her side now. I'm fine on my own. She's the most important thing to us. It's awful to see her suffer."

The debt, his mother and father, the farming—it all needed to be attended to, and Francis did not want to think of these responsibilities as burdens. If he could establish routines and more efficient ways to do them, the challenge of it could be part of his overall plan for leaving Hounslow.

He finally understood what it meant to be a late child. He was left with aging parents. He could not leave them as long as they needed him, and by staying he would inherit the Brayton debt. There was only one thing to be done: He needed to think of a way to pay off the debt. He headed for Lawton Woods.

The walk calmed his mind as he focused on the repayment of the Brayton debt at the emporium. On his side was good health and a strong body. No less was his focus on the work at hand. He was intense, not distracted by neighbors or the usual interests of sixteen-year-old youths, and his ultimate goal energized him during his daily routines. Work was his best asset. Diligence was a better way to think of it, since how he worked, where he worked, and how long he worked were the sum of his daily activity. He believed he could do more of the same.

There were several garden plots around Hounslow that were not being planted. He would ask those tenants if he could plant there in exchange for some of the produce he harvested from them. This proved to be an easy plan, since everyone he asked were very pleased to have their gardens replanted. Most were of an age that made gardening work too painful for them.

Another idea was to help tenants expand their chicken coop areas so they could increase their egg production. He was ready to talk with Clive Steadman to propose that he supply garden produce and eggs for the emporium in exchange for defraying the Brayton debt.

Francis went to Clive and told him of his plan—the produce, the eggs, and the most far-reaching of his ideas that had come to him, which was to use Lawton Woods for gathering firewood, nuts, and berries. He would need permission to go into the woods.

Clive was impressed. Such an enterprise would help his business and cut his costs. He listened as Francis added, "If I could get permission to go to Lawton Woods, I could gather stray limbs and pieces of wood that people are always needing for fireplaces, and in season I could gather nuts and pick wild berries. I know it will take a long time, but time is what I have. So will you think about it, Clive, and give me permission to go into Lawton Woods?"

Clive's first thought was, "This young man would make a good businessman!"

"I'll discuss this with Edward Childs and give you an answer on Thursday," he said. "He needs to know—especially about Lawton Woods."

Edward Childs could see how the arrangement could be a good thing for Hounslow and Lord Fulham. He knew the Fulham estate would like to see the community taking initiative toward reducing the emporium debts. All things considered, Childs decided to give Francis Brayton approval. He alerted the two scouts who roamed Lawton Woods to apprehend anyone attempting poaching and asked them to come that Thursday to meet Francis. That done, Francis would never be apprehended there.

On Thursday the agreement was finalized.

Clive said, "Let me be sure we both have the same understanding of our agreement. I will keep track of the things you bring to me to sell. I'll price them equal to what I pay vendors, and that amount will be deducted from the

Brayton debt. You get an accounting at the end of each month."

"That covers what I'm saying," Francis said. "I'll do my best to give you good products." They shook hands on April 3, 1628.

Neither of them had any idea how long it would take Francis to pay off the Brayton debt. Francis decided not to share the details of what he was doing with Thomas because he didn't want to make Thomas feel responsible for the work that he would be doing. Thomas was still busy enough with Martha and her care.

9 ~ 1629

In the Summer, Clive shared an idea he had for Francis. "I've been thinking that you wouldn't mind going to Sheffield Market to do some trading for my shop. I could make many women happy with some sharps and straight pins for sewing as well as lace and other trimmings. Tools would be good too, but maybe later for that. The market likes to get preserves from the country and potatoes too. I would suggest, if you're interested, that you go with items not so heavy and see how you do with them. Does this interest you?"

Francis was interested and only regretted he hadn't thought of it himself.

He chose Friday, since Saturday was the busiest marketing day and his items would be available and welcome for the crowd early the next morning. He had four jars of Harriet Quinlan's preserves and some onions, but that was as much weight as he could manage on his walk. He planned to arrive at Sheffield Market between ten and eleven o'clock and to wander around to see how the trading was done. Because this was his first experience with this business, he wanted to find somebody who would be helpful.

He left at dawn and arrived at half past ten. He liked the bustle of the market and walked all around to watch how the bartering worked. He approached a man who liked his preserves and onions. The man paid with coins and said, "I'm Steven Studley. You bring me your items anytime, lad. I'll buy from you."

Francis used the coins to buy pins and trimmings, and although he didn't get many for the money he had, still Clive had said they were "in demand." He put the items in his empty bag and started his walk back to Hounslow. It was two o'clock and he was hungry. He decided to stop in Ellington, a town he had hoped to visit because it had a reputation as a seat of learning. There was a boys' school in the town and a circle and a square, whatever they were. He was sure there was a good tavern too, probably by the school.

He took the Ellington Road off the Great West Road and was soon impressed with the large homes of stone and brick shaded by graceful elms and oaks. He crossed a fairly wide street and came to a circle. He went to the right onto the circle because he spotted an inn and a tavern in that direction. There he surmised that he was near the school, but trees obscured his view. The tavern had a strange name—"The Dock"—painted on its sign. He entered to find a typical English tavern, hosting a few men grouped together with mugs of ale in their hands.

Francis went to the barkeep, ordered a pint, and asked, "Are you serving hot food?"

"Indeed we are," the barkeep said. "Our specialty is shepherd's pie."

"I'll have that, please." Francis said and, having ordered, took his pint and found a seat toward the rear, near a window.

The barkeep brought the pie when it had been prepared and placing it in front of Francis. "Are you new to The Dock?" he asked.

"Yes," he answered. "I've just come from the market and am heading back to Hounslow now."

The barkeep said, "I'm Joseph, by the way."

And Francis replied, "I'm Francis Brayton."

Joseph nodded and went back to his bar.

Just then the door opened with a thud and a handsome man stood in the doorway, pausing until someone shouted, "John Anthony!" He quickly entered the room and with a flourish removed his large hat adorned with a curving feather. He greeted each man in the room as he moved toward the bar and said, "Joseph, have you been keeping these men happy?"

"That I have, John, just as you instructed me the last time you were here." Joseph smiled broadly.

The men crowded around him and there was chattering as each man tried to tell John his latest news. They covered cricket, gossip, the latest gaff of one of the group. Francis enjoyed the scene before him. It was obvious by his clothing that John was of the titled class, and yet here he was with these men, who were not.

John Anthony turned and, seeing Francis sitting alone toward the back of the tavern, walked toward him saying, "We haven't met. I'm John Anthony."

Francis grinned. How could I not know he's John Anthony, he thought. "I live in Hounslow," he said. "This is my first time at The Dock."

"Hounslow! That's Lord Fulham territory. I attended Weedon Academy with George Fulham. We started university together, but I couldn't stick it. I bet George did—he's the sticking sort. What is your name, if I may ask?"

"Of course. I'm Francis Brayton."

"Francis? That was my grandfather's name."

Francis quipped, "My grandfather Brayton's name was John!"

They laughed together then raised their mugs of ale. "To John and Francis!"

John sat at the table saying, "Brayton. I'm not familiar with that name."

Francis broke in. "John Brayton was Jean Brejon from France. He changed his name so the English could pronounce it!" They laughed again, and John began asking Francis questions, one after another, until Francis had told him all there was to tell.

John seemed satisfied and rose. "Well, Francis Brayton, this has been my pleasure, but now I must go about my business." He turned and, with the same flurry his entry had caused, he left The Dock.

Francis had never met anyone like John Anthony, and he was certain he would not see him again. Probably he had been just another diversion for this affable man. John was close in age to Francis, but he, unlike Francis, had time on his hands. This, no doubt, would be a one-time meeting, like the waves made by a single pebble thrown in a pond sending ripples to the edges of the pond, where they disappear. The Dock settled back down, and Francis paid for the pie and ale, telling Joseph he would return on his next trip to market. As he walked to Hounslow he reminded himself to ask Joseph to tell him about the circle, the square, and the strange name of the tavern. He'd also ask his family name.

Francis went to his sleeping mat behind the fireplace. As he lay thinking about his extraordinary day, he hoped he would see John Anthony again.

10 ~ 1630

Often that winter Francis was in Lawton Woods gathering kindling wood, and with Child's permission he trapped wild pigs, lured with grain. He learned that the extra time he spent in the woods was a good investment, for the customers were clamoring for the nuts, berries, and hog meat. The Brayton debt was dwindling, albeit slowly. On the home front, Thomas kept busy caring for Martha, but there was little he could do for her. Francis could not comfort his mother; the broken pieces of their relationship could not be mended.

The trips to market continued through 1631, always including a visit to The Dock on his way home. He had come to know Joseph better, and they each looked forward to the monthly visits. Francis was able to let go of family concerns, becoming at ease in Ellington. He also enjoyed learning about its history from Joseph.

"Many years ago, the Circle had been a meadow, with a copse of hardwood trees and bushes. It's now known as Weedon Park, but back then it was called Shepherd's Bush. The meadow is now known as the Weedon Green. That's where the sheep grazed while the shepherds rested on the way to market. More and more shepherds stopped in this place, and there would be flocks of sheep in the meadow. It's said that one of the shepherds remarked that the sheep grazing there looked like waves coming to shore. Another was to have said, 'That makes this the dock then.' The name stuck with them. When Lord Weedon established the Weedon Academy for Boys in 1558, the Shepherds Inn was built and beside it was this tavern, which was given the name, The Dock."

Joseph paused a moment, then added "The town has developed around the academy, supplying its needs and services. It was carefully planned, and because of the serene atmosphere, Ellington has attracted wealthy men who have built their retirement homes near the Circle.

"It also became the seat of a regional judiciary, with the magistracy—you can see it from the window there—as a part of its building. Have you been there yet?"

"No, I haven't."

Joseph continued. "One half of the Square is civil services, the other half is the magistracy. The town park is between the two. So, there you have what are known as Ellington's Circle and Square."

"This is interesting. It might be just the place for me. I want an education, and I want a steady supply of shepherd's pie. Oh yes, and good conversation with you, Joseph."

Joseph laughed, just as Francis had intended.

Francis had shared with Joseph that his mother was very ill and that his parents were older. Joseph had shared that his family name was Pebbles and he was tired of the "stone" gibes, so he rarely used it at The Dock.

The new year came, and Martha was near death by March. She lingered on, and Thomas prepared himself for the end of her care. He hated watching her suffering and did all that he could. On March 21, 1632, she died. Reverend Morton was by her side, praying for the soul he knew would be in Heaven with her God. She, his most faithful parishioner, would be a loss to him and the chapel. He praised Martha three days later at the burial site.

Thomas grieved and wandered about the house, at a loss for what to do. Francis, who was rarely at home to comfort him, was trying to think of what Thomas could possibly do at age sixty-two. It came to him in a flash—the Houndstooth Tavern! He said to Thomas, "Go to the Houndstooth, Papa. You know the fellows who go there and, they'll enjoy your company."

It was just the thing for Thomas, being with his hardworking neighbors, playing cards, and telling stories.

They were delighted to put Thomas in charge of cheerfulness.

Meanwhile, Francis was twenty and still working to pay off the Brayton debt. Marriageable women noticed him even though he paid no attention at all. He was different—not like other young men who overcompensated for their awkwardness by being cocky. Francis' indifference attracted them all the more.

John Anthony did get his attention, whenever they met by chance at The Dock. Francis was drawn to John's easiness and his assured manner, but he was not envious. He had seen how envy could lead to discontentment, as it had with Martha. John and Francis were a good match, since John enjoyed the company of a good listener with whom he could share his experiences.

John had interesting stories to tell about his family, and one day in September as they walked to Sheffield Market John began: "My grandfather, Francis, had gone to Pembroke College and became a chemist and jeweler. After much experimenting, he made an elixir of gold dust suspended in a combination of chemicals which he gave the name *Aurum Potabile.* His customers, believing it improved their health, included Queen Elizabeth I, who requested a steady supply. The medical authorities took Francis Anthony to court for quackery, where he was fined and sent to prison for a short time. His loyal wife, Susan, supported him throughout the ordeal. He continued to supply the potent, and his 'quackery' was ignored in time.

"My Father, John, became a physician, wealthy enough to be knighted. He established a manor in Hammersmith that he named 'Foxgrove,' and there my father and mother settled into the privileged life of titled gentry. They have two sons, me and my brother Charles. My mother has poor health and lives a quiet life. The elder, Charles, is the heir, for which I, the second son, am forever grateful. He has the title and I have the freedom, which perplexes my parents, but they're now accustomed to their gadabout son."

John then switched to his oft-talked-about plans to emigrate to America. Francis had not been exposed to the world, so it seemed preposterous that anyone would choose to leave the predictable life for the wilderness. However, John seemed determined to go, and he had a neighbor friend, William Brenton, who would soon sail to Boston. William was spurring John on with his own plans. Today, at the market, John would order looms to be made that could be disassembled, packed, and reassembled in Boston.

"So," thought Francis, "he really is leaving."

"Francis! John said with enthusiasm, "You must come to Foxgrove in Hammersmith for a visit. Could you come next week? I want you to meet Will Brenton before he sails for Boston."

Francis was more astonished and curious than he was apprehensive. He said that he could manage to meet him at The Dock on the following Saturday.

"That's settled then."

11 ~ 1632

The time had been set and Francis was having misgivings as he dressed in his farmer's clothing for a visit to a manor.

If the clothes weren't worry enough, he was clearly agitated about telling John that he had never ridden a horse. John had said he would bring a gentle mare for him to ride, knowing without being told that Francis was not familiar with horseback riding. John felt it was time for Francis to spread his wings.

The mare, named "Libby," was experienced and knew at once when a neophyte had climbed into her saddle. John trotted off on Dix, and Libby, ignoring "giddy-ups," grazed blithely along the side of the road.

John turned and, seeing what was happening, came back to Francis and reproached him. "Take control, boy! Put some tooth into your voice or we'll never get to Foxgrove. Use your heels, dig in, and flap the reins with some vigor. She knows her job, let her do it."

Francis would always remember that moment. It was the right advice, and in time it would be applied to other aspects of his life when firmness or resolve was required. He began to enjoy the feeling of power as the horse trotted along—such a different experience with the scenery whizzing by!—but he wasn't deluded. It wasn't the scenery whizzing by, but instead it was the horse that propelled him through space with its strength. It was very different from the effort of walking.

They arrived at Foxgrove in good time, and Francis was relieved that he would not be sitting down at table with the gentry. As they entered the gates and trotted along the curving road to the house, he took a new measure of his relationship with John. There was a much wider distance in their social standing than he imagined as he viewed

Foxgrove in the distance. Once there, they went immediately to the library to greet John's father, Sir Anthony.

It was obvious that John's father adored his son. He wore a look of joy on his face as they entered the large room. The men clasped each another and stood smiling, and then John introduced Francis. There was not a hint of hesitation as the lord met the tall handsome friend of his son. They spoke of the beautiful day and how the leaves were beginning to color, and then, shifting his tone, Sir Anthony spoke of Sarah, who was "keeping to her bed today."

John softly nodded and asked about Charles. "Oh, he's about. Probably in his study room."

They popped in to greet John's brother, who was utterly indifferent to Francis. Francis wondered how two brothers could be so dissimilar, only to remember his own brother, Charles. They went on to tour the manor, and Francis enjoyed seeing where John spent his childhood. John had decided this life was too restraining for him, just as he himself had concluded about life in Hounslow.

They went to the kitchen, where the cook, Hazel, became enlivened the moment she saw John. She immediately pulled things from the shelves and cupboards, chatting as she prepared a cold meal for them. They sat at her large work table, and John asked about her family. The two of them told favorite stories of John's childhood. Their easy relationship revealed even more about the life of this enigmatic friend.

John told Francis he was fascinated with people who had skills and who did great work with their hands. He considered himself to have been restricted to rules and manners as the son of a lord; he was rejecting such a life with his plans to emigrate to New England, where he would establish a weaving shop, living and working among freemen.

"Now let's rescue Libby from our proud stallions and go have a visit with William Brenton," he said. On the way he talked of William. "Five years my junior, but he's gone circles around me in the business world. He's already amassed substantial wealth, and he's enthusiastic about going to America. He wants me to go with him when he sails on the *Lyon* in October, but it's too soon. I'm not ready."

The friends greeted one another. When Francis was introduced, William asked, "Are you coming along to America as well?"

Francis admitted, "I'm sure I'll eventually get there. It sounds like quite an adventure."

Will turned quickly and said, as he hurried from the room, "Wait until you see what I've received!" Will soon returned and motioned them over to a table, where he unrolled a document. It was a charter with the Royal Seal of King Charles I, beautifully scripted and emblazoned with gold and purple flourishes. In part it read: "… that William Brenton be granted one acre of land for every mile surveyed in the New England Colonies."

"Will!" exclaimed John. "I hand it to you. This is a tremendous parchment and guarantees your good fortune in America."

"Indeed it does," Will said, "and I'm not wasting a bit of time. I have two surveyors who are willing to sail with me to get the surveying started as quickly as possible. King Charles is keen for the land to be claimed and secured for England. My passage is booked on the *Lyon* next month, and John, I urge you to hurry your business and get to Boston soon. By the way, our friend, Captain Isaac Headly, is building his own ship, a barque, to sail back and forth between London and Boston. He has formed the *Headly Passenger and Cargo Company* and is seeking investors. It promises to be very successful, I have no doubt. I've put some silver into it, and it would be wise for you to do the same."

John said, "I hear you. It does seem a safe place for money these days. I have no idea how many voyages have been made all together this past decade, but I know the business has continued to grow. I've heard that the pirates have stopped harassing the ships to New England since there's no cargo and the passengers have nothing of value. The seas are now only threatened by Mother Nature."

"Now, John, you aren't trying to paint a dark picture, are you?"

"Not at all! Remember, I'll be following you."

The three men—John, the oldest at twenty-eight; Will, twenty-three; and Francis twenty-one—could not see into their futures, but had they been able to do so, they would have been amazed how the events of their lives would one day intermingle in the New World.

John sailed to Boston on the *Hercules*, which left England April 16, 1634. It was six months before Francis heard from him, and by that time he'd had to exert his will to be patient with his own life. John was full of enthusiasm for New England, writing about opportunities, land that seemed never ending, and the many exceptional men who had fled England's restrictions for political freedom.

One benefit for Francis, these years after his mother's death and John's departure, was the money he was making from his business with Clive Steadman. It had taken seven years to finish paying off the Brayton debt, and it was such a grand day in 1635 when Clive informed him that it was paid in full. Since then he had continued to supply the same items to Clive and had been paid monthly. He was saving to buy new clothes and to finance his education, however he could manage it, possibly with books if they weren't too expensive. He might try being tutored if he could find the right person. Of course, he would have to find a job as quickly as possible and find a place to live too. Undaunted, he was confident he would manage it all, somehow.

America seemed a good idea for his future, but he would not go until he knew more about the world. He had heard enough to know that living the rough life would be very much like the peasant's life in England, and he did not want that. Each day he renewed his energy to fulfill his plans. Diligence was the way to get it done.

Chapter 3: Diligent Son

Diligence is the mother of good fortune. — Miguel de Cervantes

12 ~ 1637

Folks in Hounslow had a saying for the dreamers or eccentrics among them, those who often stared into space or remained on the sidelines of community activity. They were said to be "somewhere else." Such behavior was noticeable among like-minded people of Hounslow who strove to live consistently with the vagaries of nature. They understood the rules of the natural world—that there was a time for planting, a need to cultivate, and an urgency to harvest.

The tenants of Hounslow learned respect by being respected, faith by observing the faithful, orderliness by experiencing disorder, and generosity by receiving. Their families were the investment in the future, the reward for hard work and sacrifice. Francis Brayton loved the people of Hounslow, how they labored with the soil, how they cared for their families, how they accepted the responsibility of making all that possible. However, they were not the ones who owned, governed, built, or educated, and Francis Brayton wanted to be with those who did. He wanted to be "somewhere else."

Francis had decided at a young age that his persistent curiosity had found limits in Hounslow. There was limited reading material and few people who knew about the world, even fewer who *cared* to know. But Francis cared, and he would do what needed doing while his aging father was alive, so that later he could leave Hounslow. He would have to make it happen, and there was no time like the present to be prepared. For one thing, he wanted to be educated which would require books and probably a tutor. The only book he had, *Don Quixote,* was the wisest gift ever given to him. Matthew Brooks, his former teacher, would be pleased to know how many times Francis had read of the exploits of Don Quixote and his faithful servant, Sancho Panza.

Francis had a routine that began his days. He prepared a breakfast, first by slicing crusty bread from Paddy Ould's Bakery, then he slathered the slices with Harriet Quinlan's preserves. Sometimes there would be some Comstock cheese or a sausage or two from the emporium. Once all was prepared, he would wake Thomas to come for his breakfast. Francis would then sit down to eat his share and then get an early start with the chores. However, he never left until he heard Thomas stirring in the room under the eaves. Once he did, he would yell, "Bye, Papa! I'll see you at midday. You know where I'll be till then."

Francis often walked in fog to the barn to care for his ox, "Dapple," named for Sancho Panza's donkey in *Don Quixote*. He was able to buy Dapple by cleaning the barn for the estate and taking care of oxen that belonged to Lord Fulham. Having the ox was good for Francis because he could do the plowing more quickly with Dapple. He also had more time for his other chores. Everyone was happy, and eventually Francis owned the animal.

Francis, in fact, rented out Dapple to others, and the coins allowed him to buy more seed for his gardening. These projects were allowing more exposure to neighbors and residents in Hounslow. Nevertheless, the people who knew him had adjusted to his offhand behavior, how he avoided conversations and didn't attend the social gatherings at the Houndstooth Tavern. He did enjoy listening to his father repeating the tittle-tattle from his evenings there. It helped Thomas unwind before he climbed up to bed each night. Thomas occasionally repeated the good things he heard others say about his "Frankie."

Clive also would tell him, "Francis, you realize you're much respected here in Hounslow for your diligence, don't you?"

Francis didn't know what to say so he just smiled. It seemed odd to be praised for what he was doing so that he could leave Hounslow with no regrets. Would his "diligence" be so praiseworthy if they knew the cause for it, he wondered?

Thomas was aging. It would be his sixty-seventh year in December, and he was moving more slowly. Francis urged him to sleep in the bedroom by the kitchen, but it seemed to be a point of pride for him to climb the steps, just as Francis had refused when Thomas urged him to sleep in the bedroom instead of the mat behind the fireplace. Each continued in his own way, loving and caring for one another, but neither feeling obligated to the other.

Francis enjoyed his monthly visits to the Sheffield Market. Nature had smiled upon the region, and farming was flourishing, at least for a few years. All around, the landlords were pleased, and the government and the Crown were equally pleased by the income from the land taxes. Clive urged Francis to use an ox and a cart to go to market, but he convinced Clive it wasn't worth the fuss.

"I either go into the marketing business full-time, or go along as I have been. Business is not how I see my life, Clive."

And Clive had stopped urging him. He knew Francis saw a friend on his market days but, he didn't ask. Clive knew about John Anthony because Francis had been so morose for a while., He shared how he missed his friend who had gone to America. Clive began to believe that Francis would leave for America himself, once Thomas was no longer alive.

It was November 1637, and Francis was on his way to market with a letter from John in his pocket, which he planned to share with Joseph when he got to The Dock. He planned to spend less time with Steven Studley, who always bought his goods but who also liked to talk, but today he would hurry so he could spend longer with Joseph. A sharp wind blew on that overcast day, and he was thankful for his old cloak, which elderly Ida Bame had repaired for him.

It was half past eleven when he left the market. The sun warmed the air, and Francis was lost in his thoughts, anticipating the good meal and discussion he'd have with Joseph. He didn't notice three men on the road in front of him until they were immediately blocking his path. He instantly sensed the danger, knowing they meant him harm. He lunged at the man in the middle and rammed his fist into his belly. The man fell to the ground groaning, and while the other two tried to seize him, he pushed the one to his right into the ditch by the roadside. He took flight, his long legs taking him quickly beyond the third man still standing.

When he felt it safe to look back, the two men were standing over the one he had punched. He ran on until he was gasping for air, then slowed to a walk, catching his breath. He was gradually coming down from a heightened burst of energy that had alerted him to danger. He reviewed in his mind's eye what he had just experienced, how he reacted without thinking, that he had punched the man without hesitating. He wondered about his violent reaction, so unlike his usual way, which was thinking methodically when faced with problems. Was this impulse always inside him, at the ready, to protect himself? This time it may have saved his life.

Francis had heard of the dangers of the highways, that marauding thieves would come out of the woods to rob people. He never thought that it might happen to him, but it seems he had been fortunate that something like this encounter had not occurred before.

He was thinking from a new perspective. He had not considered how he had been protected by the "limited life" in Hounslow. The sameness, the like-mindedness of people, also brought security because of their desire for orderliness. In Hounslow, Lord Fulham need not order a lashing on people when they failed to produce for his profit. Instead of threats of violence, people were evicted and denied the right to remain as tenants working his land.

Francis' mind had been sent into a whirl, beyond his usual rational thinking. He debated which was worse—his being threatened, or using his strength to harm those who were a danger to himself. Violence seemed the better course than to submit, he decided. Having concluded this, he realized he was returning to himself once more. Being calmer and feeling hungry were good signs of normality.

13 ~ 1637

Joseph was standing at his bar, just where Francis usually found him. They greeted each another, then Joseph asked, "Will it be shepherd's pie, then, Francis?"

"Yes, and a larger portion, please. I'm quite hungry today."

"You're a bit early. Not much trading today?"

"Not much. But I had to run to get away from some men setting out to rob me. My long legs saved my life."

"A bit of excitement for you," Joseph said as he turned to go to the kitchen.

Francis was reassured by Joseph and by being in his familiar place in The Dock. Joseph was soon back with a mug of ale, and before returning to his customers, he said, "I hope we have time to talk together."

Francis ate and frequently looked out the window to see the buildings in the Square, not too far from The Dock, noting how those municipal buildings seemed different from the mills, shops, and foundries. He was curious how business was conducted there, or what the classroom activity was like at the academy nearby.

Joseph came back during a lull, and Francis shared news about John Anthony. "John has just met a woman, and it sounds like he's serious about her. Her name's Susanna Potter. Her family went to Boston quite a while ago, and when her father died recently, her brothers decided to leave Boston for a new settlement to the south of there. They plan to go to the new settlement when it's surveyed."

"That *is* news. I suppose it might be important to have a wife in the wilderness. I've heard stories about the hardships in America, especially in New England's climate."

"John's enthusiastic about his future. He says he'll begin a weaving business in this new settlement. It's on an island, the largest one among many in a bay. There's a settlement northwest of the island called Providence Plantations. Doesn't that sound grand? Not like a wilderness at all."

"Yes, it does seem impressive. Does he mention Indians?"

"As a matter of fact, the Indians sold the island to the people who had been organizing the settlement. A theologian named Roger Williams negotiated with the Indians to give rights to the settlers. Williams lived with the Indians when he was excommunicated from Boston. He speaks several languages and believes the Indians should be paid for giving up their right to hunt the land. John wrote at length about him. I guess he ruffles feathers wherever he goes."

"Well, I suppose John is content being in such a place. The world is in turmoil enough on our side of the Atlantic. We may see war soon enough, Francis."

"Lord Fulham will not be happy if the fight comes to his 'experiment' in Hounslow. For that matter, we'd be even *more* unhappy. We have no desire to take up arms for the powers above us."

"Is your father concerned for his welfare and yours?" Joseph asked.

"No. He's content. He's a remarkable person. Manages to fix a midday meal for me, then walks to the Houndstooth for an evening with his friends. When he comes in, we talk a bit, then he climbs up to his room. There's a bedroom on the first level, but he says it feels right to be up under the eaves."

"How old is he now? Joseph asked. "Not that age always matters."

"Sixty-seven next month."

"Do you ever go to the tavern with him?"

"No. I don't like to waste my time, and pardon me for scoffing at your occupation, Joseph, but at this time in my life I don't want to drink and chat, and chat and drink! I urged my father to go knowing it would be good for him, and I was right. He's having the best time of his life." Francis smiled broadly.

"That's good," Joseph said.

"Yes, and I also look forward to visiting with you here at The Dock."

The first part of 1638 had been uneventful, with Francis trapping birds and boars and gathering kindling in Lawton Woods. He did his work in the barn and often yoked the oxen for others, mostly tenants who were aging like Thomas. Francis picked the meats from the nuts he had gathered in the fall, those he wasn't able to get finished in December in time for Christmas baking. He worked meticulously to free the hickory nuts as whole meats. Some customers would pay a little more for them. It was his particular trademark—"Francis Brayton's whole-meat hickory nuts."

He kept a candle burning in the evenings as he reread *Don Quixote*. He was intrigued by Sancho Panza, who tried to warn his master against his dangerous pursuits. Francis could see how the lofty Don Quixote and the practical realist Sancho Panza depended upon each other, or at least they each had a mission. Francis preferred Sancho Panza's to the Don's.

In April, as usual, there was plowing to prepare for the planting in May or June, including all his gardens. Francis grappled with the timing, the weather often pushing his usual dates to a later time. He was unaware that Thomas was staying in bed most of the morning until one day he came back earlier to work in his own garden and found

Thomas still in bed. He made light of it, since Thomas was so embarrassed.

"Stay in bed as long as you want, Papa. There's nothing that bothers me. I'll be fine. Besides," he teased, "you need the rest for your evening at the tavern."

14 ~ 1638

On the sixteenth of August he called up to Thomas as usual. He sat down to eat his breakfast but realized that his father had not answered. He called again, then started up the stairs full of dread, his heart pounding because of the quiet, the absolute quiet.

Thomas was lying on his back, so still that Francis felt a chill come over him as he moved closer to the bed. He knew when he touched his father's cold hand that he was gone. He felt for the pulsing of his heart, and there was none. His next thought was unexpected. "Just like your beloved Isobel, Papa." He had been told more than once about the unexpected passing of his grandmother. It was what Thomas had hoped for himself, after witnessing the long agonizing years Martha had suffered. The tears spilled onto Francis' cheeks as he stood for a while, holding his father's hand. He was not quite ready to leave and begin the process that would end with the burial of his father. He went to the small window as if to ensure that nothing had changed in Hounslow.

Down below, it looked serene and peaceful without animal odors or the noises of work implements, so quiet and lovely. Had these two scenes always existed together, while he had been too taken up with one to notice the other? How often had he missed one perspective for being too engrossed with the other? It brought another thought: What about viewpoints themselves? Are there often more viewpoints to consider in most situations? He wanted to remember these thoughts. No doubt he would also remember his dear father when they came to mind in the future.

He stood beside the bed and looked at his father. Thomas was at peace, as if asleep. Francis thought of how he had cared for Martha and how he had made her last days tolerable. Thomas was content with his life, always seeing the brighter side. His presence had buoyed others. Francis pulled the sheet over his father's face and said, "Thank you, dear Papa. I have loved you from the moment I came to recognize you, long ago. I hope to do you honor in my life."

He left the house to do what needed to be done, beginning with Doctor Lessing, who knew why Francis was at his doorstep.

"Has your father left us, Francis?"

"Yes, doctor—Papa has died. I need you to come and see for yourself, then tell me what I need to do."

The doctor stepped across the threshold and put his arm around Francis, saying, "I am so sorry, my boy. I'll come immediately. Do you have any family to notify?"

Francis nodded and said, "Charles in Isley and Gwen in Limon. That's all."

Doctor Lessing took on the role of doctor with a patient and said, "You notify them, and I'll go to the house. Is it unlocked?"

"Yes. He's in the upper room."

"I'll notify the coroner and undertaker for you as well."

Francis went back to the house to get some coins, then on to the livery to pay a boy to take messages to Charles and Gwen. He had written Gwen, "Please bring some baked goods to serve neighbors who will come to say farewell to Thomas on the nineteenth of August." He asked the messenger to bring replies from them. He went to the chapel to see Reverend Morton, who gave Francis words of comfort and agreed to perform the brief graveside service.

Francis did not want to return to 10 Farley Lane until the body of his father had been moved. He took the path that led to Lawton Woods to walk, this time to seek solace, not firewood.

He took care of business with the undertaker and was greatly shocked by the cost of burial services and the coffin. At least he had the money. When Martha died, the expenses were paid off over time, and Francis was relieved that he would not have to do that with Thomas. Later he found a small stash of coins in Thomas' room, possibly from his monthly allowance for his ale at the tavern. Maybe others were buying ale for him, or he was more interested in the company than the ale.

On the day of the burial, Thursday, August nineteenth, Gwen and her husband John were the first to arrive. Gwen had biscuits and cakes ready to serve the neighbors. They set up the table, and Francis borrowed some wooden chairs to put in the small parlor and the kitchen area. Charles and Jane came without their sons, giving several reasons why they could not come.

Many neighbors came to honor Thomas Brayton, who was well-liked and would be missed. Gabe Bixby told some stories about funny incidents in the Houndstooth. Silas Bame spoke of Thomas as "such a good, caring man, and the best of neighbors."

Ida Bame told how Thomas had run around catching their rabbits that had escaped their hutch. Many spoke of the devotion Thomas had shown with Martha.

"Thomas never shirked a duty and was a hard worker. He will be missed in this community." This was a sentiment stated one way or the other by many of Thomas' Hounslow friends.

It was soon time to walk the short distance to the cemetery for the grave-side burial of Thomas. Reverend Morton cited verses from the Bible, ending with one that Francis found appropriate, Ecclesiastes 2:24: "I know there is nothing better than a man to be happy and to do good while he lives. That each of them may eat and drink and find satisfaction in their toil; this is the gift of God."

After the burial, the neighbors drifted away, and Francis asked his family to come to the house to settle some matters.

Once they were all seated in the parlor and before Francis could speak, Charles asked, "Francis, is there a will?"

It was so unexpected that Francis caught his breath and held it to keep from gasping. He replied, "No, but I wish you and Gwen to go through the house and divide between you whatever things you want. I've already packed my bag." Francis gestured toward his satchel by the fireplace. They all looked over at the case as Francis continued. "Once I've met with Lord Fulham's attorney, I will be leaving this home and Hounslow for Ellington."

Gwen said, "What about the field, the garden, and the animals?"

"They will return to the estate. I'll sell the animals to pay for father's funeral expenses."

Charles asked, "What about the proceeds from the estate?" Charles asked. "I trust you will share those with Gwen and me."

It took a strong will to keep his composure, but Francis said calmly, "Once seeds are planted in the ground they belong to the landlord. When the crop is ready for harvest and the tenant does the harvesting, the yield is shared equally between the landlord and the tenant. I have planted this year's crop, but I will not be harvesting it, therefore there is no income coming to our family."

"That seems unfair," Charles said, bristling. "The Brayton family has worked this land for two generations. Is there no provision for that labor and loyalty?"

"I will tell you this. Our family will leave the Fulham estate without debts, and for that we should be proud. Few families can make the same claim."

Charles was unrelenting. "Surely, there were savings, or at least some assets."

Francis could not believe that Charles was due a detailed explanation, but he had nothing to hide from him, so he explained as best he could. "I have sold some tools to pay this month's rent. We lived here year by year, only making ends meet when there was a good harvest. When there were crop failures, as we had during the 'cool years' from volcanic ash, the debts mounted. We tenants stuck together, and Lord Fulham extended our credit and we all survived. But the debts were there to be paid after all."

Charles acquiesced, and Gwen was relieved because the tension was worrying her. Charles sat back in his chair and listened very carefully to Francis.

"I have had to work to be sure I could leave the leasehold agreement. I've met the requirements and I plan to find work in Ellington until I have enough money to go to America. For now, I wish you to take what you want because on August twenty-seventh I'm leaving Hounslow, taking only my satchel. Here are two sheets of paper for you to indicate what you and Gwen each want. You need to remove the items before August twenty-fifth, giving me time to clean the house, which will be turned over to Lord Fulham's estate. I'll be available to help you load the things you want."

Francis said, "Thank you," and left the house, feeling dejected that the whole thing had not gone better. He was relieved that Thomas had not been a witness to the exchange.

Then Francis did something quite unexpected and out of character for him. He went to the Houndstooth Tavern to have ale and a bowl of soup. He had not been eating well these past three days. Of course, he was inundated by the men at the tavern, who wanted to express their sympathy and to tell anecdotes about Thomas. He listened, drank, ate, and listened some more. When it was dark, he left for Farley lane. He was reluctant to go inside and think of Thomas. It was over. His father was laid to rest, and he was left with only his memories of his dear and much beloved father.

He was rather certain that Charles would have opened his satchel to see if he had taken any family treasures. He would have seen two such items there: his father's prized brush, and his mother's King James Bible. He kept his great grandmother Elaine Brayton's gold ring in his pocket.

15 ~ 1638

The next day he helped Bill Newcomer move the chickens and coop to his place down the "row," as they called the Lane. Bill was pleased to have the hens and the ready-made coop. That afternoon Francis used his spade and turned over the herb garden. It was a symbol to him of the end of the Brayton family tenancy. His grandfather John had planted the herbs and then shared them with neighbors, giving instructions on how to use them. He loved hearing Thomas talk about John and Isobel. Francis felt akin to them and was determined he would tell his own children these Brayton stories one day.

He met with Clive, who had known this day would come. It was no secret to him that Francis would terminate the leasehold agreement. Francis said to Clive, "I'll have the barn clean before I leave. I hope you find a good home for Dapple. I'll be leaving on the twenty-seventh, and I hope my family clears it of furniture, since I can't take any with me. The house will be clean. Tomorrow, I'll bring all the produce available to you and will settle up with my garden people as well. I'll say goodbye later, Clive."

Clive looked fondly at his favorite tenant and gave him a sad smile.

As he visited each of the neighbors who had allowed him the use of their garden space, he took time to chat with them. They were pleased by this gesture, so unlike the usually reticent Francis. He asked about their families, about their health, and ended, as usual, talking about the weather. He also went to the barn to give his faithful Dapple a few pats. It was a difficult goodbye.

For the next few days, he did cleaning, said more goodbyes, and then walked to see Edward Childs, the overseer of the estate, to set an hour and day for meeting with the attorney. Edward was not there, but the clerk told him to come on the twenty-sixth at two o'clock for the final settlement. Henry Hayes, Esquire, would be available along with Edward Childs.

Monday, Gwen and John came to collect the items they had selected. She had selected fewer things since she had no children. They talked of John's weaving business and that he was doing well now that his former employer had retired. They were curious about Francis and his future, but there was little to say.

"I want to leave tenant farming for good. I hope to find work suited for me, but first I need to decide what that will be. I'll keep in touch with you, Gwen. Family is important."

"I regret I didn't come here to visit," Gwen said. "Thank you for your care of our parents. I should have shown my appreciation long before this."

"Thank you, Gwen. We'll meet again, and I look forward to that."

The next day Charles came with his sons, Henry and George. Francis was happy to meet these young men. Charles, he could tell, had worked to give them a good start in life.

Henry, the image of Thomas, said, "I work at the local bank. It's the bottom rung of the ladder, but the income is steady."

George was younger than Henry, closer in age to Francis, but George seemed younger. He was living at home with his parents and was pleased to get the bed from the upper room. Charles was proud of his boys, and the whole meeting on this day was very different from the confrontation of the previous week.

Charles also said, "I wish you well, Francis, and I do appreciate how you stayed with our parents."

"Let's keep in touch, Charles. I'll let you know my whereabouts when I get settled."

The house was empty of furniture by the twenty-fifth, and the only place for Francis to sit was on the stairs. He went to the mat earlier than usual, but he was tired enough to sleep soundly.

On the twenty-sixth of August, Edward Childs greeted Francis with an expression of sympathy. They sat together at a table where they would begin closing the Brayton leasehold contract as soon as Henry Hayes, the estate attorney, arrived. Childs complimented Francis on his years of work and added, "You've shown initiatives that have not gone unnoticed. Lord Fulham, in fact, suggested I offer you a position in the overseer's office, and I'm pleased to do so."

Francis was stunned and not prepared for such an offer. He hesitated, and Childs said, "What are your thoughts on that, Francis?"

He could not say what he was thinking, that he couldn't work for the estate, which he had come to think of as oppressive. Instead he said, "Thank Lord Fulham for me, but I have plans to go to America."

Edward Childs was about to say something when the door opened and, the attorney entered with a portfolio under his arm. Childs introduced him. "Francis, this is Henry Hayes, who is meeting with us, as you requested, to terminate the Brayton/Fulham leasehold agreement."

Henry Hayes took a seat, pulled papers from the portfolio, and carefully laid a pile in front of him, with "pomp and ceremony," Francis was thinking. He then turned to Francis. "I represent Lord Fulham in the matter of a petition for termination of the leasehold agreement between the recently deceased Thomas Brayton, by request of his son, Francis Brayton, the existing leaseholder, and the other party, Lord Edward Fulham," he said. He lowered his eyes to the pile of papers before him. "It is a necessary formality that I review the lease, but rather than reading it word by word, I will explain for better understanding."

He took a deep breath, and with the top paper he started talking and, at the same time, waving his hand up and down the page. When he had said what needed to be said with the page, he grasped the corner of the paper with his right thumb and forefinger, lifted it high, turned it quickly, and brought it down onto the table with a flourish. He then talked and waved over the next page, lifted it up and over and down, just as before, going on with each page talking and waving and lifting until all but one page was left on the table.

He turned to Francis and said, "This page is a current accounting of outstanding debts"—he paused for an intake of breath, then continued—"owed to Lord Fulham. It includes the cost of spring planting and the rent on the Farley Lane house for August, all of which amounts to two shillings and four pence."

Hayes picked up the quill from the holder in the center of the table, dipped it into the inkwell, and dramatically slashed through the figures on the last page. "However," he said with a slight increase in volume, "Lord Fulham has instructed me to write off this amount as 'paid-in-full,' as a token of his appreciation for the long service and fine character of Thomas Brayton. If you will sign here, then we will consider the business at hand to be terminated."

Francis picked up the page to be signed, read it carefully, then picked up the quill and signed where Hayes had indicated. However, he did not hand the paper back. Instead he said, "I appreciate the tribute of Lord Fulham to my father's memory, but I want to say that the seed had already been paid for, since I settled all accounts with the emporium yesterday. Also, I know that the rent for the Farley Lane house has always been paid at the beginning of the month for that month, not at the end of the month for the past month. Since we are clear of any debt to the Fulham estate, I will accept the kind offer as one of goodwill between the Brayton family and Lord Fulham, and, also agree that our business is terminated."

He handed the paper to Hayes, who was a bit flustered as he put the papers together. Hayes said, "You are to vacate the premises of 10 Farley Lane by August 31, 1638. The keys are to be handed over to the overseer."

He gathered his papers and put them into his portfolio. In so doing, all the work of two generations of Braytons was whisked away like the wave of Hayes' hand over the mysterious legal papers. Then he was gone.

Childs had said nothing during the proceedings, nor had he reacted when Francis set the record straight with Hayes. After all, he was a faithful agent of Lord Fulham and loyal to his other employees as well. Childs had witnessed a peasant who had proven to be more honorable than the Honorable Lord Fulham. It was a rare occurrence. Francis told Childs that he had arranged for a neighbor to lock the house and return the key to the estate.

Childs reminded Francis of the offer of a position with the estate and added, "If we can be of any help when you seek employment—a reference or such—I'll be happy to supply it."

"That is very kind, Mr. Childs, and I will remember the offer."

As he walked back to his house to spend his final night on the mat behind the fireplace, he was reminded again how he had been praised by others for his work, which had been done to ensure he could leave the Fulham estate. And yet, possibly in his future, the offer of a recommendation from the Fulham estate might be quite valuable.

The next morning, he rolled the canvas mat and put it by the door to the garden. He opened his satchel and checked to be sure all was in order. The large book, *Don Quixote,* took up a great deal of space, but he must have it. He dressed and brushed his hair. He got some water from the well in the garden and shaved his beard, leaving the cloth on a bush to dry. He thought for a moment, then took the cloth and wiped his boots clean.

"That will do no good, since I'm walking to Ellington," he told himself. "Just the same …"

He was ready to leave and turned to take one last look at the garden. Then he went inside to get his satchel. He put the key on the window ledge and left through the front door. He did not say goodbye to anyone, since it was too early, and, besides, he had said goodbyes enough. He walked out of Hounslow and toward the Great West Road. He did not look back as he said aloud, "I'll be living in Ellington by the end of the day."

Part Two

SOMETHING DIFFERENT

Chapter 4: Yardman

We are what we repeatedly do. Excellence then, is not an act, but a habit. — Aristotle

16 ~ 1638

Francis Brayton entered Ellington with all his earthly possessions in his satchel, its belt slung across his shoulder, bearing the weight. He was certain that this was the logical place to pursue an education, a town dedicated to learning. Francis had come eager to share his adventure with Joseph and to eat a hearty meal at The Dock.

Joseph, eyeing the bulging satchel, made a fair assumption.

"Going to market are you, Francis?"

"No, not this time. I've left Hounslow and will be living here in Ellington."

"Well, now, that is good news for me! I look forward to a steady order of ale and good conversations."

"I hope that includes shepherd's pie. I'm famished." Francis took his satchel to his usual place at the rear, by the window.

"To be sure, and I'll tell the cook right this minute." Joseph turned toward the door behind the bar and disappeared.

Francis was relieved there were no patrons—it was a bit early in the day—and now he could ask Joseph where he might find cheap lodging in Ellington.

Joseph came to his table with the usual mug of ale and asked, "What brought about this move, friend?"

My father died on the sixteenth. It wasn't unexpected—he died in his sleep, for which I'm grateful. He deserved an easy exit from a difficult life, but I can't say my father was unhappy or downtrodden. We were very close, you know, and I'll miss him every day."

"You have my sympathy," Joseph said. "To be sure, you'll miss him. So, there's no one in Hounslow to keep you there?"

Francis took a sip of ale, put the mug on the table, and looked up at Joseph.

"Not a soul. That might be the fate of a late child. My life has centered on my parents. But no, that's not the cause. I've planned a long time now to leave Hounslow because I have no interest in farming, which begs the question—what else is there for a tenant's son?"

"You, Francis, will work that out, I have no doubt. In the meantime, how about some good lamb and vegetables?"

Joseph turned to go to the kitchen to get Francis his pie. In a moment, he set it on the table before Francis, asking, "Can I get you another ale?"

"I'd better not. I have to be on my way as soon as I eat." Joseph returned to the bar, leaving Francis to his meal. Francis glanced out the window at the Square and thought, "I wish I were working in one of those buildings."

When Joseph came to remove the dish after Francis had finished eating, Joseph said, rather hesitantly, "I'm not sure this would interest you, but Chester Holmes, the owner of the Ellington Bakery, came here yesterday, quite disturbed that his yardman suddenly quit to go to America. He's trying to keep his ovens going, taking care of customers, and he's desperate for help. He wanted me to post a notice on our board for someone to work mostly in the yard, preparing wood for the ovens. That's about all I know, except that Chester is well respected in Ellington. Agreeable person too."

Francis *was* interested. "Yes, I'd like to talk to him. Is that his bakery across the Circle?"

"It is, and I'm sure he's there, since the bakery is open every day but Sunday."

Francis got up, took his satchel, and put his coins for the meal on the table, amazing Joseph with his abrupt manner.

Then Francis paused and said, "I do thank you, Joseph, and I'll be back soon to tell you more, to be sure." He walked toward the bakery feeling hopeful, his satchel back in place again over his shoulder. He wanted work that would allow him time to study, and this might be just the job.

As he approached the bakery, he heard someone chopping wood in the back and assumed it was Chester. He walked through a narrow passageway between the bakery and a creamery. In the backyard was a man, probably in his forties, with wisps of reddish, gray hair over his forehead, not plump but not slender either. He looked up at Francis, observed his satchel hanging on his upper body, and said, "Are you lost, young man?"

"I'm looking for Chester Holmes," Francis answered.

"You've found him. As you can see I'm busy."

"Joseph Pebbles at The Dock told me you needed someone to work for you, and I need work. My name is Francis Brayton from Hounslow."

"What are you doing in Ellington, if I might ask?" Chester's ax came down to split a log on the splitting stump.

"My father died recently, and I've terminated our tenant lease with Lord Fulham because I don't want to be a tenant farmer like him. I need work, and I'm ready to begin right away." Francis halted, not sure how much was enough to assure Chester he was serious.

Chester stood up and squinted as he looked at this lanky fellow, tempted to hand him the ax and tell him to "get at it" but also needing to be sure he could trust the stranger.

"Why did you come to Ellington? What do you expect to accomplish in a town that's not a farming community?"

"I was the third generation to work in Hounslow, and I worked the family allotment because my parents needed my help. Now they're gone, and I have no reason to stay in farming. What I hope to do is work, and also to study. I'm assuming this town has more ways to learn than others, and that's why I came here. Eventually, I'd like to hire a tutor."

"You might be right about that. I'd wager you could find more educated people per yard in Ellington than in all of London." He chuckled, then said, "I'll give you a proposition: Work for me a week, and then we will see if the job suits you, and I'll see if your work suits me."

"Fair enough, Mr. Holmes," Francis said, putting down his satchel, and to the amazement of the baker, he took the ax, picked up a log, set it on the splitting log, and chopped it directly down the middle.

"Hold on! Give me a minute to show you around, and don't call me mister. Chester will do. After I show you what needs doing, I'll go home to my sweet family. They haven't seen much of me lately, nor I them. I closed my shop for the first time since I bought the place five years ago. Come inside and I'll show you what needs to be done."

He entered the door, which was separated by two huge mounds of mortared stones, and led Francis into a passageway between the two baking ovens. He stopped at a large table in an open space. Knocking his fist on the table, he said, "This is my kneading table, and it's off-limits to everyone but me."

He continued through another door into the small shop where customers were served. There was a counter with a cash box out of sight of the customers, shelves for the baked goods, and a display case on the right. The area for the customers was a typical shop with a front door in the center separating two small bay windows. Chester gestured to the space and said, "This gets a good cleaning every Saturday after the shop closes at four o'clock."

Chester then walked to the alcove to the right of the ovens and pointed to the three bins fixed to the wall with shelves above the bins. "These are my flour, cornmeal, and sugar bins, and the other ingredients I use are on the shelves above. The bins are just the right size for the amount I need for my daily bakes. They have to be filled to the top each evening."

He took a key from a hook hidden from view, opened the door to the shed, and walked around a bed, saying, "I'm ashamed of the mess in here. This is the storage shed, where the flour and meal are stored, plus tools and such.

"This bed is for you, if you care to use the shed for sleeping. All my yardmen have stayed here, and you're welcome to also, if you want. There's a wash basin there and shelves for your things above. My wife, Abigail, changes the linens every week, and these are clean. There's a towel and small cloth too." He continued talking as he walked to another door in the shed.

"This door goes into the yard. This shed is rat-proof, so you must keep this door closed whenever you come and go from the yard. Here, take this key and use it to lock yourself in at night. That is, if you choose to stay."

"I will, thank you, Chester, I have no other plans. This suits me very well."

Chester turned back to the bakery and Francis followed.

Chester then pointed to the ovens. "These need kindling laid every night, so I can start my bakes first thing each morning. I begin at five to give the ovens time to heat to a proper temperature. The firebox under each oven needs to be filled, and these boxes here must be filled for the second bake. Now, I'm sure I've missed something, but you can come into the bakery at six thirty, and I can answer any questions you might have. So, I'll leave you to it, Francis, and we'll talk in the morning." He left by the back door into the yard and Francis followed. "Oh yes," Chester added. "The front door is locked, but you might want to lock the alcove door into the shed as well."

With that, he walked away from the bakery but turned at the end of the lot to say, "I live just a way down here on Linden Street. Also, this is the ash pit where you put the ashes. You need to clean out the ashes each time you lay more kindling in the ovens. A man named Tinker cleans out the pit when it's needed. Well, goodbye then, and I'll see you in the morning."

Francis took his satchel inside the shed, carefully closing the door behind him. He had to think about how to proceed. There was a window on the yard side of the shed giving light inside, and since there was still daylight to work outside later, he decided to start work first in the shed.

The shed, he figured, was about twelve by eighteen feet. It was attached to the bakery, and a brick wall shielded it from the heat of the oven on that end of the shed. There was a fireplace on the opposite side of the brick wall, and debris littered the corner on the yard side. He wondered why the bed was next to the doorway, blocking the way to the bins. He could see no reason for it to be there.

He cleared away the debris and found an almost useless broom to sweep the floor. He moved the bed to the space just cleared and then moved the barrels near the bakery door. Some buckets sat on the floor, and he decided one was for flour and the other for meal. There were scoops in each bucket—clear enough how the job was done.

Outside, he split the wood and stacked the extra logs along the back of the bakery. He found a sickle, a scythe, and a rake in the shed to clear the long grass from the yard. Once that was done, he found the ash bucket and removed the ashes from the ovens. Then he laid the kindling, chopped more logs, and filled the fire boxes. He inspected it all, then carried a bucket of ashes to the pit, closing the door behind him.

The yard was much improved. Next, he checked out the well opposite the shed, and the outhouse at the end of the shed, hidden from Linden Street by bushes and trees. In the shed, he unpacked his satchel and put his things on the shelves. He took the basin to the well, being careful to close the door after himself, got some water, and set up his water stand with his father's brush and his razor.

The sun had gone down so he lighted the candles that he'd found in the shed. There was a lantern too, with a candle in it. He had his own flint stone in his bag, not knowing what he might need this first night away from the comforts of Farley Lane. He was hungry, but he often was when he went to bed at night. Chester had asked him to come into the bakery at six thirty, so maybe he would have some bread for him.

He had found a small barrel in the shed, and this he turned upside down to sit on for a few minutes before he climbed into the rope bed. He had always slept on the floor and now hoped the bed would be not too soft to suit him. How can I be worrying about such a trivial matter? he wondered. He had a job, and even if it might be temporary, it was a beginning. He had a roof over his head and was tired enough to sleep soundly. This day had been good for him—finding Chester Holmes through Joseph Pebbles. "Would it ever have come about without Joseph?"

He crawled into bed, grateful to be where he was.

17 ~ 1638

He awoke in the morning to the delightful aroma of bread baking, so he knew it was at least six o'clock. He hurried to get ready for his meeting with Chester. He had slept well on the rope bed, though if one is tired any bed will suffice. He shaved and dressed, and at six thirty he walked through the alcove and greeted Chester. There were two chairs at the kneading table, and Chester gestured him toward one and placed a mug of hot cider in front of him. Plates of sweet buns, bread, cheese, and sausages made Francis' stomach growl.

Chester explained, "Sweet Abigail sent the cheese and sausages. She was happy to see me home early and to hear I had hired you. Thought we deserved something extra. So tie into it, Francis. The yard looks better, and all the work is satisfactory. It's a good start. Did you sleep well?"

"Yes, I'm rested. This morning I hope to clean the shed, but I'll need a better broom."

"Right! So you shall have one. I have an account at Albert Greenly's shop. I'll write you a note, and he'll put it on my account. When you're ready to set out, come in and I'll write up a list so all three of us will be straight."

The two ate and sipped, and Chester talked of his family. "Abigail is a perfect baker's wife, a good mother, and a delightful person. She keeps me supplied with eggs, milk, baking powder, soda, and the sweets I need for my bakes. As I said, she does the linens and takes care of our home and our children. We both work hard and appreciate each other."

Chester had a soft smile as he talked of Abigail, and he served more hot cider then continued to tell Francis of his children. "Our oldest is Catherine, ten; then Judith, eight; Juliet, five; and Henry, six months. The girls are very smart, and good girls too. Henry is our big boy who gets a lot of attention, you can imagine. Now, tell me about yourself."

"When I was sixteen," Francis began, "I knew I didn't want to farm for the rest of my life, but I wouldn't leave until my parents no longer needed me. My mother died two years ago, and my father scarcely two weeks ago. He was almost sixty-eight. I decided to live as I want to live, so I acted quickly and terminated the leases on the house and land."

"And do you have specific plans?" Chester asked in a kindly manner.

"Yes, I do. As I said, I want to get an education, however long it takes. Education is denied sons of peasants beyond age ten, you know. If I must learn by reading books, it could take a very long time."

"Yes," Chester said, "I'm sure it would at that. I'm prepared to offer you the job, Francis. I pay the going rate for this type of work, which is twenty pence a month. So, what do you say to that?"

"I say yes, Chester, it will suit me fine."

It was time for Chester to get to his second bake and Francis to his duties. They each turned to their work.

Francis finished splitting the logs that morning and left the cleaning of the shed until after his visit to Albert Greenly's shop to buy a broom. In the afternoon, with Chester's note of authorization in his pocket, he walked to the grocery shop.

At the grocery, he met Albert Greenly, who was pleased that Chester had found help. "He's been working too hard, and his business would have gone down, I think," Greenly said.

This was the first of many trips Francis would make to the shop, but neither was sure of that this day. Once back at the shed, he got to the cleaning. He arranged all the tools and equipment near the workbench, put the candles and flint stone on the shelf, and got water from the well so he could wash with soap using the cleaning cloths he found on the shelf. He was sure they hadn't been used in a long time. He swept the floor and scrubbed it.

He cleaned himself up a bit, putting on a clean blouse, then walked across Weedon Green to thank Joseph and get a hearty meal. Joseph was pleased to hear his good news.

"I'll be interested to see how your life unfolds here in Ellington," he said. "I doubt that you'll be living in that shed too long."

On Monday, Francis went to the tailors to order new clothes. He entered the small shop and was greeted by a man with a tape hung around his neck. Francis introduced himself and told the man he wanted a new coat, a blouse, a jerkin, and trousers. The tailor said his name was Tobias Sitwell, and Francis noted an attitude of superiority right off. "I suppose he thinks I don't have enough money for his shop," he thought.

"Could you give me an estimate of the total cost for these?" Francis asked.

"Well now, I would think at your height, it would cost ten shillings at least."

Francis was shocked. He needed boots as well, but he reminded himself of his "investment" and he took five shillings from his pocket and said, "Here's half. I'll pay the balance when the clothes are ready." The tailor smiled and proceeded to measure him. He told him to come back for a fitting on Monday, the sixth of September.

Clarence Hall, the bootmaker, was offhand but direct. The boots would be five shillings, and they would be ready Thursday, the ninth.

He walked to The Dock for a good meal and some conversation with Joseph. Today's visit was not as it usually was with Joseph, for there were two younger men who engaged Francis in conversation. Bill Travers worked as a dispatcher at the Basom Stables and Livery, keeping track of the scheduling of various coaches, drivers, and stable boys. John Templeton was a clerk for the utilities section of the town and worked in the municipal building. They seemed surprised that Francis was Chester's yardman, but they enjoyed having a good listener to hear about their exploits, especially with the ladies.

Time went along nicely the next week, since the work was routine and not challenging for someone like Francis. He enjoyed the walks around the Academic Circle, along with breakfast with Chester and his main meal at The Dock. At night he slept soundly. On the sixth of September, he had a fitting at the tailor's shop, and Tobias was a little more at ease with him this time. Afterwards, he went to the stationer's and bought quills, an inkstand, and some ink and paper so he could write a long letter to John about the excitement of his life in Ellington.

Later that week, Tinker came to make deliveries. He bustled into the yard and asked, "Who might you be?"

"I'm Francis Brayton. I work for Chester now."

"Well, that's good news. Chester deserves help—that last fellow just up and left. I'll need the keys to get my barrels into the shed."

Francis opened the door and watched as Tinker struggled through the grass with his wheelbarrow and the heavy load. He didn't offer to help him since he knew what he was doing without help. Once he had finished his delivery, Tinker asked, "So, you're new in town?

"Yes. Just came last week."

"I'm happy here," Tinker said. "Glad I came and stayed. I was tired of moving about, and this town suited me. I guess they're happy with me, because I'm sure busy. So, I'd better get on my way. Nice to meet you." He waved as he rode off with his donkey and cart.

On Sunday, Francis arranged the workbench as a desk, and, sitting on his barrel, he wrote to John. As he dated the letter September 12, 1638, he was surprised to see he had forgotten his own birthday on the fifth! He was now twenty-six years old.

The clothes were ready on Monday the thirteenth, and they were wonderful. And the boots—well, it would take time to get used to having leather to his knees. He wore them the next Sunday, and at The Dock he told Joseph, "I'm going to the bookshop tomorrow, and I hope to find some books to read that I can afford to buy. It's time I began my education."

"You'll find what you're looking for, I have no doubts," Joseph said in a tone similar to his barkeep manner.

Ever sensitive to others, Francis wondered if he had offended Joseph. It was a fleeting thought; he was too anxious about the visit to the bookshop because he didn't know what books to select and dreaded coming across as a bumpkin. At another time, Francis might have realized that, since he had moved to Ellington, all his conversations with Joseph, or at least most of them, had been about himself and his move, job, and education. That was not how it had been before, and possibly Joseph was wary of this change in Francis.

Chapter 5: Stvdent

Education is the kindling of a flame, not the filling of a vessel. —
Socrates

18 ~ 1638

When Francis entered the book and bindery shop, his first impression was of the odor—not unpleasant, just different. Possibly it was from the mixture of publisher's ink, binding glue, and seasoned leather. The windows in front provided the only light, except for a shaft from an open doorway at the back of the small room. Bookshelves covered the side walls, and Francis turned to look at the titles of the books on the nearest shelf by the door. They meant nothing to him, and in an instant, he became shy and uncomfortable.

At that moment a man came through the doorway at the back. The proprietor, Francis guessed. He looked to be in his forties, dressed conservatively in dark trousers, a jerkin, and a tailored white blouse. He greeted Francis, saying, "May I help you find something?"

The choice of words was so appropriate to Francis' purpose for being in the shop, yet he was intimidated and taken aback. Unexpectedly he blurted out honestly the real reason why he had come to the shop.

"I'm not sure you can help me, but I want to learn about history, geography, politics, and why people go to war. I'm eager to study—not to get a piece of parchment that says I'm educated but to understand the world I live in day to day."

He stopped abruptly as he had begun, and without being aware of it he bent his head toward his chest, an uncharacteristic stance for Francis, as if he were saying, "It's hopeless."

The proprietor studied the young man and surmised that he was not of the gentry even though he was wearing well-tailored clothing. No one of that class would admit to being ignorant of any subject. It was highly unlikely that he belonged to the proprietary class, since they were rarely interested in anything but their own milieu, and surely he was not a peasant, since they did not frequent bookstores and did not know what they did not know.

Francis slowly lifted his head and their eyes met with unguarded honesty—two strangers, one in desperate need and the other genuinely compassionate, coming together in a small bookshop. They were socially disparate, but they were bridging a gap between them, a gap that heroic persons from the past had been urging mankind to cross, a message most often unheeded. Stephen, the bookseller, observed this young man, and in that moment neither missed the importance of their meeting.

"I'm Stephen Smith, the proprietor of this shop, and I'd like to try to be of assistance to you."

"My name is Francis Brayton, and I wouldn't refuse your offer."

Stephen Smith was willing to share his knowledge, because at heart he was a teacher and he was witnessing an honest expression of the hopes and frustrations of Francis Brayton. From experience he knew how difficult it would be for Francis to achieve his goals on his own, and this had created a rare moment for both.

"Come with me, Francis." He turned and went through the doorway toward the rear of the shop. Francis followed. It was a larger room than the front of the shop and well-lighted by the windows on the back wall. There were shelves on the other three walls. In the center was a large table with chairs around it and a work space for Stephen's bookbinding and repairs. Stephen gestured toward one of the chairs, saying, "Have a seat. This is my bindery."

He retrieved a large book from a special shelf, carried it to the table, and placed it in front of Francis. He opened it, showing an exquisite map on the first two pages. "This is John Speed's *Prospect of the Most Famous Parts of the World.* He's an accomplished cartographer but also a tailor. At times he has been forced to take up his needle to help keep his home and hearth intact. Have a look through the pages. It's a book I treasure, and I'm pleased to share it with you. I have a book repair I must finish for a customer, so I'll return to my work."

Francis had never seen maps before, only a small globe. The large expanses of water impressed him. He could not understand how English ships could survive during the time it would take to get from one shore to another. That will be a question for Stephen, possibly.

After an hour, Stephen came beside him and, choosing a map of England, said, "Right here is where we are, do you see? It isn't named, of course, but there's London, not so far away. This is Wales, and over here is Calais across the channel. It belonged to England for a long time, but recently France repossessed it."

Francis was excited. "That's where my grandfather took a ferry to England! He was seventeen, and his name was Jean Brejon. His family, parents, and sisters all died of a pox epidemic, so he came to England. He had promised his mother, before she died, that he would go to England. My father, Thomas told me all about him. He changed his name to John Brayton."

Stephen was interested in this. "I can see we will learn from each other. I enjoyed tutoring my sons, preparing them for Oxford. I've missed teaching, now that they've finished their education. Mark is an attorney and Samuel is at Pembroke College, studying to be a physician. I have time in the afternoons, as you can see, and business is very slow these hours. If you could come here at two o'clock each day, I could help you get that education you desire—at least we can work on it together."

Francis was rendered speechless with emotion by this offer, so that Stephen finally said, "Well, think about it and let me know."

That alarmed Francis. He said quickly, "I don't need to think about it! I've hardly thought of anything else for years and years. I'll be here at two tomorrow and every day. Oh, yes—I should tell you that I work for Chester Holmes at his bakery, evenings and early mornings. If he has any special tasks for me to do, I'll let you know. I doubt it. He's been very understanding and helpful this past month. I didn't say before, but my father died not long ago. I took care of all the family business and left Hounslow at the end of August, coming straight to Ellington. It seems I made a good choice." He offered a wide smile.

Stephen also had childhood dreams and expectations which he had not yet shared with anyone except Elizabeth. He had wanted to teach and was not expecting resistance from his father, Clement Smith, a prosperous jeweler. Stephen was astonished when his father refused, saying he was not fit for academia. Instead, he bought a bookshop and set Stephen up as proprietor. Stephen felt frustrated and trapped, but he did take over the shop.

He had met Elizabeth Holden and they married. The books in his shop kept him from becoming bitter. He read and learned on his own, achieving an education his father had denied him. When his father died Stephen learned he had set up trust funds for Samuel and Mark to go to Oxford, and the old feelings of bitterness returned. Stephen's daughter, Mary Elizabeth, would inherit money, a dowry, after she married.

Mary was already twenty but had not found anyone to suit her. Stephen had allowed her to join her brothers' tutoring sessions. She was brighter than her suitors—a factor that had not helped her courting relationships. Elizabeth was not yet worrying, but time was passing, and spinsterhood was not a fate Stephen wanted for his beautiful daughter.

The next morning, Francis shared his bookshop experience with Chester, and also his plans to go there afternoons. Chester knew of Stephen Smith and had heard him praised for being helpful with his customers.

Chester said, "I know sweet Abigail will be very pleased to hear of this, and Catherine will be impressed." They both chuckled because Catherine was ten but believed herself to be twenty. Each member of the Holmes family was precious to Francis, since he had never experienced such a friendly family atmosphere. Abigail had urged him to have supper with them twice this month, and they had made him feel at home. He played with seven-month-old Henry, who even with his round angelic face had the look of Chester. Judith, eight, was creative, making something to play with out of the most unlikely items such as hollyhock blossoms as dolls. Juliet was five, and because of missing baby teeth she lisped as she told her topsy-turvy stories. Francis knew that if he listened patiently she would eventually make sense of it all. And adorable Catherine loved talking with him as if she were an adult. "Well, Francis, how was your day, and I hope all went well for you?" "Yes," he would answer, and "thank you for asking—so kind of you, young lady!"

Chester and Abigail were a picture of happy husband and wife, taking every opportunity to praise one another, and the children reflected this friendliness. Abigail had been sincerely sad for Francis when she learned he had just lost his beloved father. She didn't avoid the issue but asked questions about Thomas and encouraged the Brayton stories. She seemed to understand the issues involved in being a late child, saying, "How sad for you, not to have brothers and sisters as companions." Or, "Your mother must have been terribly frightened giving birth at age forty."

He decided that Abigail was very much like his father, and before him, Isobel—all seeing a good side to things. Chester was different from anyone he had ever met because he seemed capable of living in the present, of dealing with the moments at hand, and quite often doing it all with humor. He was thoughtful and knew each of his customer's foibles and adapted to them. Other people saw these traits in Chester, and Francis heard more than once, "Chester Holmes is a good, reliable person." High praise, Francis believed.

That afternoon he was at the bookshop precisely at two o'clock. It was September twenty-first, a beautiful day as well as the beginning of his education with a good teacher. Stephen came out to greet him. They went to the bindery, where Stephen invited Francis to take the chair where he had studied the day before.

"Well, Francis, tell me your thoughts about John Speed's maps, and your impressions from seeing the countries of the world."

Francis had not prepared for such a question and, could not remember anyone asking his opinion of anything, except when the wheat might be ripe enough to harvest. However, he had begun in honesty with Stephen and it had given him a very good result, so he cautiously answered Stephen's question.

"It astounds me to think that Englishmen are sailing all over those large areas of water, to places I cannot pronounce. I know England does trading all over the world, yet I'm not sure what it means to trade, especially where you don't speak the language. I have a friend, John Anthony, who left four years ago for Boston, and I've received several letters with his description of life there. One time it seems very normal, and then he mentions that a tribe of Indians had burned houses to the ground. I try to picture day-to-day living in such a place, but I know it is nothing that I could imagine."

Stephen said, "Before I respond to you, I know some Anthonys. Could it be Sir Anthony of Foxgrove—his son John?" Francis said it was. "He used to come into my shop while he was attending Weedon Academy," Stephen went on. "He was such a special lad. I guess I shouldn't be surprised that he emigrated to America—he had such an inquisitive nature."

"That would be John," Francis said.

"Well, back to our lesson. Can you think of any conditions that might be the same for people, no matter where they are in the world?"

Francis thought a moment and said, "I imagine everyone worries about bad weather, keeping safe in a storm, worrying about crops being destroyed by fires started by lightning. It seems to me people worry about themselves, what they own or don't own, of their families, about their health and staying alive, or whether they're under God's favor or not, trying to be good. I notice that some rarely speak of themselves, and they're looking out for others all the time. My father was like that. My mother was always thinking about herself, mostly how others had wronged her, even when there was no evidence of it. You know, I could never decide whether I had the choice to be like my father instead of my mother. I'm not one to pray, but I can tell you I fervently hoped I was like my father."

"Can you accept that maybe you weren't like either one, but possibly a bit of each of them?" Stephen paused to let Francis consider the proposition. "Let's think about how we began talking of John Speed's maps and are now thinking about how people view life. One of the duties of education is to discipline the mind, and train it to focus and explore and discover specific topics, then to integrate and relate the information with what is already known. Information can easily be taught, but helping students learn to ask useful questions, to question answers, to explore options, to seek further information: That is the real purpose of education."

Stephen paused and said, "It's now half-past three and I want to give you this paper. As you see, it has one question at the top: *What is the purpose of government?* In formulating an answer, I want to say, there is no one answer, no right or wrong answers either. This topic has been explored by some of the great intellects in history. It's a question we will think about off and on as we discuss different issues."

Stephen continued, "Use your experience, if it helps, to answer the question. Let's stop with that for today. I think it would be best to leave the paper here while you think about it until we meet tomorrow, and you can come fresh and put down your thoughts then."

Stephen could tell he had stirred his student's mind, so he stood. Francis did also, bringing the session to a close.

Francis left the shop and walked east on Market Street toward the Circle and The Dock. He was hungry, and he wanted to bring Joseph up-to-date. He took his usual place by the window, and as he glanced toward the Square, he had an inspiration. The next morning, he would go to the Square and look around at the government offices. He enjoyed his meal and time with Joseph before leaving to do his evening chores at the yard.

19 ~ 1638

The next day at mid-morning, he walked up Market Street, passing The Dock and entering the municipal building for his first visit. Inside was a wide corridor, which, he could see, had a door at the end of it opening into the town park. The town park separated the municipal building from the magistracy, which he would explore as well. To the right of the entrance was the constabulary. There was a uniformed constable at the desk, Francis approached and introduced himself.

"Hello, I'm Francis Brayton, and I'm a new resident of Ellington. I'm familiarizing myself with town services."

"Well, young man, I am a constable, and this is the constabulary of Ellington. We're the people who keep our town peaceful and orderly," he said with some pomp. "We also handle violations of town ordinances. We report to the mayor's office across the corridor."

Francis thanked him and said, "Is the fire brigade behind those doors?"

The constable said, "Yes, but no one's there. It's just equipment, since all our firemen are volunteers."

Francis thanked him again and left, crossing the corridor to the section on the left side, which according to the sign, housed the offices of the mayor, town services, and comptroller. He entered, and the first person he saw introduced himself as John Templeton.

John asked why Francis was visiting the city services building.

"I came to see government at work, John. I trust you are hard at work?"

"Of course!" he replied with a smile. "Here's my desk in the utilities section. People come here to pay their bills. I gather you haven't been here before. Let me take you around, except for Mayor Burson's office. We'll be careful to leave him in peace."

They entered a good-sized room that had tables and chairs. "This is the hearing room, and it has multiple functions, most often for Town Council meetings. Once a month, the mayor listens to complaints, and on Tuesdays he holds hearings about violations of the town codes. Besides receiving payments, I am responsible for the mayor's calendar, the post, and other clerking duties."

Francis chose to delay a visit to the office of the comptroller, which seemed self-explanatory. He thanked

John, who looked pleased to have shown Francis where he worked.

He crossed the town park to the magistracy building, identical in construction to the municipal building, and entered a similar central corridor. The right side was the magistrate's chambers and to the left was the registry. He entered the less intimidating room, the registry. It was large but included an enclosed office at the rear on the right side, with a fireplace on the left. In the open space there were three tables with chairs, and a desk positioned in front of the windows. It was quiet, with unoccupied benches along the corridor wall just inside the entrance. He asked one of the men at a table for information about the magistracy, and the man said, "It would be better for you to ask Martin Kennett—he's the registrar. He's in that office."

Francis tapped at the door.

A voice said, "Come in."

Inside Francis found a middle-aged man engulfed by a large desk piled high with papers. He was a small man, a bit hunched over, but as he looked up, Francis could see an air of authority in his glance.

"May I help you?"

Francis gave a slight bow, the custom in such circumstances, and introduced himself. "I am new to Ellington and I'm taking a tour. I hope I'm not disturbing you."

"I'm always busy, Francis. My name is Martin Kennett, and I'm the registrar. Please have a seat and tell me how I might help you?"

"I'm curious about local government, and I'm not sure how the magistracy and municipal services work together."

Kennett leaned back in his chair and said, "Well they don't work together, in actual fact. Let me explain briefly what the magistracy is. I answer to the magistrate, Judge Seymour Denison. We answer to the Crown's Judiciary, and our jurisdiction covers most of Middlesex, Ellington having been chosen as the district headquarters. The court is considered a lower court; we hear only civil cases and the judge's rulings are final. The registry is responsible for accepting petitions, which must be carefully reviewed before being submitted to the judge. All petitions are identified by number and by name and records are assiduously maintained."

Francis was thinking that Martin Kennett had delivered this orientation many times before. He acknowledged to him that the information had been useful, especially for someone from the countryside.

He added, "I'm very appreciative, and I thank you for your time, sir." Martin could not dismiss such a curious visitor without more information, so he asked, "What did you do in the countryside, Francis?"

"I was a tenant farmer working with my father until September. He died rather suddenly, and I settled my business there and moved to Ellington. I'm working at Chester Holmes' Bakery as his yardman. The hours suit me since I'm pursuing an education"—dare he say it?—"with Stephen Smith."

Francis left and sat in the town park thinking about *the purpose of government.* He organized his thoughts, and at the table that afternoon at the bookshop, he began writing his answer to the question, outlining his visits to the Square and interviews with government officials. Stephen read it and complimented him on his writing, then they turned to a discussion of government.

The session ended as it always would:

"So, will I see you tomorrow, Francis?"

"Yes, for certain, Stephen."

January 1639 was uncommonly cold from the beginning to the end of the month, with blustery winds buffeting Francis as he split wood and carried ashes to the pit. The warmth of the bindery with its fireplace was pleasant, though, and his studies were progressing satisfactorily.

Stephen had given serious consideration to his plan of study for Francis, which was difficult because he had no idea how many sessions he would have with him. They had established guidelines to keep them on course, and Stephen had a talent for simplifying complex ideas. Therefore, a world of ideas was unfolding for Francis, and his eagerness encouraged the teacher. Each day Francis came promptly, listened intently, and studied the material Stephen gave him for his evenings in the shed.

The new year continued as usual, but by springtime Francis yearned to be out of doors. He had been thinking about making a pathway for Tinker to more easily push his wheelbarrow across the yard to the shed. This would be a good time for that project. Chester approved the idea, and Francis went to the stone mason to get some gypsum. He wasn't sure that his plan would work, so he talked with Sudlow Frith, the mason, who said, "It just might do the job."

Francis began by cutting out the pathway and lifting the sod away. He separated the soil from the grass to use later. On either side of the pathway, he created a small trench to keep grass from creeping onto the path. He mixed ash with the gypsum and created a pasty sort of mix and spread it on the path, a batch at a time. He spread it even with a rake and let it set a few days.

When Tinker moved his wheel barrow across the path, as slick as skates on ice, he and Francis laughed gleefully. Tinker spread this bit of joy all around Ellington.

"That Francis Brayton is quite a fellow. He works at Holmes Bakery, and he fixed me a path to make my wheelbarrow deliveries easier. He said he did it just for me."

20 ~ 1639

As 1639 continued, Francis sometimes enjoyed summer evenings in Weedon Park before starting his studies in the shed. He sat on a bench, under a spreading elm tree, and watched the students romping about the Green. It was a rare treat for him to just sit and do nothing. There were strollers walking around the Circle, but he didn't know them, so he was left to enjoy the tranquility.

That June, he got a letter from John Anthony. John wrote:

I've been busy. I am building Susanna and me a house in Portsmouth and at the same time building a shop for my looms. One of the problems I encountered was crossing the river into Massachusetts for supplies. There is a ferry to Bristol, but it takes me out of the way from my preferred route to Boston, so I started my own ferry business. Many of our people don't have horses or wagons, so I also opened a stable, a livery, and a forge on both sides of the river so Portsmouth people could more easily travel to Boston for goods not available here. The ferry business is doing very well, and people are pleased with the services it provides.

Susanna and I were married in Boston last March 1638 by a magistrate, but we plan to have a proper wedding in Portsmouth with Roger Williams officiating, as soon as I finish our house. Susanna is staying with her mother, Martha Potter, in Boston until the Potter houses are completed here in Portsmouth. I have a batch of brothers-in-law. Martha lost her second husband a few months ago, and she plans to live with her children, one at a time, rather than living alone. It will work for that family; the Potters are loyal to one another. I better get back to work on our house. I miss Susanna, and I miss you, Francis. Come to America.

Fondly, John

John always ended his letters with "Come to America." Francis and Joseph chuckled over this, and whenever either of them became frustrated the other would say, "Go to America," and they would laugh, forgetting the frustration. Francis did continue to think about emigrating, but it was too soon. He was making progress with Stephen's lessons, but he needed more time, and he was exceedingly grateful that Stephen was still willing to teach him.

In truth, Stephen enjoyed his time with Francis, who made connections, discerned underlying issues, and always pushed himself to concentrate when thinking through difficult concepts. He let Francis know how delighted he was to have him as a student. Francis was always pleased to hear that Stephen himself enjoyed the teaching. It was uncomfortable to feel obligated to another person. Stephen, in his wisdom, promoted the relationship as mutually beneficial and, because of this generosity, Francis could swallow his pride and continue working as a yardman and sleeping in a shed.

Stephen introduced Francis to the world of heavy thinkers, men who had different perspectives and who made discoveries that resulted in benefits for all mankind. Once, when Francis was struggling, Stephen reminded him, "These are difficult matters, written by men who had years of education—Aristotle, Tacitus, Luther, Machiavelli, Galileo, Bacon, More—all have shared their genius and they have furthered man's understanding of life on Earth and beyond. I have merely given an introduction to the works of these important men, trying to give you general ideas, theories, events, and possibilities. The purpose is not to present academic studies—neither of us is prepared for that.

"From the beginning of our daily sessions, you have kept your mind open to understanding; in fact, you seem to want to be vulnerable to the stress that deep thinking can cause. You always have questions, Francis, and seldom do you assert answers. As I see the process of learning, I believe that questions open the mind, answers often close it."

"Thank you, Stephen. Sometimes I wonder how it was that I walked into your shop and was so fortunate to have been given such an opportunity. You have what I've heard people refer to as 'character.'"

"I'm not comfortable with expressions of gratitude, Francis. Just know that I understand you're grateful. As long as you work as hard as you do, we will continue."

It would be the last time they would allow gratitude to take time away from the daily lesson.

Francis had no complaints. He was learning as he intended, and he got by with earnings from the yard work. But one Saturday in September, he was feeling a need to stretch his legs and go away from the familiar routines of a day. Joseph, always attentive, asked, "Is there something on your mind, Francis?"

"No, but I do need a change of scenery. Do you have a Sunday when you don't work?"

"Yes, anytime I want," he replied. "Why do you ask?"

"How about tomorrow? Do you want to go to London with me?"

"London?" Joseph seemed surprised by Francis' suggestion, which was more spontaneous than usual for him. "You mean we would just go to London without plans?"

"Why do we need plans? Let's just do it!"

"What time do we leave? I'll be ready!"

At seven o'clock the next morning, the late September sun was on the horizon, and Joseph and Francis were walking on the Great West Road to London. Church bells chimed as they passed through hamlets, and at nine o'clock they stopped in Woburn at a tavern named The King's Curls for breakfast. They asked the wait man, "How did this place get such an unusual name?"

"Well," he said, "just so people who come here will ask that question. A few years back King Charles stopped unexpectedly with his retinue. The owner, Darby Cox, was proud to welcome the king to his humble Roaring Lion, which was the name then. The king and his group stayed the night, ate a good breakfast, and then left just as they had come without notice, but also without paying the bill. Since then they had ignored Darby's attempt to collect, so he changed the name of this establishment to The King's Curls. He welcomes the question you have just asked so that he can tell how he was stiffed by the king—him with his ridiculous curls."

Joseph offered, "King Charles is bringing back the old ways of the Crown, especially being sanctified by God to do as he wishes."

"Well, many of those have lost their heads, and doesn't God have more important matters to attend to? At least The King's Curls has been having its say," Francis added with a chuckle. History would also have its way with King Charles I, in due time.

Fortified and entertained, the two continued their jaunt and were soon crossing the Thames on the stone bridge to the central part of London. Francis stopped in the center to admire the sailing ships in the distance headed for the channel. Others were docked along the shores, probably being prepared for voyages to the Orient.

The next walk took them onto busy streets with coaches pulled by two or four horses. The streets were dotted with garbage and horse dung, so they were cautious. They found Westminster Abbey and many large buildings to admire. They went for lunch in a tavern and were shocked at the prices. They ate chowder and drank ale. From there, they found a park and settled on a bench to watch the people coming and going. They saw men dressed in finery, some with long curls like the king.

Francis was quiet, obviously lost in thought, and Joseph was quiet too. After a while Francis said, "I wonder if I am living as I ought to live. When I came to Ellington I was optimistic, but I'm still working part-time and sleeping in a place I wouldn't invite you to visit. At my age, I should be doing better."

"I have no advice, Francis. You're fortunate to have such a good opportunity to learn. Education, as you know, is your best chance for changing your family status. You'll see. It'll come out right for you. I'm certain of it."

They left London and enjoyed the walk in the cool evening. They returned to Ellington, revived from their jaunt. "I hope you enjoyed this respite as much as I did, Joseph."

"I did, and we both learned a lesson: Don't live in London."

"I agree, but we could always 'go to America.'" They laughed together.

The holiday season began as others had with a dinner at the Holmes'. Chester gave him several fruitcakes to share with his friends and acquaintances, and Abigail prepared a delicious roast beef dinner. Sweet Abigail showered her sympathies and caring nature onto Francis, "alone in the world." She was pleased that Thomas Clagget, the new apprentice at the bakery, was doing so well, allowing Chester more time with their family. He had begun August sixteenth and, very soon after that, Abigail noticed the difference in Chester, who was more relaxed.

The girls were about to leave childhood behind, especially Catherine. "Miss Catherine" was no longer acting as if she were twenty; instead she was a self-conscious eleven-year-old girl. Judith and Juliet were companions one moment and competitors the next. Henry delighted everyone while dictating life on his own terms.

Francis and Joseph sat together Christmas Eve by the fireplace at The Dock, eating a sumptuous meal prepared by James Byers, the same person who prepared the many shepherd's pies for Francis. Francis gifted James and Joseph with Chester's fruitcakes. After drinking and eating their fill together, the only time they did so during the year, they talked of this and that. They did not gossip, since Joseph had learned early on that what he heard in the bar could be, but probably was not, true. He kept it all to himself.

Francis thought it was interesting that he and Joseph enjoyed being together, yet they were so different. Joseph was content to do the same tasks day after day, and to stay at The Dock year after year. Francis, on the other hand, had a lot of John Anthony in him, and John was a link between the two of them.

Francis had no idea how the Smith family celebrated the holidays. He hadn't met any of them. The relationship between himself and Stephen remained strictly student and teacher. Francis understood this and thought of it only during holidays, which were focused on the family. Francis worked making the week go quickly by, stockpiling the kindling and firewood, giving the shed a good cleaning, and walking Weedon Circle. One place he avoided was the Square, which was closed, dark, and quiet this final week of the year. He did not want to be where it was dark and quiet.

Francis was reining in his desire to be somewhere else, doing something different, and continued to train his brain just as he had trained his muscles to do a man's work when he was still a boy. There were moments of yearning he attributed to his desire to have a family of his own.

21 ~ 1640

This new year of 1640 was a leap year. The extra day, February twenty-ninth, was not to be wasted, but to be celebrated. The ordinary folk put aside tasks and spent this special day cavorting in the streets—singing, dancing, and laughing at nothing at all except the joy of having such a day to play. Francis thought differently. He would have preferred this to be like any other Wednesday afternoon in Stephen Smith's bindery room.

He sat on the workbench in the shed and read a book provided by Stephen, struggling to understand the meaning of the writings of Cicero. Page by page he wrote his understandings. He ate bakery breads and sweets with sausage bits, but there was nothing to slake his thirst. He sucked on some hard candy, and as he lay ready to sleep he mumbled, "Cicero was very wealthy and yet he spent hours on scholarship. I doubt I will live long enough to grasp the meaning of a fraction of it. Maybe the mere effort of trying is worth something."

These days Chester had less time for breakfast with Francis, since Thomas stood by waiting to use the table to knead for the second bake. Most of the time with Chester was focused on his family, and Francis was always eager to know every tidbit. Francis did the wood-splitting in the mornings and he filled the bins then as well. On Fridays or Saturdays, Tinker came by just before the twelve o'clock Weedon chimes rang out over the town. He talked as he buzzed along with his wheelbarrow doing his tasks, and Francis listened to tales of people's medical woes and the latest decrees from the mayor's office. Tinker was the newspaper that Francis need not spend his coins to buy.

Francis went to The Dock either before his session with Stephen or just after. Every evening he studied by candlelight, sitting on his barrel by the workbench. He had the fireplace to tend during the cold season, requiring more chopping of wood and more cleaning. He spent a modicum of time on himself—only what was necessary for a decent appearance and good health.

In June he received a letter from John Anthony. He wrote:

> Susanna is expecting a child. We are delighted and Martha, Susanna's mother, is on schedule to be with her during the birth and for six weeks after. Martha has thirteen children, most of them married, so she keeps track of when she should be where, to keep peace in the Potter family. All of the Potters are fortunate that Martha loves children, a good thing for her since she has a rather large portion of Portsmouth's grandchildren. If I haven't mentioned it before, Francis, Portsmouth is a community of families. Those of us living here now will always be known as the first generation since some children are now nearing an age to be marrying their neighbors, so to speak. So far, we are a like-minded community, promoting tolerance, but we do expect residents to serve the community, since there is much to be done.
>
> We have codes and regulations that our officials attempt to enforce, but we will soon need more than our town meetings to keep tabs on all the community requirements. We are loath to do away with the grassroots governing system we have enjoyed. It would not be viable without the written Compact to guide us. John Clarke is a genius, now

> living in Newport and working to get a charter to give our own area status as a colony. It is important to have the might of the English behind us for protection with all our shorelines, especially in Newport.
>
> Enough of the Anthonys and Portsmouth. I trust you are studying and working long days as you always have. We need you here, so I'll say it once more, 'Come to America.'

Life in England in 1640 was precarious. There was the threat of war, and King Charles was putting pressure on Parliament to supply the funds he needed to enforce others to bow to his will. That was not going well for him, and the people who could were going on with life as they needed to do.

Stephen was presenting materials that challenged Francis but also were not beyond his abilities. That skill was what made Stephen a master teacher. In late September, Stephen did a recap of the studies the two of them had undertaken, and it was uplifting to see the progress they had realized in just two years. It had motivated and invigorated them to continue just as they had begun.

They were teacher and student, friendly with one another, but not friends. Francis knew of his sons Samuel and Mark because Stephen had from time to time spoken of his tutoring them for their Oxford exams. He had mentioned his wife Elizabeth too, and how she worried over their daughter Mary, who had rebuffed so many suitors. But that was all he knew about the Smith family after two years of almost daily meetings. It was wise of Stephen, since he did not want to establish a pattern of taking time from their studies by retelling family or social events.

Joseph, oddly enough, was like Stephen in this regard. He also was mum on his background and what he did or who he knew beyond the walls of The Dock. He listened like a sponge taking on water, soaking it up during his work at the bar. Joseph also wondered about Francis, and where he fit in English society. For a young man, Francis seemed rather dull to Joseph. The truth was, Francis did not miss what he never had experienced in the first place.

The beautiful weather of September always enticed Francis to walk, and it was no different this year. He decided he would walk to Limon on Sunday and visit his sister, Gwen, and her husband John. He decided to arrive at one o'clock on the twenty-third, stay a couple of hours, then return to Ellington. So he had planned. When Gwen opened the door to him, however, he could see a group of people inside.

"I should have sent a message, Gwen. I see you're busy—I'll come again, maybe next week?"

"Nonsense, Francis. Come in, these are our friends in the separatist group. I think I mentioned that John and I met at one of their meetings." She ushered Francis into the room, where John had already stood to greet him.

"Well, my goodness, Francis, how nice to see you. Everyone, this is Gwen's younger brother, Francis Brayton, who lives in Ellington." Gwen found a seat for Francis.

"We're almost finished with our time together. I'm sure they'll welcome you as Gwen and I do."

The group were all saying yes, of course, that will be fine and such, until Francis was seated in the chair provided by Gwen.

"Francis," John continued, "we don't have a leader, but together we select what book of the Bible we will study. We're just beginning Paul's letter to the Romans. We never rush our study, instead we seek a good understanding. We've progressed to Chapter 1, verse 16, so we will continue. We always start each Sunday at noon and break away at two o'clock to return to our families."

"Let me reread the verse. 'For I am not ashamed of the gospel, because it is God's power for salvation to everyone who believes, first the Jew and, also the Greek.' Would anybody like to comment?"

It was quiet, possibly because Francis was a stranger among them.

A man spoke up. "God's word is written for the Jew and the Gentile." Another man asked, "Why, William, do you think Paul has written this to the Christians in Rome?"

William hesitated a moment then said, "God wants his word to be heard and understood by all people, so they will feel God's power to give salvation to all who believe. I didn't really understand that power until I began to read his word myself. Jesus was talking to everyone, encouraging them to listen to God's promise of salvation."

Betty said, "Do you think Paul mentions the Jew and the Gentile for a reason, instead of just saying, 'everybody, listen to my word'?"

John said, "That's a good question because Paul had some knowledge that the newly converted Christians in Rome were reluctant to reach out to the Jews and Gentiles."

A man named Judson was quick to say, "Yes, Paul even said 'first the Jew,' reminding them that the Word had been given first to the Jews by Jesus."

Betty said, "Maybe so, but they didn't accept what they heard. In fact, they crucified Jesus."

"Maybe," William said, "that's why Paul said, 'I am not ashamed of God's words.' He was a Jew, or part Jew himself. Paul was, or is, more interested that everyone hears and believes so God's power of salvation will be seen within them."

John said, "Even though the Jew and Gentile are mentioned here as significant, do you think it is also as William has said, that it includes everyone who believes?"

There was a chorus of yeses to be heard. William added, "I think this is a good stopping point. We will now repeat our prayer as always before we depart."

Together they prayed aloud:

Heavenly Father of our Lord and Savior Jesus Christ, we humbly thank you for your Holy Word and for the privilege of our gathering together to gain a deeper understanding.

Be with us until we meet again, and O Lord, keep our hearts and minds in your word in this week before us. In Jesus' name we pray. Amen.

The men and women said their goodbyes and expressed their pleasure to have met Gwen's brother. There were no lingering goodbyes, probably the custom for this group since off and on they have had to meet secretly, depending on the inclination and the power of the ruling government.

Gwen asked Francis if she could offer him some hot cider and he gladly accepted. John had shown Francis samples from his weaving business, they sat together supping and eating, asking and answering each other's questions. Neither of them had recently heard from Charles.

"I hope to visit him yet this year, before the weather gets nasty," Francis said.

"So, you haven't gone to America, Francis?"

"No, I have been studying with a tutor, and for two years I have enjoyed my hours with Stephen Smith. He's the proprietor of Ellington's bookshop and has graciously given his time for me. He's still willing, which he assures me is to his benefit, but how he can say that I do not know."

"I'm sure he feels that way. What did you think of our meeting?"

"I'd welcome the opportunity to study the Bible like your group is doing. It's difficult to read without guidance."

John said, "I believe it is, but not so hard with the power of God's understanding in your heart. That's how we believe, and many others have come to believe that every individual can seek God's saving grace and live daily by and in His word. The Puritans have others believing this too, even though they use different names to describe their faith. Many of that group have gone to America to escape persecution. We've escaped it here because we meet privately and boast to no one, as Paul says."

Francis had listened carefully and responded with a reticence that came from his nature, or from his tendency to speak only when he was certain of the subject. "It seems that the faith of such people is testimony to something worthy. I haven't come to such an understanding for myself, I admit. There seems to be a need inside, a yearning for understanding about what purpose there is for my life and for the living of it. I do know, I'm going to need to learn a lot more before I understand it, if ever I will."

Chapter 6: Clerk

Speak up for those who cannot speak for themselves. Speak up and judge fairly; defend the rights of others. — Proverbs 31:8-9

22 ~ 1640

Circumstances swerved in a different direction beginning October twenty-ninth, when Elizabeth and Mary Smith came to the bookshop that Monday afternoon. Elizabeth came into the bindery, surprising both Francis and Stephen. Francis stood as Elizabeth said, "Hello, don't let us interrupt you. We'll be here only a moment. Stephen, may I speak with you?"

They went into the shop, and Mary came to the table and stood opposite Francis, who was not sure what to do. Mary, not unlike her mother, spoke first. "Hello. So you're Francis Brayton."

It seemed to Francis a strange way to address him, but he couldn't have known that she had seen him once before walking on Weedon Circle. She was with her friend, Lydia

Lytle, and Mary had said to her, "I wonder who he is—isn't he handsome? He's quite a walker. See how he strides!"

Lydia answered, "I've not seen him before, but I can see he has your eye."

She now looked at him until he blushed, and she asked, "What are you studying?" She sat at the table, and he followed her lead and sat as well.

"I'm reading an essay by Francis Bacon—'Of Nature and Men.' Your father and I have been studying that theme."

"Hmm ..." She almost said something but instead got up and walked to the windows. Just as suddenly she came back to the table and inspected Stephen's binding work, glancing at Francis and meeting his eyes. Before she could comment, Elizabeth called to her "Come along, Mary. We must be going."

Mary made a slight wave of her hand to Francis and said, "I'm happy to finally meet you Francis." She smiled as she turned to leave the bindery. He was nonplussed. He had never seen a woman like her.

He walked over and looked through the door into the shop..

Mary was saying goodbye to her father, and he was reminded of the day at Foxgrove when he had witnessed John and Sir Anthony meeting one another. This was another special filial relationship. He returned to his chair and tried to focus on Francis Bacon. Once the women had left, Stephen returned.

"I hope that hasn't disturbed your concentration," he said.

What could he say? He wanted to say, "Yes, I am disturbed—I am distracted by your beautiful daughter! In fact, I may never feel myself again." Instead, he muttered, "No, not at all."

Stephen made no comment and returned to his binding work.

The truth was, Francis had become quite distracted. Mary had reached some place deep inside him that he had not known existed until he saw her. She didn't have a prettiness about her or any artifice; she displayed no pouting mouth or fluttering eyelashes. Nor was there any predominant feature that took away from the whole of her face, not even her hair, which was pulled to the back, emphasizing the symmetry of her beauty. Her complexion was neither milky nor rosy—instead it had the appearance of good health. Her eyes—well, how could he forget that she had peered so steadily into his own?

He had taken a measure of her that did not compare to any woman he knew in his life. He was yearning, and he did not like it. He hadn't allowed any such indulgence to overtake his reasonable approach to his daily routine. Now he was walking, thinking of Mary, and going beyond his destination. He was studying Francis Bacon, and the print on the page became two large brown eyes staring at him. He was lying in bed, ready to sleep, and he yearned to be near her. He couldn't keep his mind from wandering back to that brief time with Mary.

A week later, Mary was back in the shop, this time with her friend Lydia who was seeking a book of poetry. Stephen went to help Lydia, and Mary came into the bindery. Francis broke into a brilliant smile, and Mary thought, "A man with two faces."

She said, "Hello, Francis. How are the ancient studies going for you?"

"It goes well, thanks to your patient father."

Stephen and Lydia came into the bindery much too soon to suit Mary and Francis. Mary said, "Lydia, I'd like you to meet Francis Brayton."

He stood. Lydia tilted her head to the side as if she was scrutinizing Francis and said, "I'm happy to meet you, Francis." She smiled, as if he had passed her inspection.

"The pleasure is mine," Francis said.

"You two better get on your way," Stephen said. "Francis has a lesson to complete."

Stephen made no comment once they'd left, but Francis was convinced that Mary wanted to see him. The visit had fanned the flames he had tried desperately to smother.

On November the fifteenth, he decided to vary his routine and go to the bookshop at one o'clock to do some research. When he approached the shop, Mary was coming from the opposite direction and he waited for her. It was a surprise meeting, and they hesitated, then both started speaking at once, causing them to laugh.

Mary explained, "I took too long browsing, and I'm meeting mother here, at the bookshop."

Francis, delighted to be standing next to his adorable Mary, said, "I'm glad you're here, Mary."

The tone of his voice was unmistakable, and their defenses were down. "And I am glad to be here, Francis."

They looked at each another, content for the moment, unable to look away, but were startled when Elizabeth came to the door and said, "Ah, you've finally arrived. We must be on our way."

She and Stephen had observed the meeting from inside the shop and could see the attraction Mary and Francis had for each other. Elizabeth said, "I need to speak to Mary." Stephen agreed.

They left, and Francis went into the shop. Stephen was in the bindery and said to Francis, "You're early today. Is there a problem?"

"No, no problem. I wanted to finish my reading of Martin Luther. I worry about getting behind."

"You shouldn't worry, Francis," Stephen said, with a tenseness not usually in his voice. "We can proceed when you're ready."

Elizabeth, however, was the harbinger of events about to unfold in the lives of Francis and Mary.

The mother and father of this beloved daughter had become alarmed by the scene they had witnessed outside the bookshop between their daughter and the son of a tenant farmer.

Elizabeth said to Stephen later in their home, "This will not do, Stephen."

"No, it's gotten out of hand, I can see that. Mary should understand without being told that Francis is not a probable suitor, not a suitable match for her future husband."

"And to be sure she *does* understand," Elizabeth said, "I will talk with her."

"Let's discuss the best approach. We both know how willful Mary is when she gets an idea in her head, and how uncooperative she had been with suitors."

"Yes, you're right, we need to open her eyes to what future she might have with Francis. He has hardly any income, and he will not be able to overcome his humble beginnings or the disparity between the two of them."

Elizabeth considered the problem for several days, then went to Mary's room. "I need to speak with you, dear," she said. "It's concerning Francis Brayton. You're aware, are you not, that these studies are very precious to him? He did not have the same advantages of education as you or your brothers have had. Do you remember how adamant you were to be included in the tutoring sessions with Mark and Samuel? Your father has generously offered to tutor Francis because he so very much wants to learn." She went closer to her daughter and continued. "Without your father's help, he would not be studying as he is now. It would be very unfair of you to interfere with this opportunity. Your father and I are asking you to stop visiting the bookshop. Please don't risk this one chance Francis has, and we ask you to do the right thing for his sake. Will you do that Mary?"

Mary had been feeling an array of emotions as her mother spoke, beginning with shock going on to defensiveness, then panic, and finally a deep-seated feeling of sadness. She had nothing to say to her mother that would not sound frivolous or even false. Barely able to speak, she finally said, "Yes, Mother, you're right. I will not go to the shop any longer."

Elizabeth was relieved, but later when she heard muffled sobs coming from Mary's room, she felt a pang in her heart, conflicted by what she knew to be best for Mary and her daughter's attraction to a handsome man.

Francis was anticipating seeing Mary again, but the days became weeks, until he finally approached Stephen. "Is Mary all right? She hasn't been here for some time."

"Yes," he answered. "She's fine. She's busy helping Lydia prepare for her wedding, and they're about to set a date. Lydia is marrying Gavin Longway. An instructor at the Academy."

Francis was certain that Stephen and Elizabeth were intentionally influencing Mary to stay away from the shop. He had no defense except that he wanted to get to know Mary. He felt humiliated, and knew he had no disgrace to overcome or a failing in character, yet he had nothing to recommend himself as a suitor. He had no steady income and was still sleeping in a shed. Without encouragement from Stephen, how could he assert himself?

It was hopeless.

23 ~ 1640

It was December 1640 when Stephen asked Francis to go to the Square and visit the comptroller's office for tax information he needed. Francis was happy to stretch his legs, and while at the Square he might visit the judge's chambers at the magistracy.

He got the information in the municipal building and saw John Templeton also, whose job at the utilities office was close to the comptroller. After a brief chat, Francis went to the magistracy. Once in the corridor, he saw a posting on a board outside the registry that read "Opening for a Records Custodian—Inquire Within." He was pleased by the prospect, so he entered the registry office.

He asked the only man there, "Where do I inquire about the position in the registry?"

He glanced at Francis impatiently. "Go talk to Martin Kennett. His office is there, on the right."

Francis remembered his visit with Kennett earlier, and he knocked on the door. "Come in," Kennett said, and when he saw who it was added, "Well, Francis Brayton. Are you doing more investigating?"

Francis smiled. "I'm inquiring about the Records Custodian position."

Kennett waved him to a seat. "Are you inquiring for yourself?"

"Yes, Mr. Kennett, I am."

"Please call me Kennett. In the magistracy, we refer to one another by surnames, except the judge, of course. About the job: It's a new position that we're establishing to offer some relief to the clerks who process petitions. We have difficulty now tracking the petitions as they progress from the registry to the judge's chambers. It has become quite time-consuming. We need someone who can maintain a record of the petitions in our registry."

He leaned forward in his chair and continued. "The judge is concerned because of the time. As a lower court, it's our duty to resolve these civil matters as soon as possible for the welfare of the community. The clerks who work in the registry have the responsibility to review petitions of relief to be sure it's a matter for our jurisdiction and then to determine if it's appropriate for the judge to order remedial action. It does not take full knowledge of the law but requires an ability to sort out the issues of the petition and a dedication to serve the individual and the community.

"Those are demanding requirements, and now our clerks spend an inordinate amount of time just looking for a petition in the magistracy. We want somebody to remedy that problem, and he would need organizational skills."

Francis was apprehensive about the question he anticipated, and it did come. "What experience have you had with record-keeping, Francis?"

Hoping he appeared calmer than he was feeling, Francis said, "I've always considered details to be very important, since careless mistakes can cause delays and unnecessary work and expense. I've been studying with Stephen Smith at his bookshop over the last two years, and he has taught me the importance of investigation, analysis, and discernment in a variety of disciplines. I'm eager to put those methods to good use. One aspect of the service here in the magistracy that I remember you telling me of when I was here before is the need for sensitivity toward petitioners. I believe I have such a sensitivity."

"How is that?" Kennett interjected. "Can you explain?"

"I'm not familiar with the intricacies of our system of justice, but I have seen what happens if it isn't serving its purpose. A person who takes the risk of coming to court seeking help should be given serious consideration. Besides showing his neighbors how justice works in his town, he might also be showing how it fails to serve as it's intended. It's important that the system serves rightly."

Kennett caught a tone of enthusiasm, even a bit of desperation, but even more importantly he noted intelligence. Francis was also responding without having prepared for the question and Kennett felt confident to ask, "Do you have two persons who would vouch for you? Judge Denison would be interviewing, and he requires two written recommendations."

Francis answered thoughtfully, "There is Stephen Smith for one, and I remember that Edward Childs, overseer of Fulham estate, offered me a position two years ago. I had other plans, but he offered to write a recommendation for me if I ever needed one. I think he understood how difficult it would be for me as a tenant farmer to leave farming."

"What were these plans?" Kennett's tone was not intimidating but did show a keen interest in a young man so earnest in his quest to leave the tradition of the family.

"I want to continue learning, to be challenged mentally, not just physically. I'm grateful to Stephen Smith for enlarging my world. The first day I met him, he showed me a copy of John Speed's atlas. Imagine seeing maps for the first time in your life, and a world that is so vast, then to learn that the maps were made by a cartographer who also worked as a tailor. That was a moment I shall never forget."

Kennett stood and said, "Very well, Brayton. Have those written recommendations sent to me at the registry. Judge Denison and I will review them along with other applications. If the judge wants to interview you, we'll let you know. Should I contact you at the bookshop?"

"Yes, please. I appreciate your considering my interest and application."

Francis had taken longer on his errand for Stephen than he should, but Stephen was enthusiastic about what he heard from Francis when he returned.

"I know Martin Kennett by reputation," he said. "He's been in the registry for years. Judge Denison is revered in Ellington. As an attorney, he could go to a higher court—everyone knows that—but he chooses to stay here in Ellington. I've heard that he believes the law is better served by the lower courts. I'll be pleased to write you a recommendation. This sounds like a perfect job for you, Francis."

"Thank you!" Francis cried. "If you don't mind, tomorrow I'll go to Hounslow to see Edward Childs, who offered to make a recommendation when I left the tenancy."

"He would be an excellent person to speak for you. You'll get this job. I just know you will."

"If I do, it'll be your doing. I've learned so much from you. In fact, I believe it would have taken me eight years at Weedon Academy to learn what I've learned from you."

"You're more intelligent than you could know, since you haven't been in competition with other students these two years. It's been a pleasure to teach you. But go on to Hounslow and get Child's letter or we will have been wasting our breath here with our congratulatory talk."

Francis arrived at the overseer's office early. Childs was obviously pleased to see him. After catching up with what Francis had been doing since he left Hounslow, he reminded Francis, "I had hoped you would join our staff, so I'll gladly write to Judge Denison. It sounds like the place for you. I'll get it done right away. We don't want another chap taking the job from you."

As he walked back to Ellington, he hardly thought of his years in Hounslow, or of Clive Steadman, Farley Lane, and of course, his parents, Thomas and Martha. Instead he was thinking that he needed to move from the shed to a boarding house. He thought about leaving Chester and how he would miss his family, and even Tinker. He allowed himself to think of the Square and how he had yearned to work in such a place, and as he glanced up and saw Weedon Tower, he thought, "It is good to be back in Ellington, back to my duties and my studies."

He received a notice from Kennett that Judge Denison would like him to come to his chambers for an interview on Thursday, December twentieth. It asked for confirmation as well. Francis did confirm the date and arrived on the twentieth. The judge greeted him (Kennett was there as well), and once they were all seated, the judge spoke.

"I'm happy to meet you, Brayton. Kennett has praised you, so let's see what you have to say for yourself. Why should we consider you for a position in the magistracy?"

"I have attended to what was expected of me with diligence and dedication," Francis began, "whether I was working with my father on the tenant farm in Hounslow or helping Chester Holmes at the bakery. When I was sixteen, I began to pay off the debt the Braytons owed to the Fulham estate. I provided produce to the estate emporium by planting garden plots that were available in the area. I took on other ways to supply the emporium and to reduce the debt. It took me seven years, but it was a good feeling to have paid our debts."

The judge listened intently, impressed with this young man's demeanor of confidence and enthusiasm.

Francis continued: "I knew at a young age that I wanted to leave farming. I was fortunate that Stephen Smith agreed to tutor me, and he has taught me how to think through situations using assessment and alternative solutions to solve problems. He has exposed me to many writings about justice, beginning with Plato and Aristotle. I've had practical experience with the importance of justice."

At that the judge interrupted and asked, "How is that?"

"A system of justice is a way for the community to test the response to the concerns of its residents," Francis explained. "Often there are larger issues in small disputes, like a man's frustration or personal pride. I think we are fortunate that England has developed a system that offers an avenue of redress that is civil. When a man comes to court to seek a remedy to a problem, he is representing the community, and when it's handled properly, we in the community witness that; when it's improperly handled, we see that as well. I have seen people discouraged by delays in processing their petitions, which I've learned about from conversations I heard in town."

Once he stopped, Francis saw the judge look at Kennett with his eyebrows raised.

He turned to Francis. "That's very interesting and certainly unique," he said. "Kennett has told me of your background, and I've received the letters of Edward Childs and Stephen Smith. I have heard nothing that refutes their assessments, therefore I support your application going forward. I thank you for your interest in our magistracy."

He rose and said to Kennett, "In my opinion, Kennett, I think we should put this young man to work."

Walking back to the registry, Kennett said, "Well done, Francis!"

Once they were in his office, Kennett made the offer official. The pay would be ten shillings a month, paid at the end of the month. The hours were eight thirty to five Monday through Friday, but only until one o'clock on Saturdays.

"All the magistracy offices will be closed from the twenty-fourth of December until the second of January. I think it would be best to have you begin on the second of January. That will give you time to settle other matters that may need attending to as well."

"That suits me fine. I'll see you then at eight thirty. Thank you, Kennett, for this wonderful opportunity."

"No need to thank me, Brayton. Have a good holiday."

24 ~ 1640

Francis went immediately to Grace Towson's boarding house on the corner of Market Street and Ellington Road. Grace Towson had been a widow for several years, and Joseph had said, "It's the best boarding house in Ellington." Francis was happy to find her available that afternoon, since he was determined to move before Saturday. She was very businesslike and asked many questions about Francis, reminiscent of John Anthony. She had many regulations she expected to be honored.

"What is your monthly rate for room and board?"

"I charge two shillings a month and require the first month in advance. Do you have references?"

"I was just hired at the magistracy, and I gave them written recommendations from Stephen Smith and Edward Childs, the overseer of the Fulham estate. I was told that both were very favorable regarding my character. If need be, I could request them again."

"I'm a pretty good judge of character myself, so we'll leave it at that. Come, I'll show you the room."

It was satisfactory and featured a small table that could be used as a desk. "Fine, Mrs. Towson. It's good."

He went to the bookshop to share his good news with Stephen.

"I say, Francis, that is splendid. I can imagine you have many arrangements to keep you busy in the next two weeks."

"Yes, I want to have plenty of wood ready for Chester's ovens. I'm moving to Towson's in a day or so. Stephen, I'm going to miss our sessions." Suddenly the drastic change in his daily routines came upon him in a rush. He would, he knew, miss Stephen terribly.

"I as well, but this is a good result, don't you think, Francis?"

"Yes, of course, and I'll be working on the Square, at the magistracy. And Stephen ..."

Stephen broke in, saying, "No need, Francis. I've been doing what I believe I was meant to do. Please drop by whenever you can."

"I shall. For certain."

He went to The Dock, where Joseph exclaimed, "Didn't I tell you this would happen? You'll be close by too, so I'll keep Byers on alert!"

The next morning, he told Chester, who did not hesitate to even take a breath before congratulating him. "And Miss Catherine will be so pleased!" They laughed together out of a fondness they both felt for this young lady. Each member of the Holmes family was like the family he would want for himself.

"You are not going far, so we'll see you from time to time."

"Indeed. I have a room at Grace Towson's house, so I'll be moving in a day or so. I'll also leave you a good stock of wood, and the shed will be clean."

Chester got up, went into the shop, and came back with the coins he owed for the month's work.

"This has been a good arrangement, and that's enough said on the matter, except that you know the Holmes family wishes you well, Francis."

The rest of the day was busy as Francis shopped for gifts. He went to the stationer and bought a journal for himself, and for Stephen he purchased a wooden inkstand with blotter and inkwell he had been eyeing. He stopped by the shop to give it to Stephen, since he wasn't sure if he would be open on the twenty-fourth.

He went to Greenly's on Friday and bought toys and games for the Holmes children. He bought lavender scent for Abigail. He picked a wool scarf for Tinker and leather gloves for Chester. He got a manicure tool kit for Joseph and hoped it was the right thing to do. Francis did not like that he was unsure of himself in his relationships with others. He preferred being given tasks or a challenge and then left alone to do it. But now that wasn't what mattered the most in his life. Relationships were more satisfying, and he had been learning that from Chester and Stephen—well, even with Tinker—and from Mary, the person he felt most deeply for, but that relationship had not gone as he wished.

He moved to Towson's the next day and rearranged the furniture slightly. He placed the small table next to the window to take full advantage of the light and set his ink and quills on top. On the spur of the moment, he started a letter to John. In a while, he left for the bakery, wanting to be there when Tinker came. He chopped and split wood while he waited. The shed was already clean and orderly. When Francis gave Tinker his gift, he was so surprised and grateful that he could hardly wait to tell others.

It was quiet at The Dock. Francis supposed people were busy with Christmas preparations. He told Joseph he would be at The Dock on the twenty-fourth if that would suit him.

"Yes, we must not disappoint Byers. He's already begun cooking our usual feast."

"I'm going to Isley tomorrow to see my brother and his family. I sent a message last week, and they're expecting me. I learned my lesson about dropping by unannounced with John and Gwen."

"No more prayer meetings, eh, Francis?"

Charles and Jane were very welcoming, and they beamed as they introduced their grandchild, Tommy, who was toddling around, excited with a visitor to impress. George had married, and he and his wife Belinda were living with Charles and Jane. It appeared that all were satisfactorily managing the arrangement. Francis noted that Charles was aging, but that could be expected of one approaching age fifty. He told his brother about his new position in the magistracy.

"That's wonderful, Francis!" he said "Our father would have been so proud to hear such news."

Charles was interested in knowing about the work Francis would be doing. The conversation went along between that and other family news. Henry had moved up at the bank and was engaged to marry Felicity Morrow. Charles was still at the foundry and was not in the best of health because of the strain of the work. Francis told them of his visit with Gwen and John and the separatists' meeting.

"I don't get the fuss about the Church. We attend our church here, and for us it's a comforting ending to a week. Jane is one of the church's willing volunteers, but not like our mother."

"No, I suppose not," Francis said.

Monday the twenty-fourth, he finished his letter to John and told him he would be eager to hear news of the baby. He did not share the disappointment of his relationship with Mary.

On the twenty-fourth, he thought of the book he was going to buy for Catherine Holmes at Stephen's shop. He hurried to the shop, and luckily Stephen had kept it open for the last-minute shoppers. Stephen suggested a book of Shakespeare's sonnets. He left the shop with a "Merry Christmas" wish for the Smith family.

He delivered the gifts to the Holmes family, and Catherine was pleased with her sonnets but teary about Francis leaving the yard work. "I want to say don't go," she said, "but that's not fair. I'm pleased for you, Francis."

"Thank you, Catherine." He was thinking how pretty she was at thirteen. Judith had learned to crochet and had made him a scarf.

"I will always treasure this, Judith."

The family gave him a book of essays. It was a brief but cheery time together, and Abigail reminded him of his invitation to dinner on Wednesday. "Come at five. We're looking forward to it."

"Me too, Abigail."

His evening with Joseph was relaxing and good fun. They seemed to find conversation to keep them cheerful. Francis wished that John Anthony was there with them.

The dinner with the Holmes, always delightful, was nevertheless mixed with melancholia for Francis. Mary belonged there with him in this lovely family setting.

The rest of 1640 was spent preparing for his new life in the magistracy. He spent some time with the other "roomers" at Towson's. The four men were instructors at the Weedon Academy. Francis listened to them and became somewhat disillusioned as they denigrated the students.

How could they be at cross-purposes with their life's work? he wondered. The Weedon Academy could benefit from a few Stephen Smiths on their faculty.

On New Year's Eve he was alone in his room. This was the busiest night of the year for Joseph, and Francis had no other reason to go to The Dock. He sat at his desk reading from his book of essays on ethics, trying to get into the issues of the good life but thinking more of what it will be like to work in an office for the first time in his twenty-eight years.

25 ~ 1641

Francis entered the registry a few minutes before eight thirty and saw a group of men standing near the blazing fireplace around a cart with biscuits and coffee. Kennett came forward and greeted him.

"Come in, Brayton, and meet the clerks," he said. Among the five men of different ages, Francis recognized only Morrison.

Kennett raised his voice slightly, saying, "Gentlemen, this is Francis Brayton, who begins today as our records custodian." He pointed to the one Francis recognized. "This is Luke Morrison, and next to him Victor Russell and Robert Pendale; they are clerks of the registry." He gestured to the other men, "And here are Owen Lovell and Ishmael Stone, senior clerks of the magistrate's chambers. The deputy magistrate, Otis Ranger, and our magistrate, Judge Denison, are not in their offices this morning."

The introductions and greetings having been performed, the men sipped coffee and feasted on biscuits until eight thirty, when everyone turned to begin the day's work at their desks. Kennett led Francis to his office.

Inside, he handed Francis a small journal and a printed parchment. "This book is for you, Brayton, to take notes of meetings and arrangements. The parchment is a Petition for Relief, a printed application form which is the basic tool of our service. It has been used since 1600 when the magistracy in Ellington first began operation. We are a district of the King's Council, which takes in all of this part of Middlesex. The petitions are signed by the District Magistrate, who is now Judge Denison. He is respected here in Ellington and has been called judge as long as I can remember.

"Once the petition is signed, the case is concluded. There is no appeal in this lower court. The petition is stored in the designated box in the library. Judge Denison has written the final summation of the hearing on the back of the petition. Once you've organized the petitions, the judge would like to have some information gathered from them, but that is for a later date." Kennet smiled as Francis took a deep breath. "Come along, Brayton. We'll go to the library now."

They crossed the corridor that separated the registry from the magistrate's chambers, and Kennett opened the door to another passageway. Francis received a quick orientation of the facility—the three doors to the left were to the offices of the Judge's staff, and the two on the right were entrances to the hearing room and the library. When Francis entered the library, he was pleased to think he would be working in this room. There was a wall of windows with a view of the town park just beyond. Light flooded the room. The remaining walls had shelves except for the space for the entrance and the small fireplace. There were five tables with chairs in the open space.

Kennett began, "These boxes contain the petitions. They're filed by the dates. Brayton, if you would, note that the Petition for Relief, which includes the cause and remedy that the petitioner expects from a hearing, the names of the respondents, and the assigned number in the upper right corner. That is simply the date, plus the last number, which identifies the petitioner.

"I would like you to begin by organizing each box with the most recent petition on top of the stack in each box. It would be good to read several as you organize them—write questions in the book I gave you. This afternoon we'll meet at four to review your work. Of course you know where I am if you need me before then."

"Of course, sir."

"Oh yes—we all take lunch at twelve, and no longer than an hour during the winter months, but longer when we have longer daylight hours."

Francis nodded.

After Kennett left him alone, Francis pulled the most recent year, 1640, to review. It was almost bulging with petitions, and he organized and counted a total of sixty-five petitions. Of those, ten plaintiffs had failed to appear for their hearing. That seemed excessive to Francis, considering the time and cost of arranging a hearing. He decided he would keep track of the cancelled hearings as he sorted the other boxes. He had gone through half of the thirteen boxes. The fourteenth, 1641, had already been prepared for the new year.

At noon he hurried to The Dock for a bowl of soup, which Byers scooped up for him right away as Joseph supplied his mug of ale.

"How was your first morning, Francis?"

"I met the five clerks and worked in the library—a room I'll certainly enjoy if this morning is a sample. It was quiet, I was alone, there's plenty of light, and I was busy. That's the most important part. I like to be busy."

"True. Now you've finished your soup but how much time do you have for lunch? Is the time the same for everyone?"

"It's one hour and, yes, everyone has from twelve to one. Kennett said it's longer when the days are longer. I want to finish my assignment before four, so that's my hurry today."

He returned and did manage to sort all the boxes and tally the number of cancelled hearings. There were 730 petitions with an average of eighteen per year, of the total ninety-eight had not been held, cancelled because the plaintiff failed to appear for the scheduled hearing.

At four, in his meeting with Kennett, he reported on his assignment. All boxes and petitions were now in proper order. He read his numbers from his notebook and added a question: "Is there a concern that one in four persons have failed to appear at his own hearing?"

"We had no facts on the cancelled hearings," Kennett responded, "and one out of four seems excessive by the numbers. Possibly the general opinion is that it's, not unexpected, considering the lack of experience with the judicial process. These numbers do not reflect the number of petitioners who gave legitimate reasons for being unable to attend on the scheduled dates. Those are rescheduled, and they're not reflected in the archives. As you work with the process, you might gain some insights about this issue. I would encourage your sharing those with me, Brayton. I also want to say that I had not expected you to complete this task today. Tomorrow I want you to sit alongside the three clerks to observe the processing of petitions. I will alert them that you are doing it merely to understand the movement of the petition in the magistracy. I'm sure you understand that, as an observer, you will make no comments."

"Yes, I understand how disruptive and rude that would be."

During the remainder of the meeting, Francis asked about the petition—who authorizes it, for example—and (he had noted) there were some changes in the form since 1634, when Judge Denison became the District Magistrate, and whether they had been authorized by a higher court.

"The printed form was designed by a committee of attorneys in the Middlesex Court, Kennett said. "The alteration was initiated by Judge Denison and approved in Middlesex. Morrison is responsible for keeping a count of the number of petitions stored in our cupboard, the one located by the fireplace, and I take care of ordering more petitions and clerical supplies.

"In case you were unaware of it, Judge Denison has a law practice in Ellington, so his role in the magistracy is an extra duty for him, one he enjoys I might add. He comes and goes by his schedule, which is coordinated by his clerks. Presently that is Lovell's responsibility. Otis Ranger is at the judge's right hand, keeping him up to date with the hearings and preparing summaries as well. I am, as the registrar, the judge's left hand, so to speak."

The meeting ended just before five, and Francis went to the library and wrote in his notebook: "Organizing archive boxes completed … will complete some record numbers when appropriate … sharing with Kennett. Work tomorrow as observer in registry. Quite comfortable in library. Learned that Otis Ranger is judge's right-hand help and Kennett his left hand, as registrar. January 2, 1641 ~ F.B."

Writing in his own journal had begun to form a pattern: the date and day; the weather; his job assignment and its outcome; The Dock and Joseph; any unusual conversations with the Towson roomers. Oddly, and for his own reasons, he had begun ending each entry with "Mary …"

It had been two months since he last saw Mary Smith. He had no useful reason to continue thinking of her, but his feelings were beyond utility, and certainly too often out of control to suppress. His work at the registry was interesting and challenging in some ways but disappointing in others. He had grasped the idea of petitioning and understood the importance of keeping records straight and of keeping the petitions moving along in a reasonable time. The clerks were not officious with him nor at ease either, but Kennett seemed pleased with his job performance.

However, he had a concern that was delicate. He didn't feel the men who came to seek redress were being shown respect. He decided it was mainly due to the low expectations they harbored and also societal barriers, neither of which should be part of any judicial function. The attitude was subtle, but for vulnerable petitioners it was easily discerned and possibly exaggerated. Francis rarely had direct communication with the petitioners. Occasionally he would start a casual conversation with one of the men who was waiting. Something like, "Have you ever experienced such a long winter as this?" It would start a series of experiences on the weather, difficulties, survival, triumphs, and information that humanized him, giving him a depth beyond a mere number on a petition for relief.

Most of the petitioners came early in the day, and Francis made a habit of being in the registry then. If any of them began talking of their grievance, he immediately deferred them to one of the clerks.

By March, he was writing reports on his findings from the petitions. He would present his ideas to Kennett and then hand him his written figures. He sensed the clerks were wary of his approach, maybe even suspicious, therefore he was careful to keep them informed of what he was working on and his reason for it. He continued to interact with the waiting petitioners and believed this brief encounter changed the tenor of the subsequent meeting with the clerk. At least it seemed so from his point of view.

He was formulating a flow chart and protocols for the petitioners and Francis expected the clerks to be wary and resistant to adopting them. He was careful of their need to debate, knowing that good came from the discussions over the issues in the grievances. Gradually the petitions were going through the magistracy in a more timely manner.

Then he was astonished one day to be asked to do the work for Pendale, who had taken ill and would probably not return for a week or two. This was late April, and he had no difficulties with the interviews with petitioners. The issues were not complicated and the causes and remedies straightforward. Whenever he had a question about the remedy he would consult with either Morrison or Russell.

He received a letter from John in May 1641. Susanna had delivered twin boys in January, first John and then Joseph. They were doing well at four months, and John wrote:

> Thank heaven for Martha, otherwise we would be in such a muddle. They are identical—twice the delight and both healthy. My life is surely changed now, Francis. My looms are strung, and I have a long list of orders. I have fields of flax here and there and I am worn from the traveling back and forth to supervise the process. I hope to start the weaving in June. I have two qualified weavers and they are affordable, as well. The ferry business is flourishing and so is my darling Susanna. Twins! Who would have imagined? You must meet these fellows. Come to America,
>
> Fondly, John

He heard that Lydia Lytle would marry Gavin Longway on the first of June, and he was tempted to go to the chapel but could not risk a disrupting scene. He could not allow that to happen. He knew it would be difficult for Mary to have Lydia married and not having so much time with her good friend. Lydia, he had been told, was the last of Mary's friends to be wed.

His work in the magistracy was going well. He had done an acceptable job with the petition interviews. He had learned, in an offhand way, that his work had been appreciated by the petitioners and by Judge Denison. The rest of 1641 slipped by very much in the manner it had in the years before, with lovely autumn days, hectic holidays, and a grateful New Year.

26 ~ 1642

Changes were brewing in the magistracy, noticeable to all the staff by the numerous meetings of Judge Denison, Registrar Kennett, and Deputy Ranger. On January 15, 1642, a meeting of the entire staff was led by Kennett in the registry. He began, "It is my pleasure to announce to the staff that Judge Denison will be retiring at the end of the month." He paused until he could get the attention of the men, then he continued. "His leaving will be felt for some time as we fill the void of his leadership." He turned to Judge Denison and said, "I know I speak for all of us when I say that we are dedicated to continuing in the ways you have taught us, and we will do our best to maintain the high standards you have established." The men applauded in agreement.

"We have decided on staff changes and have discussed them with those who are being promoted, and we have learned that Ranger will move into Judge Denison's chambers as district magistrate."

The men applauded heartily since he was respected as the workhorse of the magistracy.

"His position will be filled by Clerk Stone, who will serve as deputy magistrate. Junior clerk Morrison is to be promoted to senior clerk." Applause again, and Kennett continued, "Here in the registry, Pendale will be the desk clerk and Brayton will replace Pendale as junior clerk."

More applause followed, but Kennett quieted the men to close the meeting with words of encouragement and praise.

Francis had been asked the day before if he would accept the junior clerk position. He was elated, of course, and surprised because it was so unexpected. His salary was increased to thirteen shillings a month effective January the first. That was also good news. Kennett told everyone that Judge Denison planned to continue with his law practice in Ellington.

It had been challenging to keep the promotion to himself for the days before it was announced. He had written in his journal that evening, "Mary, my Mary, how I long to share my good news with you." He was mindful that his silent conversations with her might be skewing reality. Was he molding his idea of Mary into someone quite different than who she was? He hoped at least this thought might keep him alert to this possibility.

He shared his good news with Stephen, Joseph, Chester, and Grace, and they were genuinely pleased for him. He wrote to John, which helped him release the joy he so safely guarded from others. Francis had a quirk in his nature—he was a bit superstitious and feared the power that allowed his good fortune might be poised to take it away on a whim.

Francis gained assurance from his title and he proceeded in the role as he had imagined it could be. He stood when a petitioner approached his table with the petition form in his hand. He shook his hand, smiled, and offered a seat. He asked him, "I'm sorry, I didn't get your name. Well, Daniel, how can I help you?" He would listen to the grievant as long as he wanted to talk, unless he was repeating himself for the third time. Then Francis would address the emotion:

"I can see you are quite angry—" (sad, resentful or worried) "—and I know you're looking for help." Then he would take the form and ask the man what he hoped to have happen as a result of a hearing with the judge.

Most of the requests were for some sort of compensation for damages. Once that was established, the precipitating cause of the damage usually involved another person or persons. Questions would bring forth underlying information, maybe a history of offenses, grudges, or humiliations, and these would be helpful for the judge in the hearing. Francis would complete the form, making certain the grievant's words and demands were clearly stated. With the grievant and his signature in place, together they went to the desk clerk and Pendale signed and accepted the petition as a matter of record.

Francis assured the Petitioner that it would be reviewed and that he would be informed of the outcome of the review.

Before greeting another petitioner, Francis would make notes of anything that had not been written on the form, but which might be helpful for the Magistrate. These points helped bring about peace in the community, civil respect for the citizens, and an atmosphere of civility.

The third week in January, Francis got tragic news. Charles had been seriously injured in the foundry and had died of the injuries before he could be taken for medical aid. As soon as Francis received the message on the twenty-first, he made arrangements to go to Isley. He had no difficulty getting days off work. He had ample money available, and that evening he informed Grace and then Joseph that he would be gone the rest of the week.

He got a westbound coach to Isley and arrived at Charles' home the afternoon of the twenty-second. Jane was bereft, and Henry and George shocked. Henry had taken hold of the situation and arrangements were in place when Francis arrived. The accident had been a typical foundry danger, and after all these years, Charles had made a fatal wrong move and his body was horribly burned. Many foundry workers and their families gathered to comfort Jane. The funeral was sad but unlike any of the burials Francis had attended. So many people had lost a father, uncle, grandfather, brother, or nephew, all taken too soon from this earth. Francis recalled how Charles had talked so happily of retiring. Of course, there was no income for Jane, but at least the funeral expenses were paid, as was the custom after a death within the foundry. Gwen and John were there too, and Gwen wept the entire time.

Francis learned that the sons and wives had decided that George and Belinda would continue to live with their mother, Jane, and Henry would contribute a certain amount each week. There were some savings, but not enough for Jane to live independently. Francis slipped a crown in Jane's pocket before he left for Ellington. At least the coin would be her own. How sad that she would be dependent on the generosity of her sons and their wives for the rest of her life.

Gwen invited Jane to come stay with them anytime she wanted, and to stay however long she cared to stay. Francis knew they were sincere. It was actually an anomaly, to be getting involved in his family after such a long while. He thought of the hackneyed saying, "better late than never." It seemed the time had come for the Braytons.

Part Three

HERE AND THERE

Chapter 7: Suitor

When I saw you I fell in love, and you smiled because you knew. —
William Shakespeare

27 ~ 1642

It was January 25, 1642, and daylight was dwindling as snowflakes danced around Francis Brayton, who was deep in thought. He was walking on Academy Circle examining his feelings, and he was unused to being introspective. He was frustrated because his former strategies of patience and diligence were not as effective as they had been before. "Before what?" he asked himself. "Before Mary," he answered.

A year of separation had not quelled his desire to be with her. His restlessness was not a matter of his work which had been progressing satisfactorily. It was not financial difficulties, since he had adequate income now, and he had made significant changes in his living arrangements. Most of all, he was not living like a tenant farmer; he did not feel like one nor did he think like one. He asked himself why was he not able to be content with these accomplishments and put Mary out of his mind? Again, he knew the answer. His accomplishments were not meaningful without Mary with him to enjoy them. Reason was failing him miserably.

He had been considered an unacceptable suitor by her parents. On its face, the English tradition of arranged marriages was absurd. The practice of shackling sons and selling daughters was couched in a language of suitability, good manners, and, heaven forbid, protecting blood lines. In reality, it was a system for increasing and assuring the wealth of the middle- and upper-class families.

Francis had experienced humility, had even tried being humble, but now he just felt rebellious. What he wanted was an opportunity to talk with Mary, to see if she was interested in being courted by him. He would not create a scene by deliberately placing himself in her path. He could have gone to Sunday chapel services, for example, but there he would be at great disadvantage. The same would be true of going to their home uninvited. He already had walked the streets hoping to meet her, but it had come to nothing. Somehow he would have to find a way to be alone with Mary.

Mary and her friend, Lydia Lytle, were walking at this same time, on this same snowy Saturday afternoon. Mary had insisted that Lydia walk with her. It was useless to resist Mary.

"I need to talk to you." Lydia knew what the topic would be—Francis Brayton. Month after month, Mary had been anguishing about her lost love. It was a bit annoying to Lydia, since she had recently become engaged to Gavin Longway, and she had many things to discuss about her upcoming wedding.

Mary declared in a rush of words, "I am ready to be brash, Lydia. I must know if Francis is thinking of me, if he cares about me. I was thinking of the one place I might get information—the Holmes bakery. "What do you think? We could go there and get into a conversation with Chester Holmes and mention Francis. I'm sure I could find out where he works, and possibly where he is living now. Would you go there with me on Monday?"

"Mary, your parents would not approve …"

"I'm almost twenty-two years old, Lydia, and I must know how Francis …"

Mary stopped mid-sentence because she had glanced up toward Academy Circle. "Francis! There he is!"

Lydia saw him and said, "I'm leaving you, Mary." She turned and walked back to Elm Street.

Mary hesitated a moment, and when Francis saw her they hurried toward each other, meeting in front of the Holmes bakery. Francis pulled her into his arms and she clung to him, in the snow, in the gathering dusk, in resounding joy.

"Mary, Mary, here you are, after all this time. I have been searching for you wherever I go."

"Yes, Francis. Here I am just when I had almost given up hope of seeing you."

Francis made a rash decision. He took her arm and led her through the narrow passageway to Chester Holmes' yard behind the bakery. In the yard, he kissed her with all his yearning and desire. Mary responded, and they leaned against the shed kissing with their pent-up passion. The snowfall had increased, and they were soon covered with it. Francis had things that he must say, and he pulled away, then looked into her beautiful face and said, "I love you, Mary. I've loved you from the moment I met you. I must know how you feel about me. It's very important, Mary."

"Surely, Francis, you know that I love you! I've been trying to find a way to see you. I never gave up hope."

Francis wanted to shout with joy, but instead he said, "We will marry, have a wonderful family, and be together forever, my Mary!"

Mary laughed and said, "You will ask me, won't you, Francis?"

At first, he didn't understand and then he laughed too, "Yes, yes of course. Will you marry me?"

"Yes, Francis. I will marry you."

He put his cheek next to hers and it felt like ice. "You're too cold! We must start walking." He led her back to the Circle, and they turned toward Market Street. He said, "We need to meet tomorrow so we can talk. Somehow we need to tell your parents because we are not going to meet in secret, Mary."

"I agree. The best place in this weather would be the Confectionary Shop. Lydia and I go there on Sunday afternoons. Could you come at three o'clock?"

"Yes, of course. I'll be there."

"I may be a bit late, so be sure to wait for me. I have to work out the details without alerting my parents. We need to have this go our way, Francis. We've waited long enough."

She looked up at Francis, and he tightened his arm around her. They were soon in front of the Smith home, where he had not been invited. Francis said, "I'm living at Towson's boarding house in case you need to leave a message." She nodded, blew him a kiss, and walked into her house.

He could not go back to Towson's, so he walked on to The Dock. He assumed Joseph would be there, even though the town was quiet, even more quiet than usual with the cover of snow curtailing the usual activities of Saturday evenings in Ellington.

"Francis! Come and keep me company!" Joseph was obviously happy to see Francis. The tavern was empty of patrons, and Joseph began filling a mug of ale for his friend, who blurted out his news. "I've just proposed to Mary Smith and she said yes!"

Joseph was stunned, and Francis was almost babbling about his happiness.

"I'm speechless," said Joseph. "How did this come about?"

"It's a long story, and I want to share it, but could you get me some of Byer's good soup?"

"Of course." When Joseph returned with the soup, Francis began his story. "It started on the twenty-ninth of October, two years ago." Joseph's eyebrows shot up. His eyes were wide with surprise, and Francis said, "Yes, I know. It's really a long story."

They sat together for a few more hours talking of the events that led up to this remarkable day in Francis' life. Joseph, as usual, gave his encouragement whenever Francis talked of his upcoming meeting with Stephen and Elizabeth Smith. "Keep me informed, Francis. I'll be here."

Francis was not comfortable as he waited at the shop for Mary the next day. But the moment she came in, he thought, "She is so beautiful, and she has waited for me, committed herself to me." They smiled at one another.

"I think my parents are suspicious that I'm meeting someone other than Lydia, but they are in truth a bit afraid of me, Francis, so here I am."

"Are you saying that I need not worry about my meeting with them?"

"No—I'm not. I don't think they realize how serious I have been about you. They've seen my lack of enthusiasm for other suitors who have been calling in the past, but they're hoping I will find one of their liking on my own. Let me say, Francis, that when we make our declaration, I will be supporting you and leaving no doubt of it with my parents."

Francis, anxious about her parents' attitude, was fortified by her saying that she was resolute. They agreed that Francis would come to see her parents on the third of February at three o'clock, just seven days away. He would be prepared.

• ❖ •

He knocked on the Smiths' front door at the appointed time. Stephen answered and showed surprise at the unexpected visitor.

"Francis, is anything amiss? Please come in." He led Francis into the parlor and offered him a seat. Francis removed his cloak, holding it in his lap.

"No, everything is fine." Francis wanted Mary in the room before they made their declaration. "I suppose you remember that I've just been promoted, and it would not have been possible without …" At this point Mary and her mother came to see who was in the parlor with Stephen. Francis stood, and Elizabeth came straight to the point.

"What brings you out in this cold Sunday afternoon?"

Mary was not happy with her mother. Francis could see this. "I've come to say something to you and Stephen on a matter of utmost importance to me. Last week Mary and I met by chance—the first time we've seen each other in over a year. It was a complete surprise for both of us, and we expressed what has been in our hearts all these months. We are deeply in love—" (Elizabeth gasped, and Stephen sat straighter) "—and we are committed to being together. We have decided to see each other, to become better acquainted before making any announcements, but we will not meet in secret. We ask only that you give us an opportunity to demonstrate our love. We love and respect you, and it would be distressing to not have your approval."

"You know I stood by my agreement, at your urging," Mary said with emotion, "to allow Francis to study with Father without my interruptions, and Francis out of respect for you has not pursued me. But now we want to see each other, get to know one another, and we shall."

Elizabeth and Stephen said nothing.

Francis took his cloak, and no one spoke as he and Mary went to the front door. They smiled, and he kissed her quickly, saying, "I'll see you next Sunday under the elm."

It was a difficult week, but at least he had his work to occupy his mind. He worried that he had said too much. Then he worried that he had not said enough. His anxiety would not be lessened until he heard from Mary that she had not been persuaded in some way by her parents to back away from him.

On Sunday as he was waiting, he saw her walking on the Circle. Mary was taller than most women and walked gracefully with a steady pace, her shoulders straight but not stiffened. When she saw Francis, she quickened her steps. They embraced briefly, then Mary began to talk, and he listened anxiously.

"As soon as you left Father said, 'Well, that was quite a speech,' and Mother said, 'I'll say it was!'"

Mary continued, "That's all I heard said on the matter, but I believe they have decided to give us time to see it isn't working, because they do not believe my resolve with you, Francis, and my strategy is to give them time to adjust to the inevitability of our marrying."

They walked on the Circle around to The Dock as they had planned, so Joseph could meet Mary. They recognized one another because Joseph attended chapel every Sunday and he had seen Mary, not knowing she was *the* Mary. She had seen Joseph, as well, but there was no occasion for them to meet. What dismayed Francis was not having known that Joseph attended chapel every Sunday. Why had he assumed Joseph would not be religious? There was only one time he had been with Joseph on a Sunday morning—the day they went to London.

Mary and Joseph were very easy with each other, and it was an enjoyable time. Joseph had shown them to a special place for privacy and arranged for James Byers to attend patrons who might come in out of the cold on Sunday evenings. This became a weekly ritual.

28 ~ 1642

Work was going well for Francis, which caused him to think more about emigrating rather than less. The lack of opportunities was discouraging for him. He had nowhere to advance in the magistracy, and other office positions that he might qualify for didn't become available. He could see that he had been fortunate to be with Kennett and Denison, both being so liberal-minded and willing to go with their intuition rather than insisting on experience. They gave him a chance to do some creative work in a very dull and routine process. He felt, however, such an opportunity would not come his way again.

Mary was pressing for a wedding date, and his reluctance was the issue of emigrating, which he had not yet mentioned. He was actually fearful of talking to Mary about his desire to go to New England. In his own mind, Mary would be a perfect candidate for this new form of government. She liked change and was very confident. He wasn't convinced that she saw the same spirit in herself that he saw in her personality. He knew he would never give her up to go to America, but nevertheless he had a hard time giving up the idea of emigrating.

One day in early April, he rented a horse and cart from the Basom Stables. Mary filled a picnic basket and off they trotted to a popular place along the Thames. They had a wonderful time, and Francis was pleased with himself for doing well with Dobbin. He had hoped to be alone to talk to Mary about emigrating, but he didn't find the right moment. He took John's letters and read them to her, trying to balance the Indian problems with the excitement of democratic government. He pointed out the opportunities, and that too excited Francis more than Mary.

He shared with her the work he aspired to do. He liked office work and had proven to have good ideas about improving processes and systems in the magistracy. He often mentioned the lack of opportunity for him in England—so often, in fact, that he could tell it was an overdone topic. They did not discuss finances at all, possibly because it was a bit premature to discuss expenses. The word "pioneer" did not come up, and John's letters were more positive than negative, yet Francis had delayed telling Mary about his emigration plans.

Later in April, while in Weedon Park sitting on the usual bench, she again brought up the subject of a wedding date. Francis felt anxious and was also needing to get the matter settled. He decided to broach the delicate subject.

"Mary, I want to talk with you about something I have been contemplating for a long time," he said. "I'm doing well at the magistracy, but even with the good pay it is as much as I can hope to earn there, or anywhere else. I know I'm capable of more challenging work, but in England I won't be allowed to work up to my abilities. That's how it is in England for my class." He paused and looked at her, and she knew he was wanting so much to convince her. Then he said, "Your parents were reluctant to invite me into your home. I don't resent them for it, but I'm realistic about our future in England. I want to emigrate to Portsmouth in New England, and I've been saving money for the voyage for a long time"

Mary's eyes became so wide he was frightened. He knew she was shocked. "Please Mary, listen to me. I want to be responsible for myself. I want to be allowed to work as I choose without others telling me where I should work or cannot work. I'm willing to take responsibility for my choices. It must be hard for you to see that, since your life has been so different."

She stood, clearly angry, and said, "You think I can make my own choices? You think I could take care of myself with dignity when I have no legal rights or educational opportunities available to me? I got some education by asserting myself, but what can I do with it? My life is restricted by rules of decorum and traditions."

"Mary, Mary, please, I'm so sorry. I'm only thinking about how I can provide for you, give you a decent life, and be somewhere we would be accepted for our own merits, not what others prescribe. I feel responsible for having been born a peasant's son and not of your family's status in society. I don't want to be limited by my heritage. I want to own property, and most of all I want to make you contented and happy with me. You love life and have a spirit of adventure. You need a larger stage to live your life—a new country would be good for you to give you space and opportunities. I've hesitated to talk of emigration because I would never take you away from your parents without their approval. What am I to do?"

"I'm confused," she said, "and thinking of emigrating has me on shaky ground with my own feelings. I know with certainty how my parents would take the idea of me leaving England for America, so I need time to think! Francis, I will take this week to sort it out, then next Sunday we will talk together. I cannot be reasonable now, I'm too unsettled."

She left without touching him or saying goodbye, and Francis was bereft.

He berated himself for having brought up emigration with her. Would she not have come up with the idea herself, in time? He had been worrying about their ages, thinking and believing the new world was for young people. He was soon to be thirty years old, and Mary was already twenty-two. What if, by postponing the conversation, Mary would become even more convinced that they belonged in England?

He felt conflicted. He remembered what Stephen told him about deus ex machina, a Greek invention for plays to retrieve a hero who has been put into an impossible situation. A machine would swoop down, as a God, and pull the hero out of his dilemma. Francis could use such a God-machine, right now!

The week's separation had given Mary and Francis time to step back and take a new look at their situation, which had changed in spite of their devotion and love. Commitment to one another had a new landscape, and it was unknown and fearful for different reasons. The fear was not about where or how they would live together but rather how they would come together to decide how and where they would live. It was not just a matter of influencing, persuading, compromising, and sweeping away expectations but deciding what they wanted from their marriage and identifying the values necessary to attain and preserve it. Mary and Francis were both rational in their approach to complexities, and now they were challenged to preserve their relationship for the sake of their love.

The next week, as they came together under the elm, they were overpoweringly reassured as they embraced and looked into each other's faces and eyes. "I see two thorny problems," Mary began. "The first is with my parents. As difficult as saying goodbye to them will be, it is nothing compared to my leaving without their blessings. That would taint my life forever. The other issue is what sort of life will we have if we were to stay in Ellington? We could find another village, I suppose, where our family's status could be glossed over, but that would be a small matter compared to your not having the freedom to work as you choose, Francis. It seems to me that there's more hope of overcoming my parents' resistance to emigrating than there is in finding a place in England for you to achieve all you're capable of achieving."

Francis found himself consumed with love as she continued. "I can see what we're facing together, but I must admit to something that is not obvious to others. I am reluctant to be involved in anything I dislike doing, and I think being in a wilderness is beyond my capabilities. I believe we hate to do what we are not good at, or trained to do, and I would not, could not, be prepared for life in an unsettled country. I haven't worked, Francis. I play a lot, at this and that, but work seems like drudgery."

Francis was taken aback. He had not considered this for a moment. He had pictured Mary as charming herself into being and doing whatever would be needed. And how absurd was that thinking?

"Mary, all I can say is that I enjoy work," he said. "I find great satisfaction in learning how to do something, especially from someone who knows what they're doing, and then seeing the results of having exerted myself. Then come the benefits of having a body that responds to demands made upon it. That is better than any prize!"

He took a deep breath.

"I've always looked for more efficient ways that work can be done, and I've never minded starting out every morning with chores that had to be done the same way, day after day. I do admit, though, I like being in control, and maybe that's why I take charge of situations—offering better procedures, for example, because that gives me control of them."

Mary was thinking about this as Francis spoke of work. She knew his work on the tenant farm had been taxing, every day, all day long, and she had never considered that he enjoyed doing it. She was a competitive person, she knew it, and had been called "plucky" more than once, so maybe she could come to enjoy at least some of the housekeeping tasks.

Suddenly she had an inspiration. "You know, Francis. I'm thinking that if I began learning to cook, sew, launder, houseclean, and such, Mother would see that I'm very serious about marrying you. That's what I will do. I also believe we shouldn't speak of emigration to them for a while. Who knows what could happen in the next few months? I may even become a good housekeeper!"

Francis felt like they had a starting point with Mary getting some experience with the work she would have to do in America. They would see what came of it.

It came about as they planned but not overnight. Mary progressed and demonstrated her determination, but some things did not go well—baking was a waste of good ingredients.

In September, the young couple told Elizabeth and Stephen of the emigration plans and they were devastated, knowing they no longer had a way to influence Mary. In truth, they never had been able to influence Mary. She had rejected suitors who would have provided her a comfortable and financially secure life, a life she had been accustomed to with them. She had refused to learn domestic skills and insisted on being allowed to sit in on the tutoring sessions of her brothers, and now they believed Mary was not prepared to live in a wilderness. Stephen and Elizabeth asserted that romantic notions would not do the work of survival.

Their arguments were useless, and they could not claim the couple were being impulsive. Francis was thirty and Mary twenty-three, and yet they had not rushed their wedding plans and had even allowed more time after the wedding before their planned departure for New England.

Elizabeth had convinced Stephen to cooperate and enjoy the time with Mary before she left them. It was the wiser choice. Elizabeth offered to help with the wedding arrangements, and Mary was quite happy to relinquish them. She continued to make progress with learning the housekeeping, gardening, and needlework tasks she would need for life in New England.

Francis was impressed with Mary's resolve. She was thorough and as thoughtful as a carpenter building a house.

In October, they conferred with Pastor Thomas and set the date for the wedding ceremony in St. Albans Chapel for Sunday December 28, 1642, at two thirty. The banns would be announced on the seventh, fourteenth, and twenty-first of December. Mary and Francis would attend catechism with Pastor Thomas for several Saturdays prior to the wedding. Mary had asked this of Francis and he had agreed, believing it would be good to know what Mary already knew, that which, it seemed to Francis, had benefited her.

It was difficult to convince Joseph he was needed as best man. He was just as convinced that he was not suitable for such a situation. Francis said with a laugh, "Well, neither am I, and that is why I need you!" Francis sent messages to Gwen, John, Jane, and her sons. Jane answered that she would stay at home with the grandchildren, but the other Braytons were planning to attend.

Christmas was almost overlooked by the business of preparing for the wedding, and the impending emigration ran as leitmotif throughout the festivities. Francis had his usual holiday week off from work, and he helped prepare for their move to Towson's. They had gone there earlier to see if Grace had space for them somewhere in her large house. She took a week to decide then offered a space on the third level, saying, "It has light enough, a good enough bed, and enough space. So, if 'enough' will do you, then I'll make it ready. You said New Year's Eve, right? I wanted to be sure since that's an odd time to move in."

Grace talked like that, and it was best to wait until she stopped before responding. "Plenty good enough, Grace, thank you very much," Francis said. "Yes, New Year's Eve is when we will be arriving. If you don't mind, we'll bring Mary's things in the middle of the week before."

John had written as soon as he learned that the Braytons would be emigrating. He had already conferred with Captain Ike Headly about voyages, and the logical date for Mary and Francis was the voyage leaving London on July 1, 1643. He had reserved two passages, but the booking needed to be confirmed as soon as possible—there were waiting lists for all of Ike Headly's voyages. He had other information to tell Francis about the voyage. John had told Ike that Francis would be a good person to fill one of the passenger liaison positions on the voyage. John wrote:

> I told him of your work at the magistracy, of our friendship and of your character. He was impressed and said he would appoint you. All you need to do is go to London to Longwharf Street. That is where the Headly Passenger and Cargo Company is located. If you sign the letter of appointment, Headly said that you and Mary will be given free passage to Boston on the Courser. I know that will be good news for you, Francis. No doubt you will earn the fare, and I am sure you will make an excellent Liaison. Hurrah! You are coming to America.
>
> Fondly, John

When he told Joseph about emigrating, the barkeep was quiet but obviously disturbed, and he said, "I'm happy for both you and John, that you're pursuing your special lives of adventure, but I do not envy you. I'm content in my predictable world of The Dock. If the people come for a while and then move on, that is also predictable. You might be the exception, since no one in my life has given me more time or a more lasting friendship than you have."

Francis smiled but said nothing as he stood looking with a strong feeling of affection at his good friend. There would be farewells in the months ahead, but Joseph had experience with farewells and knew better than Francis how permanent theirs would be.

Work was a relief for Francis and he spent hours reviewing petitions and debating them with Pendale. He wrote summaries for the senior clerks and Ranger, and they found this helpful. He attended the scheduled hearings and learned about procedures, courtesies, and central issues. As he listened to the judge conducting the hearings, he was reassured to see how often his suggestions made it into the arguments and settlements of the cases. Francis was eager to help settle disputes and he hoped he could pursue such work in New England.

Before he left England, there were people he wanted to see, but most of these visits would have to wait until after the New Year—except for one person. Chester was quite surprised when Francis arrived one morning at six thirty. It was a cold November Wednesday, the one day of the week that was not as busy as the other five.

Chester grinned broadly. "Come in, Francis!" he said. "Just in time for some hot cider and a bun. What brings you to our side of the Circle?"

"You do, Chester. It's been too long since I've had the pleasure of your company, not to mention the buns. I also wanted to personally invite you, Abigail, and the girls to my wedding. Have you heard that Mary and I are emigrating to New England?"

"Yes, yes I had heard. You know this town—we thrive on the news of comings and goings. I heard of the wedding, of course. Elizabeth has given me precise instructions on the cakes, and we have received the invitation. Abigail loves weddings, but I warn you she cries through all of them. The girls are excited and talk of what they will wear as if you two were the king and queen of England. Thank God you aren't, eh? Here's Tom Claggett, you remember him, don't you, Francis?"

"Yes. Hello, Tom. I see you two are doing very well, and I'd better be on my way so you can get to that second bake."

He and Mary were in a whirl of activity, each in their separate ways. He had made a hurried trip to London to sign the necessary papers for the voyage. He didn't see a single person he knew, coming or going, but it did help to be alone, if only for a day, and gain a modicum of his usual equilibrium. Mary seemed to thrive on the demands for her attention. All in all, Mary's life was much more complicated than his had ever been. Mary was simply Mary, a beautiful person to whom people gravitated, hoping to soak up some of her enthusiasm for life.

Francis had shown Mary his grandmother Elaine's gold ring that had been passed on first to Isobel, then to Martha, and now he wanted Mary to have it. She was delighted with the gift and said, "I will wait until the ceremony in the chapel to wear it. Such a symbol of our marriage! It's so fitting that I should be joined by the other Brayton brides. Thank you, Francis." She kissed him, and he felt that this had been ceremony enough for him.

"Francis!" Mary exclaimed as she had a habit of doing when she wished to alert him that she would be revealing a plan that involved him. "Why don't we plan a visit to Calais and Ardeau? I would enjoy seeing where the Braytons lived in France."

"Certainly, but when could we do that?"

"April! April would be a lovely time to go to France."

"We shall see, Mary, in due time. Let's get the wedding behind us, and then we'll talk of France."

"You are, so … well, *orderly*."

"I hope that's a good thing, Mary. I'm not quite sure sometimes."

"It's a good thing for me. I'm filled with fancy," she said, and they both laughed.

The Christmas celebration was especially wonderful. The Smiths scheduled the festivities over the three days so that everyone could be feted personally instead of all noise and confusion. This was Elizabeth's idea, and each of the groups included Francis and Mary. The first was Elizabeth's family, the Holdens, who were meeting Francis and saying farewell too. The second was with the Smiths' sons and their families, who were curious about the emigration. Everyone had an opinion, and in truth no one knew what Mary and Francis would be encountering.

The gifts reflected their leaving: Mary received a special bonnet with ribbons to tie under her chin during storms at sea, and Francis a long wool scarf to wrap around his cloak on the deck of the ship. Their gift to Elizabeth was a gold locket with a miniature painting of Mary and to Stephen a pair of leather gloves. Francis gave Mary a cameo. Mary had made a vest for Francis, meticulously hand-sewn herself.

On Christmas Day, after a splendid celebration of Christ's birth at St. Albans, they returned to the Smiths' home and feasted on traditional food the rest of the day. Chester Holmes' fruitcake was a special treat.

29 ~ 1642

The wedding was glorious, with flowers and boughs of pine, friends and family, and a beautiful bride. Everyone had gathered at the Shepherd's Inn and walked the short distance to St. Albans on the Circle. It was a joyous parade of people dressed in their winter cloaks with scarves fluttering about and cheerful bantering until all were inside and quieted for the solemn ceremony. Pastor Thomas repeated the traditional words and the bride and groom were serious and aware of the importance of the moment.

Afterward, everyone walked back to the inn, showering the bride and groom with wheat as they walked. The inn was prepared, and Francis and Mary received their guests as they were ushered into the dining room, which was decorated with colorful festoons woven with ribbons, holly, and flowers

Francis was delighted to see Chester and his beautiful bevy of women. Francis was astonished to see the young maidens. Catherine had fully grown into her own image of herself—sedate, mature, and very pretty. Judith was like her mother in every detail, and Juliet was adorable. Abigail was tearful.

Henry and Felicia, George and Belinda, and Gwen and John were there, pleasing Francis by having Braytons at his wedding celebration.

Mary and Francis were a beautiful couple, both tall and straight and yet relaxed too. They were gracious hosts and made people feel they had provided them the greatest gift by being with them on their special day. People had given the couple coins, knowing they could not take many items along to America.

Elizabeth's efforts were worthwhile. Everyone had a grand time. There was music and dancing as people mixed and mingled together. The rejoicing continued until most of the guests had left. As Mary and Francis walked up the stairs to their reserved room they had to endure the hoots and hollers of those below until they had entered the hallway, out of sight.

Mary and Francis were shy, having no familiarity with naked intimacy, but it was soon a thing of the past as they embraced with ardor and yearning. The excitement they felt as they let go of their self-consciousness was different from anything they had ever imagined. They were right for each other, and together theirs was an intimacy all their own. How they united on this first night would be how they would go on together. They knew without a doubt that they were special, and from this night on they would become extraordinary.

No one knew, but Mary and Francis had made plans for the next two days. They hired a horse and covered cart to go to Woburn on Monday and stay two nights at the Kings

Curl's Inn. On the thirty-first, they would return and move into their own place at Towson's.

On January 2, 1643, Francis left Towson's in time to get to work, but certainly more reluctantly than he had ever done before.

"Go, Francis." Mary had said. "I will be busy enough. Go."

Soon Mary and Grace began a ritual, just as most routines get started, by having breakfast together every morning. The timing was right for Grace, once her "boys" were off for their day's work, and once she had cleaned up after them. She started breakfast for herself and Mary.

Mary confided that she was determined to learn how to do housework efficiently because they would not have the means to hire help. "I know you have enough work," she said, "and I promise I will step aside any time I've intruded too much, but would you allow me to help you with your work, so I can learn how to keep a home?"

Grace wasn't sure what to say or do. Mary was a lady in her eyes, and Mary sensed her dilemma. "Think of the bother I would be to Francis in New England if I couldn't even make breakfast," Mary said. "I need your help and if I confuse the situation for you, I'll understand that I need to step back and let you get your work done."

"What's the harm in trying?" Grace said. "Come with me and I'll show you how to make beds, and after that I'll show you what I do on Mondays."

That was a beginning of an opportunity for Mary. She and Grace got on well when she learned that Grace was not complicated. She said what she wanted and what she didn't want. Mary liked that approach, and Grace, who had no time for theatrics, was not easily upset. Mary often thought of what Francis had said about enjoying work once he got started with it, finding ways to do the ordinary more quickly or more easily than before. Mary knew she was getting somewhere, and when Francis came home from work she enjoyed sharing with him what she had learned. He was amused, but above all he was pleased.

Francis got a letter from John in early March.

> By your last letter I can see that you are curious about this liaison's position you signed on for the voyage. This is what Ike explained to me when he started the program. He said he devised a system to improve the conditions for passengers and the crew during ocean voyages. Ike had seen how the neglect of passengers created many problems. The voyages were very hazardous, uncomfortable and annoying. He decided that with a little extra expense, he could improve these situations. Ike decided to appoint five men with leadership qualities to serve as liaisons during the voyage. Each of these men is assigned twenty passengers, and the passengers are advised to talk with the liaison about their problems or

concerns. Most of the complaints can be handled by the liaison, and if not, the issue can be taken to the steward. The day before the ship sets sail, Ike meets with the five men to explain the program and to answer questions.

When you wrote that you and Mary were sailing in in the middle of the year, I was convinced this program was for you. Susanna and I are delighted to know you will be here by the next autumn. I know you are enjoying your wedded bliss, and I will toast you both in Boston when I come to meet the Courser. You are coming to America!

Fondly, John

Francis tried to get over to see Joseph, and since it got complicated juggling his work, the Towsons, and the Smiths, he and Mary continued to visit The Dock in the early evening each Sunday. That was a quiet time, and James Byers was prepared with a good hearty soup and Chester's good bread. They were surprised how easily the three of them conversed together. Joseph was a good listener, and he and Francis had accumulated enough experiences together for plenty of laughter and good fun at every meeting. It was another of those coincidences that Francis could not explain.

He and Mary talked of faith, especially after going to chapel on Sundays. Sometimes they would have a discussion at The Dock with Joseph about some thorny issues from the morning's sermon. Mary was not a student of the Bible. She was an Anglican, and she had her prayer book and was comforted by the service each Sunday. Francis had given her Martha's King James Bible, and she was reading verses from it, mostly the Psalms.

Francis could not understand that. What good came from doing something from habit if you did not have a reason for doing it? Mary said, "My reason is that I feel comforted, knowing God is in charge, that he is the Creator." This was, after all, answer enough for Francis. Why should he disturb something as reassuring as that?

When May came, Mary was in a dither about packing. They were allowed only one trunk on the *Courser*. Rose Marie Diller had been to America on a barque, and Mary went to her house and asked if she would help her prepare for the voyage. Rose Marie had said at a party that she had returned to England—that she "couldn't stick it," a paraphrase from one of William Shakespeare's plays: "Screw your courage to the sticking place."

Rose Marie said, "We sewed small items in the hems of our dresses and under gowns—needles pins, coins, and jewelry. Be sure to take dry food—meats, fruits, nuts, and even corn meal. You will get hungry and you don't get food on the voyage, but once in a while some meat from the captain. We were allowed some small crates in our space on board in the passenger level. Clothing is bulky so try to wear layers if you're able. It's cold on the ocean. We never got too warm."

Mary had not thought about food! She went to Greenly's, and he helped her, knowing more about dried food items. He suggested rolled mats for sitting and sleeping and one blanket too. He had talked to customers and knew more than most about sailing on the ocean. It was easier for Francis. He had new clothes and a set of older ones, his old faithful boots, and his cloak. Mary got a new cloak and a practical, plain woolen dress.

As the weeks went by and June came, she was more prepared. Grace had been a wonderful help, showing her "tricks of the trade," as she referred to her cooking, cleaning, and such. Elizabeth stood by respectfully as Grace helped Mary, but she did feel jealousy and some resentment. She decided it would be best to forget it, since the time was going, and soon Mary would be gone.

Francis went to Judge Denison's office in Ellington to see him before he left England. The former judge offered, "I wish you well. I also feel some envy. England is in a sorry state now, and it won't improve with King Charles and his tirades. He's stirring a very large pot. Let's see what the American colonies do with their land. They will use *you* to good advantage, I suppose."

He got up from his desk and came to sit closer to Francis. "You are the most focused young man I have encountered in some time. You see situations the way they are and in time how they could be improved. We're losing too many intelligent men to the New World, and you will probably encounter some of them." He paused, then asked, "Where did you say you were going?"

"We sail to Boston, but we'll be settling in Portsmouth, near Roger Williams' plantation."

The judge laughed and said, "Talk about stirring pots! Williams has been giving the Anglican Church a good stir.

He has some fanatical ideas, but most of them are thought-provoking. As I said, I'm envious, and if I were younger, I might consider emigration, just as you have, Francis. I wish you good luck, and congratulations, by the way. Word gets around. The Smith family has a fine reputation."

The office gave Francis a grand send-off as they gathered together at the biscuit cart. He got emotional and even more moved by the comments and praises he heard in these, his last few minutes at the magistracy. They gifted him with a leather journal which made him feel indulged, as it was the only frivolous item he had ever been given. Kennett was gracious but showed his sadness when they parted. "If you ever want it, you always have a position here, Francis." Francis looked at this dear man, and, before tears came, they both turned away to keep their composure.

Francis received a long letter from John Anthony in May. He wrote:

> My dear Francis. So, you've taken a bite from the apple. From what you have written, I believe you and Mary are of the adventuresome sort, which I found in my own dear Susanna.
>
> I have been involved with Portsmouth government, as is everyone in the area. It is quite something to see, Francis, how this settlement is developing into a strong community from a scheme devised by several people in Boston, none more so than John Clarke. He wrote the Portsmouth Compact, which is the basis for our governing. It is thoroughly thought through with purpose and

methods defined. The Compact is designed to continue in perpetuity. Twenty-three men signed the document, but the authority for governing rests in the written Compact, not with the men who signed it or wrote it.

We have built a Town Hall, and at least twice a year we meet to carry out our government business by majority rule. The first town meeting was April 19, 1639, and it was well attended. The key is commitment to this experiment in democracy; it is the belief that common men can rule themselves. Susanna and I were not part of the original twenty-three families who came to Aquidneck Island, but we have heard the founding story over and over and I never tire of hearing it. Roger Williams' plantation is a couple of hours distance by water. He played an important part in our settlement. John Clarke wisely consulted with him and asked his help to locate a place to settle. Williams consulted with the Indians, and together Aquidneck Island was selected, which is fifteen miles north-to-south and three to five miles east-to-west. The Narragansett Indians used the island for hunting but did not reside on it permanently. A treaty was signed with the Indians agreeing to vacate the island forever at a cost of beads, hoes, and men's coats.

Williams also welcomed the women and children of the Compact to stay on his plantation while the land was surveyed and allotments drawn. Then trees were felled and stones cleared from the soil. These stones were used to build charming low rock walls, while some were used to define property lines. The houses were built one at a time, and slowly the families came from the plantation to set up housekeeping in their new homes. One of the themes of this oft-told story is "community." Everyone cooperated with whatever was decided, and leaders were elected by majority vote. We have eventually had an English official take up residence, but from the beginning, Portsmouth has been a democratically organized government.

Susanna and I came a few months after the second meeting in November 1639, and we are feeling blessed to be in this community. I have two looms working every day, one with flax and the other with wool. Several farmers are supplying flax and there are several flocks of sheep here too. We can't keep up with the demand, so I'm thinking of ordering more looms.

One surprising thing occurred that included our friend William Brenton. He and eight other men left Portsmouth in 1639 to establish a settlement in a fine harbor at the southern tip of Aquidneck. It was seen as a necessity to keep outsiders from coming to claim land or invade that part of the island, which is open to the Atlantic. I have visited the settlement, which they named Newport, and it is, well, remarkable. Life there is thriving, with a commitment to democracy, to law and order, to developing businesses, and to trading. Generally, all is in service to the community.

One last thing that I believe will interest you (as it has many others): Portsmouth has a land-grant contract available to those who sign an agreement to serve the government. They receive two acres of land granted to them for each year of service. This has been a successful and valued contract, since land is the preferred reason that people emigrate to America. We find that in the return payment of government service, we have people using their talents to build roads, clear land, review petitions, develop regulations, mediate squabbles, and on goes the list. It has been important to me that I let you know what living in Portsmouth is all about. Do you now understand why I have been saying, "Come to America?

Fondly, John

The time had come. Francis and Mary moved from Towson's and said a teary goodbye to Grace before moving into the Smiths' house. The four of them did their best to put a good face on the situation. To their great surprise, Stephen presented the couple with fifteen pounds, which Clement Smith had left in trust for his granddaughter. It was a special moment, and Mary wept as she expressed her appreciation. It was a very moving moment for these four people who had invested so much in human caring and kindness to one another. Such moments were played out over and over in homes and on the docks as loved ones said their sad farewells.

There were people coming and going amid the last-minute tasks, but at least the trunk had already been sent to the wharf. Elizabeth was red-eyed, and Mary was tender with her. Francis and Stephen had not been able to recapture their student/teacher rapport, and he was now the father-in-law witnessing this young man, who was not only taking his daughter from his house, but who was taking her to another continent. Francis, in his joy with his new bride, had pushed their relationship from his mind until he came to this moment, standing before Stephen to say goodbye. The remembrance of years of study with this generous, gentle man overwhelmed him and Francis was too emotional to speak. It was unfair of him to seek approval from a man who had given so much; he turned away, sparing Stephen from a gesture of any sort, and allowing Stephen his own pain and loss.

On the way to London, Mary said with animation, "Francis! We forgot to go to France! Now we'll never know what the Brayton homeland was like. Did you forget too?"

Francis smiled and said, "I did. Unfortunately, we had so much more to attend to than we expected."

In London, Francis attended the liaison orientation with Captain Headly, and he met the other men who were serving as liaisons. All these men would become well acquainted in the next nine weeks.

Somehow, Elizabeth and Stephen had learned of the sailing date, and they were there as Francis and Mary were about to go aboard. It was a gracious gesture that, in spite of their pain, they had come to express their devotion, love, and goodwill to their daughter and her husband. They had reinforced the family bond despite the deep ocean that was soon to separate them.

There were promises of letters to be exchanged, thereby keeping the love and interests of one another in their hearts.

Chapter 8: Voyager

Anyone can hold the helm in a calm sea. — Publilius Syrus

30 ~ 1643

The barque *Courser* was sailing toward Boston Harbor, plowing its way through the North Atlantic waters by the power of a favorable wind. Francis Brayton clutched the rail on the main deck, looking up at the taut sails, and his spirits lifted, as if his will had caused all of nature to work in concert to get him and Mary to the New World and a new life. His feeling of urgency reminded him of how a horse, sensing its stall is near, picks up speed and despite the pull on the reins gallops toward the barn. Francis had not acquired a romance of the sea on this his first voyage, and he was certain he would never again take for granted the reassuring feeling of solid ground beneath his feet. Nor would he forget that for eight weeks he had made the most of being confined on a vessel of noxious odors.

Worst of all, he had been restricted to a walking distance of one hundred by twenty-five feet.

Francis looked toward Captain Isaac Headly, who stood at the helm, noting how his commanding stature gave importance to the uniform rather than the other way around. His overhanging eyebrows and leather-like complexion, exposed to sea mist and harsh sunlight, gave him a scowling appearance that belied his generous nature and his commitment to his crew and passengers. John Anthony had met "Ike" Headly through William Brenton, and they had begun meeting at The Golden Plate restaurant in Boston whenever busy schedules would allow. It was a meeting of minds of three men who were entrepreneurial—one at sea, one establishing settlements in New England, and the third a proprietor on Aquidneck Island. William and John had invested in Ike's company, and all three had profited from emigrants from England who were clamoring for land in New England.

Francis and Captain Headly met in London during the overseer's training before the *Courser* had embarked for Boston. During the voyage, they engaged in conversations on the main deck when they were free from their respective duties. The captain, like many before him, was encouraged by the rapt attention of his younger companion, and Francis was likewise intrigued by the exciting tales of life on the high seas. As the weeks went by, Francis never tired of hearing the captain's opinions of the New World or of his plans for retiring in Bermuda after his next voyage.

"Twenty-six voyages I've made to Boston, and even more before the passenger trade became more profitable, and safer, than transporting cargo. The pirates stopped bothering with our ships, and I could see the future. I formed a company, got investors, and designed a ship that was more accommodating for passengers. I always have more people signed for voyages than space for them.

"I've kept my toe in the trade business by making a swing south to the West Indies. Fell in love with a spot in Bermuda, where I bought a few acres and built a house on a small cove. It's suitable for docking the *Courser* while I relax every January, and it will be forever after when I retire. I'm fanatical for horse racing, and my favorite breed is the courser, which explains the name of my ship. I have a grand horse I named Revelation and expect to win races with him."

Francis thought, "Everyone has a story and here is a sea captain who loves horse racing!" Headly had become intimately acquainted with the North Atlantic waters, the weather, and how to maneuver during storms. With his new ship, his reputation for safe voyages had spread by word of mouth, and he had made a handsome profit from his company and also for his investors. He had met many interesting people, some passengers, and others while on layovers in Boston and Bermuda. One day, standing with Francis, he talked about the future of New England.

"All through the 1620s, we carried thousands of people. Most of them were Puritans who stayed together, obeying their leader, praying and studying the Bible for hours every day. I noticed how calm they were during storms. I didn't have my own ship then and was fascinated by people who would invest their lives so completely in another person, a church leader, and I wondered if I was missing something. I talked with some, briefly—I hadn't the time for them then or now. They never relent. I can't tell if they are trying to convert me or to save me from Hell's fire. Probably both! They came ill-prepared for the harsh winters, and in 1620 they would have starved if it hadn't been for the friendly Indians. Puritans are now everywhere in eastern Massachusetts, and their leadership has taken them wrong, as I see it. They came here to escape persecution, and now they persecute others who preach contrary to their faith."

Francis said, "You mentioned the Indians. I'm curious about them."

Headly was quick to respond with, "I'm no authority on Indians, but let me say this—we all talk of the Indians, and there is no such entity. There are hundreds of tribes of people as different from one another as Italians are from Englishmen. They are humans trying to survive in the natural world. They respect nature and have no concept of owning land. That's what's caused the strife that has come to these people who live in nature. European culture, on the other hand, has developed around the rights of property, land particularly, and it has been their basic means of survival.

"When the English came to New England, they claimed the land, and eventually denied all the tribes hunting privileges. The tribes have no effective way to stop the encroachment on their hunting grounds because they are not united, and in fact some tribes are constantly at war with each other. They continue to desperately fight for the right to roam wherever there are animals to hunt, for the food they need to survive." Headly seemed moved by this and added, "They're doomed, but they don't yet know that."

Francis treasured a particular conversation with Headly about people who were escaping England for a better life in New England. Ike had said, "I've observed many emigrants on these voyages who were leaving desperate lives to come to New England for something better, but they only thought of what they did not want. Once in New England they were not prepared to pursue a livelihood on their own, instead of that which others had either done for them or to them. Those persons do not do well and are no better off than they were in England.

"Others come, having heard how wonderful America is, and they are not prepared for the demands of the New England life. Some work through it, others return to England. The third group are those who seem to have a candle lit inside with the idea of America as a land of political independence and freedom to choose to live as they desire, especially to own land. They succeed because it is their land and their investment. The next lesson they learn in this developing country is that it takes the help of others to make a decent life for their families. Cooperating together, they have built houses, established law and order, built places of worship, town halls, and many proprietary enterprises, and the cooperation is leading to the establishment of communities."

Francis said, "John Anthony wrote to me about Portsmouth, saying the same about settlers. I think John knew a long time ago how much I yearned to be able to work as I choose to work, not as others said I would or should work. He has always encouraged me to come to New England, even after he was settled and had experienced the challenges. I covet independence, but I believe in community too. I've often thought, 'If anyone else is not free, neither am I.'"

Headly looked at Francis and saw why John had recommended him for one of his liaison positions for this voyage.

"That reminds me, Francis. How are you getting along with your flock of passengers?"

Francis paused then said, "I've learned much these past eight weeks. Such a valuable experience. It's a challenge, and I'm relieved to have time on the main deck. I was interested in your observations about people coming to America because it becomes apparent in such close quarters how humans behave under stressful conditions. The most fearful and disruptive passengers are those whose expectations are unrealistic. They expect comforts that others all around them do not have, and they are the last to be calmed during the storms, but the first in line for handouts, and rarely are they satisfied with anything."

Captain Headly was nodding while Francis spoke. He asked, "How have you dealt with those people?"

Francis chuckled and said, "It's usually out of my hands. When anyone behaves like I've described, others are quick to jump on them, and I believe the majority get the sense of community and the importance of civility. They grasp the importance of sacrifice for the sake of something more important later. The most useful strategy I've developed on this voyage, and as a liaison … is to ask questions. I might ask a complainer, 'And where do you think that is going to come from?' or 'Why do you deserve to be an exception?' That's safe, since they rarely have done anything to deserve an exception. I find asking questions helps when someone is very fearful too, since no matter what they say, I have another question for them, and answering usually calms them. I also want to say the parlor has been a lifesaver more than once."

Headly asked, "The parlor?"

"Katie Bodman gave that name to the area between the berths and the port side," Francis said. "People gather there all through the day, and we have two with good strong voices who get the people singing. I remember one time when Phillip Havershall was ill and wasn't expected to live. Ruby Styles started a familiar hymn, and everyone sang softly, one hymn after another, until Felicity Havershall came over and whispered, 'He's asleep.' The next morning, he was still alive and eventually he was well again. I was deeply moved by how one hundred people could act as one, out of respect for one person in need."

Reminded of the good in people, Francis said, "My Mary has been a great help. Every morning she sits with the children reading or playing games. She tells her own stories and often stops with questions, like 'And what do you think Grandpa did then?' They come up with some fanciful answers. In the afternoons, she soothes babies so mothers can rest, she tends the sick and ailing, she cleans up messes during rough seas, and keeps me contented." He smiled fondly, thinking of his wife.

He and Mary had discovered much about each other during their daily struggle to adapt to life aboard ship. Mary had settled into routines, unlike her impulsive nature, and Francis had learned what it was like to lose control of daily circumstances. Mary and Francis would benefit in Portsmouth from these adjustments.

31 ~ 1643

Francis and Mary slept like two spoons nestled together, anchored despite the swaying ship. Every morning, Francis awoke first and put his face in Mary's hair and pulled her even closer to him, feeling safe and secure. Mary stirred then, and sensing his need to be reassured, whispered, "I'm here, Francis." He usually said, "I will always be thankful that I went to Weedon Park all sad and lonely that January evening." She would raise his hand to her lips and kiss it. It was difficult for the newlywed couple to be intimate in such close quarters, but they lost their embarrassment as had others. They did not, however, join the others who jested. It was not their way.

Their daily routine began when Francis took their chamber pot to the porthole and waited his turn for the bucket (there were three portholes and three buckets). Then, he lowered the filled bucket by a specially rigged rope, pulled one rope to tilt the bucket to empty the contents, then another to lower it into the water to clean the bucket and then raise it out of the water. This process was precarious when the sea was swelling.

In the meantime, Mary was fetching their wooden bowls and spoons out of the food box along with barley meal, or corn meal, some dried meat, and fruit. These items could be purchased from the steward, and on rare occasions they bought milk from the Teffs, who had a cow on the third level. Once the breakfast items were out, Mary pushed the boxes to the center of their four-by-six berth, put the sleeping mat on top of the low boxes, and that was their sitting space.

They had to wait for their beer ration, which they used to soak the corn meal. Francis had the aggravation of being six feet two inches in a ceiling height of five feet. He was the tallest man on board and was forgiven for spending more time on the main deck than the other liaisons.

Mary usually read the Bible while they waited for the beer. It was the only time they spent alone, if one could say they were alone among a hundred other passengers. They talked about Elizabeth and Stephen, the future, and religion. Mary had taken her spiritual life for granted since her earliest memories, and it was strange to love someone who had practically no spiritual experience at all. However, Francis was always open to learning, so he listened to Mary. Once they had finished their breakfast, she would gather the children for games, reading, or storytelling.

As a diversion during the monotonous days, passengers enjoyed the company of others as they gathered in the parlor. By happenstance, most people made a circular route of the space, talking, stretching their legs, and exercising their lungs as they walked round and round. Mary enjoyed this time with those who were her close friends—Sarah

Trumbel, Prunella Patterson, Elizabeth Wilcox, and Rebecca Gordon. They gathered between three and six most days unless there was a stormy patch. Francis would join the men after he had been topside. Only liaisons were allowed on the main deck, since besides being a busy area, it could be dangerous. The stories of people being swept out to sea made the rounds. In reality it was rare, and on the *Courser* no such accidents had ever occurred.

As Mary and her friends circled the parlor, they exchanged their hopes, dreams, and anxieties: The Trumbels were going to Newport, where family members had opened a mill; the Pattersons were going to New Hampshire, where Bill was going to be a wheelwright; the Gordons were Puritans and had many family members in the Boston area; and the Wilcoxes were—like the Braytons—going to Portsmouth, at the urging of family members. Mary and her friends were prepared to be inconvenienced and uncomfortable, but they were not anxious. Mary had talked to several wives who were fearful and dreading the unknown life in the New World. If nothing could be said to assuage their fears, she would utter the irrefutable, "Put your trust in the Lord."

On August eighteenth, Francis took John's latest letter topside to reread. John wrote:

> My dear friend, it is with great joy that I anticipate seeing you and Mary in Boston. Susanna is eager to meet and welcome you to our home. We both remember the challenges of a crossing, so there will be ample food awaiting your arrival. I have written

many letters these past nine years and I began to be concerned that my optimistic outlook may have misled you about life in New England. I remember the years of farming you managed so well, and even after your father's health failed and the burdens increased, you managed. I saw the heroic in you Francis, that you were a very strong person. It is because of that view that I continually urged you to come to America.

I left England because I believed there had to be a better way for government to improve life. England seemed to keep on the same track, repeating the same struggles, and now, once again, they are on the verge of armed conflict. I could see how both of us were trapped by the system, even though we were each snared in a completely different manner. I have appreciated your patience, I have appreciated your hard work, and I can only hope that Portsmouth meets your expectations. I know you will find it vastly different from England, despite our status as an English colony. We who live on Aquidneck Island are secure, thanks in a large part to William Brenton.

He was instrumental in convincing eight of our Portsmouth residents to move south to the tip of the island to set up a government and a port to forestall invasions from other nations. Those men had already built homes here in Portsmouth, including William, but now we all see in about five years how both settlements have flourished. Even though

Roger Williams has his own settlement, northwest of Aquidneck, he always stepped up to offer his leadership when the area was threatened. Just recently, the Pequot Indian tribe persuaded other tribes to join in an alliance to push the English out of New England. They were defeated just months ago when Williams persuaded the Narragansett Indians to side with the colonists against the Pequots.

Williams has a vision and his ideas are radical, which frighten many, and yet he is a person that others call upon when they need help with the Indians. There are no Indians on Aquidneck, but the Narragansetts have come to work for pay and it has helped us immensely, both here and in Newport. We give them things they desire, and they work, removing rocks, making roads, building sea walls, and other labor-intensive work. The settlers have improved transportation, started trading, and opened shops. We are looking like a town. A good result for us in just five years.

The Compact I wrote about earlier is finally in place and serving as the authority in every aspect of community life. You mentioned that you were interested in the land grants, and I have investigated the lots that are still available. I am relieved that there are several, so you will have some choice. As soon as your sea legs are adjusted, we will go to Town Hall and submit a petition for a grant. I am told there will be a meeting in November where your petition could come up for a vote.

You asked how Susanna and I met. We were both in Boston, and we attended a meeting that John Clarke was leading. Susanna came with her widowed mother, Martha, along with her brothers, Nathaniel, Abel, and Robert. They were attending to gather information about new settlements south of Boston. Susanna's father, John Potter, had died a few months before, and the rest of the Potter family had decided to move away from Puritan rule, which meant going south of the Sekonnet River. I was impressed with Susanna, who was so caring with her mother and who asked good questions at the meetings. I approached her later because I knew I wanted to see her again, which I did … again and again. The Potters joined the Portsmouth Compact; George signed in 1638 for the family. Subsequently, they followed the families who left Boston for Roger Williams' Providence Plantations. They stayed at the plantation until the settlement on Aquidneck Island was ready to be occupied.

Susanna stayed in Boston with me, and we were married by a magistrate that October. Once I had tied up some pending matters in my business, we left for Portsmouth. We had another wedding ceremony in May 1639, officiated by Roger Williams; it was a grand day. John Clarke and Roger Williams are two peas in a pod, but they are competitive even though they are both pastors. Maybe competition is good for the soul. John Clarke is four years younger than I and a lot smarter. He lives in Newport now and has started his own church. Both he and Roger are called Baptists, which you will come to know about once you are in Portsmouth.

Susanna and the boys are doing well. I'm happy that Martha is nearby to help with the twins, especially since another baby is due any day now. Be prepared for bedlam! Godspeed, my good friend.

As always, John

Francis folded the letter and put it in the inside pocket of his cloak which he always wore on the deck where the winds chilled him to the bone. He sat and pondered over his circumstances. He had been dependent on a captain and his crew for his welfare for several weeks, as had Mary too—oh yes, Mary too. After all, he had persuaded her to go on this voyage to America, away from her loving parents and all that was familiar and comfortable. They and the other passengers had put their future hopes and expectations at risk in this solitary vessel. He shuddered as if to shake off the momentary loss of trust, faith, and hope in providence.

He could hear John Anthony scolding him, "Francis, just think of the wonder of man learning how to transport people across vast expanses of water. Think of the hundreds, no thousands who have already arrived safely in America. You are just another one of those."

Returning to the second level, he went to the parlor and listened as others talked about who they would see in Boston—family or friends waiting to welcome them into the fold. Others were talking of what they needed to do to get on with their adventures. Francis wondered how they would think of the extraordinary experience on this voyage—would it be a memory of discomfort and depravation, or one of companionship and a community of diverse personalities evened and leveled by a shared experience? As liaison, he had been given another opportunity to be tested on his ability to influence others, to seek their cooperation and urge them to adapt to strange and often frightening circumstances. He was reminded that John Anthony and Isaac Headly had entrusted him with that responsibility.

32 ~ 1643

The last days dragged along and when the ship turned in toward the Boston Harbor, the euphoria dampened as they waited, hour after hour for the ship to be docked. Getting off the *Courser* was even more tedious because the docking facilities were not as commodious as in London. In the excitement of disembarking, they hardly remembered that this was Francis' thirty-first birthday.

Francis and Mary were told their trunk would not be available for two days and then could be retrieved at the Headly warehouse next to the company office. Two days! They looked at one another and smiled, both thinking of privacy, good food, and solid ground. There was a hubbub of farewells all around, and they walked toward the Wayfarer Hotel with satchels in hand. The captain had told them, "The hotel is adequate, but before you go there, stop at my office—you'll pass it on the way. Check to see if there is a message from John Anthony. I wish you well! It has been my pleasure to have you aboard."

There was a message from John. "Welcome! I'll be there on the eighth day of September as early as possible. We will celebrate!" They walked the short distance to the Wayfarer Hotel and were given the key to their room on the second floor. They snickered together, Mary saying, "From the second level to the second floor. At least it won't be rolling."

When they opened the door, they were delighted to see a water pitcher, a basin, a comfortable bed, and space to walk around. Mary bounced on the bed, and Francis came to her and pushed her back, and together they fumbled to remove clothing that had not been off their bodies for over nine weeks.

The next delight awaiting them was a good hot meal. They left the hotel and soon found a decent restaurant. They ate meat, potatoes, sauce, vegetables, drank water, ale, and later a delicious cake for dessert. They were getting too full and tried taking their time, but the flavor was too good to take time to savor. After the meal, they walked the streets to help their digestion and were careful of the garbage and horse droppings. Before long they were ready to return to their privacy with no responsibilities or cares, just wedded bliss. They slept soundly and spooned by habit.

In the morning, they refreshed their clothing as best they could and went to the breakfast room of the hotel. The coffee was glorious, and they drank two pots. The toast and jam seemed as if it were made for royalty and was quickly devoured. They left and went for a walking tour of "the city of rivers," as Boston was called. They walked along the Charles River, crossed a bridge, and were soon on the grounds of the Harvard College, in an area called Cambridge.

"The English don't leave much behind, do they?" Francis asked. Mary agreed, then smiled, adding, "Let's hope they bring only the good."

They walked back across the bridge and got directions to the Boston Commons, which they had been told was the charm of the city. They were delighted as they entered, for here was a park, much larger than Weedon Park, with a pond where children were floating toy boats, and geese were squawking and splashing as they went in and out of the water. They wandered the path, and both stopped, unbelieving, as before them was a bench under a beautiful elm tree. They sat with the midday September sun warming them as they soaked it all in with satisfaction.

They sat until they were hungry and walked to a nearby restaurant to dine on fish, almost as good as in England. As they enjoyed the meal, they talked of Elizabeth and Stephen, who were probably picturing Francis and Mary in a wilderness, which brought laughter. They continued to talk of Ellington for a bit and then returned to the streets of Boston.

The next day, they checked in the office of the Headly Company, but there were no messages. They visited some shops and noted the differences between London and Boston shops. Boston shops were selling more practical items, and Mary figured these businesses were suppliers for people who were used to a rugged life. Mary remembered the Anthony children, and they found a shop with toys, where they bought pull toys for Joseph and John and a silver rattle for the baby. They had no word about the newborn, but a rattle would do nicely.

The day was pleasant, and they were told many times that in New England, autumn was the best weather of the year. They ate another satisfying meal, walked in the early evening, then returned to the Wayfarer. Francis used Thomas' brush on his clothes, and Mary gave her clothes a thorough brushing as well. They carefully laid them out and had no trouble sleeping after the long walks of the day. The next morning, they were awakened by loud pounding on the door. Francis said, "That's John." He pulled on his trousers and opened the door.

"Francis! You're here!" They hugged, pounding each other on their backs like schoolboys. It was wise that Mary had wrapped herself in the coverlet because John came into the room and gave her a kiss. "Mary, you are beautiful!" He turned to Francis and said, "Why didn't you tell me, you sly fellow?" Then turning back to Mary, he said, "My Susanna is preparing for you as I speak and looking forward to meeting you. You know we have a third child—Hannah Mary, born on July fourth. She's a beauty like her mother."

John's presence spread about the room, just as Francis had described him: "John fills every room he enters."

John began giving orders. "You need to dress, and after breakfast we'll do some touring. Later I have a nice dinner planned at my favorite Boston restaurant. I'll be down in the breakfast room. Hurry!"

Then he was gone, and neither of them had been given a chance to speak. Francis looked happy. "He hasn't changed a bit."

At the table, John asked questions about the voyage and listened intently to what they had to say. He asked about Ike, and Francis told him of their meetings on top deck. John added, "He's such an interesting man. I suppose he told you of his retirement plan: Bermuda!"

They then asked John about the Anthony children. "The boys are great fun. They're so alike that we were happy that one was born with a mole above his right eyebrow—he's Joseph. And that was good because Susanna was worried she would feed one twice and the other would starve! Hannah Mary is a good baby, but then she has no choice, since the boys demand so much care. Martha comes over often to help with her grandbabies. She's a jewel."

Earlier Mary had told Francis while they were dressing, "He is handsome but has none of the artifice or conceit one sees in many handsome men."

Francis agreed. "He's known for his generosity and his ability to sense the needs of others," he said. "He's focused outwardly and rarely calls attention to himself, but it comes to him because of his personality. He doesn't seek glory. He's interested in life, as if he truly understands what it means *to live* rather than exist. I value him, Mary, as a friend and as a human being."

Mary listened quietly. She was more understanding of Francis' relationship with John, hearing this assessment. She could see that Francis had not been flattered by the attention of a titled gentleman but instead that he saw other, more esteemed qualities in his friend. She was reassured.

John hired a horse and an enclosed carriage for their tour of the business side of Boston. "We depend on Boston in Portsmouth, since we've been developing for only five years. I set up a livery business here and in Portsmouth to help our men who come to Boston to get materials. They can exchange horses and sometimes wagons if need be, and often two men will do a round trip without a stay in Boston. They sleep in the wagon during the dark hours and can make the fifty-mile trip in less than three days, unless they have a stay in Boston. In Portsmouth we have no way to make doors or windows and our bricks have been inferior to what Boston kilns can supply. However, we do have plenty of stones on Aquidneck."

John drove the horse into the mill district, and there they saw an astounding array of enterprises, all teeming with activity. John continued, "Many of the immigrants find work here in Boston. The Indians are not afraid of hard work, but they do not adjust to our schedules. They're nomads and therefore cannot accumulate things. They live day-to-day and are not encumbered. They have disdain for our avarice and how we misuse nature. I've been outspoken about the fate of the Indians, which hasn't been well received by my neighbors. Few Englishmen see any meeting ground between our cultures."

They went up the steep hills overlooking the harbor and the ocean beyond. There were beautiful homes in this part of Boston, and the cobblestone streets had been laid more closely and were more comfortable for people in carriages.

John halted in front of a restaurant, handed the reins to Francis, and said, "Stay quiet and it will be fine." They both knew that he was remembering their horseback trip to Foxgrove. He went in and soon returned saying, "The proprietor, a friend of mine, has agreed to set a special table for five this evening."

They returned to the hotel to rest for the evening. Mary had told John about Francis having a birthday on the fifth, which they had ignored in the excitement of disembarking. John whispered, "We'll have a surprise for him, Mary."

At six, John picked them up—who knew where he had been while they had rested?—and they returned, up the steep hill to The Golden Plate. They entered a dining room lit with candles from a chandelier and wall sconces, and with tables covered with linen cloths and china adorned with swirly gold designs. The host took them to a table set for five, and there was William Brenton smiling at them as they were being seated.

Francis said, "William how nice to see you. Let me introduce Mary to you."

William stood, bowed, and kissed Mary's hand. She could not hide her pleasure. "I'm so pleased to meet you, Mary," William said. "I hope someday you will meet my Martha. We are betrothed and plan to marry next year."

Mary replied, “It would be my pleasure, William.”

At that moment, Ike Headly joined the foursome and was equally as gallant as William had been on seeing her once again, under quite different circumstances. Once Ike was seated, the toasts began: Francis for his thirty-first birthday, John’s new daughter Hannah Mary, William’s new business adventure, Ike’s safe passage and future retirement, and Mary’s gracious presence. The conversation was lively and stayed on a positive note. The men did not neglect Mary. In fact, they delighted in her intelligent quick wit.

The most important conversation of the evening came from William, who said, “You know, Francis, I’ve been thinking about my house in Portsmouth. It’s been sitting vacant for five years. I’m fond of that house and how well it turned out under the circumstances. Everything was rushed in that year, as I’m sure you’ve heard. Anyway, the house sits on twelve acres. John Brightman has the keys. Have a look at it, you two, and if it suits you we can get together to discuss a way for you to buy it.

“I’ll be in Newport the beginning of December, and I’d very much like to make a reasonable offer to you. You see how positive I am that you’ll be as enthusiastic about my house as I am?”

John was beaming. “That is an astounding offer! Francis, you’ll be astonished.”

Francis, who was not unused to being given opportunities, had to admit this was something quite different. He was moved.

Brenton said, "Have a look, Francis and Mary, then we will talk."

Later that evening, Francis asked John, "How could I ever afford such a house? And twelve acres! It's clearly beyond our means."

John said, "Believe William when he says he'll find a way for you to have his house—if it suits you."

Even at such a late hour, the merry group were reluctant to part company. They agreed to meet again, some way, and their farewells were heartfelt. Back in the hotel room Mary and Francis agreed that life in the New World had a wonderful beginning. They were being swiftly carried along into a new way of living among people of their own heritage yet, somehow, wholly different.

The next morning, the trunk was loaded onto John's wagon and the three of them were on their way southwest along one of two main thoroughfares from Boston, one to Providence Plantations and the other farther east. From Providence there they would be ferried to Portsmouth Landing, not far from John and Susanna's home. The road was one of the better byways in New England, but still it was a bumpy ride on a wagon seat, behind two horses.

John came to Boston several times a year, and this journey was very like the others, with an overnight at the Plantation Inn accommodating travelers and other casual visitors. Roger Williams was not currently at the plantation, since he and John Clarke had recently sailed for London to petition Parliament for a charter. He would, no doubt, create turmoil while he was there. John Clarke, on the other hand, was a diplomat and he might fare better for the four towns that were asking Parliament for chartered protection.

Providence Plantations was a village of sorts, smaller than Portsmouth, and there were log houses and even Indian tents, but Portsmouth had two water mills that produced saw-hewn boards for their homes. The Plantation Inn was typical of inns in New England, and the Braytons were pleased with their accommodations. Since John was such a frequent guest of the inn, a room was reserved for him as a courtesy. They ate a good meal and before dark toured the village.

Indians came and went as they walked on paths. John said they were friends of Roger Williams. They heard that prayer gatherings were held every evening on the plantation. Many people had come to the plantation who later moved on because of the erratic behavior of Williams, who had been developing a faith on beliefs that were frequently amended, or one belief supplementing another. Nonetheless, Williams was held in esteem for his stance of having a "wall of separation" between church and state.

John spoke of the struggles of many religious leaders in New England and how the Sekonnet River had been the dividing line between the Puritans and those who advocated religious freedom.

John said, "Williams was one of the early separatists to flee from Puritan persecution. Roger Williams' banishment was Massachusetts' loss and our gain; we have four towns that have risen beyond the pale of Puritan acceptance, and there's a movement to unite these towns into a colony. Williams and Clarke are good advocates, but we expect that it will take some time. With Charles I on the throne and England embroiled in a Civil War, I'm relieved that you have escaped it. Who knows? You might have been caught up in the armed conflict."

Francis listened and thought of his early days in Ellington when he discovered how naïve he had been about politics. He was thinking that he still was. They said goodnight to John in the foyer and agreed to meet in the morning at seven o'clock. Tomorrow, they would arrive in Portsmouth, and John said, "Be prepared for our raucous household and some happy smiles to greet you." Upstairs, on the second level, they were delighted to be alone for a few hours. They found comfort and ease together. The next few months would be a challenge with so many decisions to be made.

They were more than ready.

Chapter 9: Inhabitant

Pleasure in the job puts perfection in the work. — Aristotle

33 ~ 1643

It was another beautiful September day in the place that locals were calling Rhode Island. Migratory geese flew high in the blue sky. The air below was so clear that everything appeared sharper, more detailed, and more colorful than in other seasons. It was too early for the leaves to change into bright colors, the hallmark of New England autumns. The Braytons would soon be in the Anthonys' home, which was a long-awaited event for both couples. Francis thought of his friend, Joseph, wishing he would "come to America" and join the celebration.

Their arrival had obviously been anticipated, since, when they pulled in front of a lovely two-story house with mill-hewn boards and shuttered windows, the front door opened, and Susanna came running to greet them. She took Mary's hands and helped her from the carriage.

"Mary, welcome!" she cried. "I'm so delighted you have safely arrived. We've been anticipating this day more than I can say." Then she turned to Francis, and he bent down for her hug. "Francis! You have finally come to America."

She and John embraced, and together they turned to usher their guests into the house. A young man came, and John nodded to him smiling, "Hello, Peter." Peter bowed his head and took over the care of the horse, as if this was his usual duty.

As soon as they were inside, two identical boys came running as quickly as two-year-olds could run. John grabbed one and then the other, settling them in his arms. The proud grandmother, introduced as Martha Potter, stood to the side with a grin as she watched the joyful scene. John put the boys down and said, "This is your Aunt Mary and Uncle Francis."

They suddenly became shy, and Martha stepped in steering them toward their toys. Susanna led the way into the parlor, just as Peter brought in the satchels, putting them by the staircase.

"Are you hungry?" asked Susanna.

John answered for them, "Yes we are! We had breakfast at the plantation, but it was a hurried affair."

Martha had begun dishing up food and soon they were seated around a large table in the dining room. The kitchen and a playroom were behind the parlor and dining room. The house was pleasantly appointed with drapes, upholstered chairs, tables made of walnut, and floors covered with carpets. It was anything but a wilderness, Mary noted to herself, thinking of Elizabeth and Stephen.

They began with a seafood chowder, and both Francis and Mary thought it delicious and could have made a meal of it, but succulent meat came next with potatoes, sauce, and spiced pickles. They were told the meat was venison, which they would no doubt be having quite often, as it was a staple in New England. Martha kept the coffee cups filled and later served dessert, which was pie filled with spiced apples, a novelty to the Braytons. The travelers were shown to their room on the second level, and they got a peek at baby Hannah Mary, who was sleeping.

Mary whispered, "She's beautiful, and I do see you in her face, Susanna."

In the guest bedroom, Francis and Mary stretched out for a nap that lengthened into two hours. When they woke, they were still feeling tired, tempted to sleep on, but they thought of John and Susanna and joined them in the parlor.

The twins were in bed. Martha had gone to stay the night at Nathaniel and Betty Potter's home. He was Susanna's oldest brother in Portsmouth, and the family lived close by the Anthonys. The Potter families welcomed the widow Martha into their homes, since she did not want to live alone. She was helpful no matter which family hosted her.

John poured a brandy, and he and Francis sipped as they discussed plans for the next day.

"First, we need to go to Town Hall," John began. "I'd say at nine o'clock, to meet with John Brightman, our attorney. Since it's Friday, it should be a good time for John. He can help us with the petition for residency that you need to complete so it can be reviewed before our next Town Hall meeting in November. It's important that it be presented at that meeting because there isn't another meeting until next spring. After that, we can study the map of tracts to see which land grants are available. In the afternoon, I think you and Mary should view Will's house—it's across the ravine there. I'll show you in the morning."

Francis thought, "Quite an eventful first day!"

"I'd like to share with you what Will has in mind to offer you for his house," John said. "His price is much lower than he would offer to anyone else. He's willing to set terms of payment over seven years and to make the house available to you and Mary in December. I'm sure it's a price you can manage, and you have a year between each payment. You must compare that with what it would cost to build a house on your own, and remember that it would take time to clear the land before you could even begin to build. It's good business to buy an existing home, especially Will Brenton's." John was simmering with enthusiasm.

"If you are accepted for a land grant," he went on, "you'll have to work one year for every two acres you acquire. Most of the land grant lots are twelve acres, but I'm not sure how much time each day is involved in public service. Your skills will be matched with the town's needs, so I've been told. I was one of several who paid for my land rather than taking a grant, and I was able to immediately clear my land and build this house and the weaving shops. Then I cleared the land to grow the flax I needed for my business. The remarkable thing about Portsmouth's grants is that you can have use of the land immediately as your own.

"Cleared land is higher in value in Portsmouth because removing the stones is hard work. The stones are separated for use in various ways. I wrote to you already about our rock walls. We have two men who are expert at laying the stones, but first you must sort the stones that are good for the walls. They've taught many of us how to do it on our own. The larger stones are used for fireplaces, drains, and such. Clearing trees is one of the easier tasks, but there's also dredging. We have a lot of swampland all over the island."

Susanna interrupted, "John, it's late. We need to be thinking of bedtime, but first tell them about Portsmouth's temporary quarters."

John dipped his head down, saying, "I'm sorry. I get carried away when I talk about our town. There's a place a bit like an inn except it isn't staffed. It has, I think, eight small bedrooms on the second level—adequate, and that's about it. Below is a large communal kitchen, a fireplace, and a gathering area with tables and chairs. It has some storage space for food and such, all of which is available for the occupants. It's called the Resident Inn, and staying there requires a sponsor to vouch that you are intending to be a resident and have applied for a grant and residency. You'll need someplace to be as independent as possible for such a lengthy time as you're facing."

Francis nodded as John continued. "We checked for you, and there's only one couple there now. They're due to move into their new home in two weeks. We could look at it tomorrow to see if it would suit you—maybe before we meet with John Brightman, since he's the person who will handle your application. The inn is close by, as is everything for us, here in the original land grant area. Everything was laid out and surveyed before land was granted or sold. You'll see, Francis, that you have come to live with people who like order as you always have."

Susanna gave the couple candles to light their way and, saying their "good nights," they went to their bedroom. So much information, so much planning, and so many decisions to be made. They had more than food to digest.

In the morning, the Braytons were ready, having had a good sleep, and the day began in a bustle of activity with Joey and Johnny already playing. Martha was there, and she and Susanna moved about in the kitchen and children's room, immersed in the tasks at hand. Mary held Hannah Mary until it was time to sit at the table.

Francis and Mary were surprised by the many choices of food for breakfast. There was ham, boiled eggs, and potato cakes made of shredded potatoes fried in butter. Susann also set out bread with blueberry preserves and muffins.

John said, "We eat hearty in New England, probably because many early settlers starved to death, and food took on an almost sacred meaning in this harsh climate. I must say, we are healthy, our children are surviving childhood, and all of us work up a sweat doing a day's labor. We sleep soundly."

Just an hour later, the Braytons were at the Resident Inn, meeting William and Eva Delle Gatchell, who had a small lot up by Sanford's Cove. They were clearing it and building a house and a shed. Bill was going to make canoes to sell or lease to residents. He had learned his trade in Massachusetts and figured there would be a need for canoes on this island. He had come from England in 1635, met Eva Delle a couple of years later, and they were married just six months before the Braytons arrived. Francis and Mary agreed that the Resident Inn was adequate as an interim place to live, so the next step was to make arrangements with John Brightman. Mary and Susanna went back to the Anthony home, and John and Francis went to Town Hall.

At Town Hall, Brightman greeted Francis and welcomed him into the fold. John Brightman was younger than Francis expected, but he realized he had to get used to that here in America.

Brightman suddenly became serious and invited the men to have a seat. "We've just received tragic news from William and Samuel Hutchinson. Their mother and six of their younger brothers and sisters have been massacred by the Lenape Indian tribe in Slippery Rock, at New Netherlands. Anne Hutchinson and her husband William were among the founders of Portsmouth. William was so helpful as we were instituting our plans for the settlement, as were their older sons, William and Samuel. Anne had begun her ministry, for which she was put on trial in Boston, and within a year, William Senior died suddenly. Anne grieved and was not faring with her ministry as well as she had hoped, so she soon left for Slippery Rock. The sons told us she had a home in a remote area and had simply been in the pathway of Indians doing battle with the army of Willem Kieft."

John sat quietly a moment. "Anne was a remarkable person," he said. "Unrelenting in her beliefs and radical as they may seem, she had influenced many to her way of thinking."

John Anthony said, "Yes, I've heard of her in both places—Boston and here in Portsmouth. The Hutchinsons are fine people, and I'm sure the sons are bereft. When did this happen?"

"Early August. We're planning a prayer service soon, probably at the end of the month. The sons are trying to settle the estate, which is very complicated. Their father was a wealthy man who was unerringly devoted to Anne. I heard there were fifteen children altogether. There will be a notice of the service when it has been arranged. There is no doubt that Roger Williams and John Clarke would be taking part in the service if they weren't in England. Tragic, so tragic."

Francis was thinking, "Possibly, but this is a wilderness, after all."

Brightman stood and walked to a large map on the wall. "Well, then. To our own business," he said. "This shows the tracts of land in Portsmouth. Those already claimed have the owner's name on them."

John stood beside him, looking carefully at the available lots. He and Brightman were talking about the features and locations of various lots as they pointed here and there.

John then turned to Francis. "There are three good locations to see, but first we should ask about the petition for residency and grants."

Brightman went to his desk and got a printed form from a drawer. "Yes, the petition is the first requirement. You can select a land grant, but please return the petition soon."

Francis assured him in his usual earnest way. "I'll have it back by tomorrow."

"Another thing," John Anthony said. "We've just had a look at the Resident Inn, and the Braytons need accommodations for at least three months. It suits them, and I will vouch for them."

"Yes, of course," Brightman said. He reached above his desk for a key and added, "There's a list of housekeeping requirements in the kitchen, and I'm here if you have any questions. Well, you two. I hope you find a satisfactory tract, and I think I mentioned that each are twelve acres, and you'll see they are not uniformly divided. When you've decided, come back to me and I'll reserve it for you. The next step is for us to review the contract, possibly when you submit your petition."

Leaving Town Hall, John and Francis walked around Portsmouth until they found the tract that suited Francis and had John's approval. It was in the northern section just south of the area the residents called the "Neck," where Aquidneck Island curved easterly around Sanford's Cove. The tract lay on higher ground with views of both Narragansett Bay to the west and the Sekonnet River to the east.

As Francis looked around he was reminded of Hounslow because many of the lots had houses with gardens, chicken coops, sheds, beehives, and tethered cows. But there was a difference in the properties: Hounslow properties were uniform, while Portsmouth tracts conformed to the natural landscape having less of man's will in their design.

While the land to the south gently sloped, his lot was almost level. He asked John, "Are there strong winds from the Atlantic?"

"Surprisingly," John answered, "most of our weather comes from the north, so we blame the Canadians for all the foul weather."

"How about horse stables?" Francis asked. "I don't see many from here."

"We have fewer horses within our small community, since most of what we need is within walking distance. The Porter family has stables with many horses and livery for hire. The cost is reasonable, and it frees the land for planting."

As they walked back toward Anthony Way to their home, Francis asked, "Are there many Puritans here?"

"No. Maybe a few Society of Friends members. In fact, William Brenton has become one of them. Martha, whom he is soon to marry, belongs to the Society, and he has followed suit. William's first wife, Dorothy, died shortly after their son, Barnabas, was born. Will has a busy life, as occupied as I am, taking care of business. He has a home in the Boston area, and that's where Martha is living now. Of course, his famous "Four Chimneys" is in Newport. He calls it Hammersmith Farm, but the locals are very impressed with its four chimneys, thus the name fits."

34 ~ 1643

Back at the Anthonys', the "girls," as John called them, were waiting to hear about the tract and the Resident Inn. John waved the key and grinned, so they knew that all had gone well. Francis hugged Mary and told her she would approve of their land. They had ale, ham with bread, and some cheese with fruit, and while eating they talked of the morning's events.

"Hannah Mary and I are better acquainted," Mary said, "and the twins are entertaining to watch as they interact with each other. They talk together in a language each seems to understand, but adults don't understand a single word of it."

Susanna persuaded Martha to sit and eat with the adults for a change, and they talked of England until she got up to attend to either Joey or Johnny or both.

Soon after lunch, the four of them walked to William Brenton's house. It was located behind the Anthony house, across a ravine in which ran a stream the locals called Town Run. Ben Smiton owned the property behind John's land, but he had yet to build on it. They crossed over the Run on stepping stones up the sloping land to the front of the Brenton house. It faced East Main Road, whereas the Anthony house faced West Road, the two major roads of Portsmouth. The front elevation was impressive, with siding of mill-hewn wood painted white; it was two stories with double windows up and down, six altogether, three on either side of the entrance door.

Francis unlocked the door and the four, for the first time, saw why this house was referred to as "the finest in Portsmouth." Inside the entrance was a small foyer facing a staircase up to the second level. There were identical rooms to the left and the right, and each appeared to be twelve-by-fourteen with nine-foot ceilings. Each room had two front facing windows and two side facing windows, all with twelve leaded-glass panes. These rooms had fireplaces along the wall of the staircase. Also in each room were identical doorways into the kitchen on the back wall.

Entering the kitchen, they were impressed by its size. It was eighteen feet deep and twenty-four feet in length, with a nine-foot ceiling. There was a large walk-in pantry with a ten- foot extension to include a "mudroom," which had a door to the outside area in the back of the house. The kitchen was large enough for informal living of a family. The fireplace located under the staircase had two ovens on either side, and the equipment needed for tending fires was on the apron, including a swinging arm pot-holder. All six fireplaces, three up and three down, were serviced by one large chimney. The three rooms on the upper level were identical in size with the three below.

The woodwork in the front rooms was polished walnut, and the supporting beams were stained oak, as was the flooring. The walls were lath and plaster, and the foundation was of mortared stone.

The four toured this marvel of architectural design, too impressed for words beyond, "Oh, see this!" and "Oh, my goodness look here!"

Francis and Mary were both thinking, "Is this not too grand for us?"

Susanna could imagine what was on Mary's mind—furniture, drapery treatments, beds, kitchen utensils, to name a few. "Mary think ahead," she said with cheer in her voice, "how lovely this home will be, with room for a family, so solid and light, so well insulated."

"And large," Mary said.

"You two deserve this house, believe me. Francis, I urge you to go to William Brenton and talk with him to see what he offers you."

"I value your opinion," said Francis, acknowledging his friend's optimism, "and even more your faith in me. I'll meet with William. I can see that it's an extraordinary house."

In the evening Francis prepared the petition, writing, "I have walked your streets and roads, and I feel encouraged by all that the citizens of Portsmouth have accomplished. My wife, Mary, and I have come to Rhode Island because we are eager to be part of a democratic community and will support it with our services and enthusiasm. I request a land grant and will work as required to satisfy payment thereof."

The next day, Sunday, September 13, 1643, they moved with their satchels to their temporary home at the inn. The Gatchells were preparing to move to their nearly completed new home. Next, Mary and Francis walked to Town Hall, where Mary met John Brightman for the first time. Francis gave John the signed petition as he had promised. He informed John that he and John Anthony would be by at four to sign the land grant papers. On the way back to the inn from there, they stopped at a small park near Town Hall, where they sat on the only bench available, which happened to be under an oak tree.

"Do you think we should accept a reasonable offer for the house?" Francis asked his wife.

"We have fifteen pounds from my parents, plus your savings and the wedding coins, but that won't buy a house," she said. "Don't you think it all depends what Will offers us?"

"Yes, I do. We need to limit the amount of each payment, even if it takes a longer time to pay it off. Will is a very wealthy business man. I've heard he owns thousands of acres, and rich people don't get that way by giving away land and houses."

He continued after they both smiled, saying, "We have time before we meet with him, so I want to work here in Portsmouth doing odd jobs if you have no objection. I need to stay busy, and maybe we can find something for you to do as well. I think we're together about the house, aren't we? If the price is within our means, we should invest now. It's perfect and something we could never build on our own. Is that what you are thinking too, Mary?"

"I do think we should buy it if we can. It'll take time to furnish it, but we aren't fussy, either of us, so we can do that at our own pace. Can you imagine what my parents would think, seeing us living in a house like that?—in the wilderness, mind you!"

They left the bench to go to the Anthony's for their midday meal.

Susanna and Mary were congenial, both being strong women with a bent toward independence. As they worked, they shared the events of their lives. The twins kept them entertained but also alert since there were hazards all about them—fireplaces, stony surfaces, hardwood staircases, and furniture too large for babies. Mary and Susanna took turns with the household tasks like carrying water, toting wood for the fireplace, skinning rabbits, and other animals to cook, carrying garbage to the pit behind the house (which the men would bury later), and cleaning, scrubbing, washing, tending the fires, and ironing, only to face the same the next day, and the next.

Each day John left home at seven after a quick breakfast, then returned for the midday meal at two, and then back to his work until six, sometimes later. The children were fed before six and in bed by seven each evening. Supper for adults was usually at seven, and all were in bed no later than ten o'clock.

Susanna was up at five thirty each morning to tend to the fires and the children, then she cooked porridge over the fire, swinging the finished pot of cereal away from the heat to stay warm over the embers. The morning ritual was interrupted when a child was ill, cross from teething, or mischievous.

Mary walked over to the Anthony's at eight, and if Francis did not have piecemeal work to do, he would come and help "the girls" with the heavier work. He was extraordinarily skilled at chopping wood in the back, cutting down weeds, and scrubbing mud from the front and back steps. As time passed, however, he obtained piecemeal work in fields, or he would clear stones from the Brayton tract. Mary loved watching him, so intent on the task at hand, working with strength and precision. His long body was like a work of art.

Francis had learned something about the stones when he helped Bill Gatchell build a modified sea wall around his pond. He learned that a stone was not just a stone and that the shapes, the fitting, and the stacking all came together to keep stones in place. When he began working on rock walls on his own tract, it was satisfying to clean a stone of soil and see them stacked into a wall of stones. He often had to tear out a morning's work on a rock wall, but he did improve. Using a rake and hoe, he loosened the soil one section at a time. Soon he would have a field ready for planting.

He was getting acquainted with many Portsmouth men, including James Wicker, whose land was close to the Brenton property, and he was working well with John Brightman at Town Hall. It was obvious to Brightman that Francis would be valuable in government service. When John learned of his experience with petitions in the magistracy in Ellington and observed him at work at Town Hall—his discernment, how impartially he viewed the petitions, always looking for the positive points rather than enlarging the negatives—he wanted to get him involved in government service, as soon as possible.

Francis met several in the Tripp and Mott families, and also Benjamin Smiton, whose strip of land was near the Town Run. He worked for Richard Borden, who was clearing another lot he hoped to get ready for spring planting. Borden saw the strength of Francis and his diligence, so he asked him to help dredge a tract of swampland he recently acquired. That was tedious, back-breaking work, but Francis learned to step through the marshy land, to lift the soil aside, allowing the water to drain into a proper stream. It was slow work, but he and Richard made good progress, and this was another essential skill that Francis acquired. The people he helped, some with several days' work, others for just an hour or two, gave him either promissory notes for work "in kind" or, eggs, milk, garden produce, or a meal.

Mary had thought she might be pregnant, but it turned out not to be so. They were both saddened, but they also knew the timing for a baby was not convenient. As time passed, they felt welcomed into the community, and John frequently reminded Francis that all would get even better once he had the matters of the petition and the Brenton house settled. Because the residency decision depended on a majority vote, this unusual state of affairs caused Francis much unaccustomed anxiety. However, neither he nor Mary spoke of what they would do if his petition should be rejected. Instead, he threw himself into work and let John's confidence carry him along.

And then it was late November, and soon the town meeting would be held to determine their status in Portsmouth.

35 ~ 1643

The twenty-eighth of November came, and as he walked to Town Hall, the cold wind penetrated his heavy wool cloak. Francis pulled the scarf around his neck more tightly as he went the short distance along the West Road. It was mid-afternoon, and others were making their way to the meeting that was so important for the Braytons and their future in New England. He was to join John, and he looked for him as he came close to the hall. Everywhere men chatted with one another in good humor and familiarity.

Francis spotted John with a group of men, and, as usual, he was talking and the men were listening to what he was saying. John looked over, and saw Francis, excused himself, and turned to greet him. "So here you are—just in time too! We need to get inside quickly to get a seat."

Francis had been in Town Hall many times, but it took on a different atmosphere as he and John greeted their neighbors and fellow residents. A long table stood in front of the benches.

"The white-haired man is Judge William Baulston," John said. "He's the leader today."

The judge said, raising his voice, "Quiet, please, and everyone take a seat. It's time to get started, and Thomas Fish will open the meeting with a word of prayer."

Thomas came to the front, and everybody stood as he began. "Our Savior, we gather together to consider the matters of concern to this community unto which we have committed our persons to remain faithful to You, Lord, and to the principles of Your Holy Word of Truth, to be guided and judged thereby. Grant to us wisdom, tolerance, and a forgiving spirit as we conduct our meeting. With humble reverence, we invoke your presence. In Your name we pray. Amen."

The men settled on the benches and the judge said, "Thank you, Thomas. The first order of business of this meeting of the Portsmouth community is to respond to three petitions for residency and land grants. Once the introductions, discussion, and voting on the petitions is completed, the floor will be open for discussion on other issues submitted to the Town Council for consideration by the residents. To get started, I ask John Anthony to come forward to say a few words about Francis Brayton, our first petitioner on the agenda."

John faced the group. "I have known Francis Brayton since we met by chance in England over twelve years ago," he said. "I have been urging Francis to move to Portsmouth for several years, but he would not leave as long as his parents needed his help on their tenant farm. Soon after his parents died, he met and married Mary Smith, which was a good thing because she is a woman very capable of dealing with this rough life. Many of you have worked with Francis and know he is a hard worker and trustworthy. I propose that you accept him today as an inhabitant of Portsmouth with your yea vote. Thank you."

There had been some positive murmurings during John's introduction, and before Francis could recover from the embarrassment he felt as the center of attention, he heard the judge announce, "All in favor of accepting Francis Brayton as an inhabitant of our town, and granting him a tract of land, indicate by voicing a yea." The yea votes rang out, but, when called for, not a single nay vote was heard. Francis was grateful for such an affirmation from the citizens of Portsmouth. The other petitions were presented and approved as well.

There followed a heated discussion on a motion to withdraw Portsmouth from a proposal being presented to Parliament for a charter that would unite Newport, Providence, Warwick, and Portsmouth into a colony. The motion did not carry, which was expected because the majority had already approved the union. Committee reports followed, and then some matters that were being referred to a committee to be acted upon. It was a long meeting, and when it was adjourned, the men, including John and Francis, did not linger, since the November sky had already darkened. Men were lighting torches and walking the West and East Roads to their homes.

When Francis commented on the serious business that had been addressed in one afternoon, John said, "Time is of the essence. The weather will soon turn very nasty, and there's always work to be done with less sunlight to get it done. Well, here we are. The girls will be eager to hear the good news."

The husbands were greeted with a roaring fire, bowls of chowder, and hot biscuits. There were congratulations all around.

After eating they sat before the fire talking of many things and with an ease that comes when unfinished business is finally resolved. Before Mary and Francis returned to the inn, John reminded Francis of the meeting with Brightman at Town Hall set for ten o'clock in the morning. Francis did not need a reminder, but he nodded his assent.

Mary would be back to the Anthonys as usual in the morning. She was sewing a piece of canvas to make a tote for carrying wood, which she thought might be helpful for Susanna. Mary had become quite skillful with her sewing needles. She was also good with her knitting when she could get the yarn. John had been giving her bits from his shop, and she'd even been experimenting with dyes.

Once the formal contract had been reviewed by Brightman, the temporary contract was voided and the agreement that stated the terms of the land grant and government service was given to Francis for signature. There was silence while Francis signed his name, almost as a ritual of respect for something very meaningful. It was a debt, for certain, but the one provision that was unusual was that if Francis were to renege on his service to the community, he would relinquish his right to the property without punishment or payment. However, the town would take possession of the property along with any improvements that had been made to it. Francis and John walked to the tract, determined to stand on Brayton land in the New World.

Francis and John were to go to Newport on the tenth of December to see William Brenton. Will happily anticipated their visit and insisted they stay at Hammersmith Farm, saying, "I would be deeply disappointed if you were to turn down my hospitality." John believed the best way to travel in the winter was by horseback. Horses are more adroit at maneuvering on frozen ground, he explained to Francis. "We should make the fifteen miles in good time."

They had saddlebags to carry dried foods and extra clothing and left on horseback at first light on December tenth. The horses were from the Porter Stables, located where owner, John Porter, had a large tract of land for grazing on Round Meadow, facing Narragansett Bay. John was riding Pilgrim and Francis rode Nanny. The names made them scoff, but the horses were well-trained and made the journey to Newport enjoyable.

Having started just before the light of dawn, they followed an Indian trail, formed by years of hunting the island. Much of the area had been burned off, which the Indians did frequently to make it easier to get close to their prey.

"We're getting close to Newport," John said hours later. "You'll see the excellent harbor as we approach. This town will have a different history from Portsmouth. It will attract ships from all parts of the world, I believe."

After a while John spoke again. "Will's farm is south of the harbor, located on a promontory that affords a grand view, but it's also open to the wind. Have I mentioned that he has three residences now? He goes to Boston more often these days, since he's courting Martha Burton. I'm happy for him—he deserves to be happy. He's so generous with his wealth. More so than most."

They reached a narrow point where they could see water on either side, and as they rode on they caught glimpses of tall masts of ships in the harbor ahead. John said they would tour the harbor later as he veered them away from it and onto higher ground for quite a distance. They came to a pasture with sheep grazing among the briars that had snagged the wool until the whole pasture looked like white flags waving in the breeze. "This is known as Wooly Hill," John said, "and for good reason!" They rode down and around until they were on a wider road and could see far ahead the famous "four chimneys."

They rode into a driveway leading to Hammersmith Farm, and a man greeted them, as if he had been waiting for their arrival. "Let me take your horses to the barn and I'll care for them during your stay, Mr. Anthony."

John thanked him, told him the horses' names, and introduced Francis. They walked to the front door, and John hit the knocker. A woman dressed in livery answered. "Master Brenton is expecting you in the library," she said. "Follow me, please."

Before they could enter the room, they heard Will saying, "Come in you fellows! Welcome to Hammersmith." There he was, all smiles. He seated them by a large array of windows overlooking the water. He fixed them drinks, and they talked and enjoyed each other's company. The fireplaces were blazing, and later, when they walked about the lovely "country home," they saw fireplaces glowing all around them.

They ate a delicious meal and then returned to the library for brandy.

"So, Francis," Will continued, "how do you like Portsmouth?"

"Very much," Francis said, "and I am pleased to say we're officially residents now. Mary is also happy, and she and Susanna are like sisters."

"Have you seen the house?"

"Yes. Such a beautiful, solid home, and one of the finest I've ever seen."

"I put my heart and soul in that house, I'll confess. Strange that I never lived in it, but you see—and probably know already—many of us in Portsmouth decided we would have a very wary future if the port to the south were left open to anyone. You can see what has developed here in just a few years. It was a good thing that nine of us agreed to leave our investments in Portsmouth to come and establish Newport. It was a sound decision. I don't know why I haven't sold the house in Portsmouth before. Perhaps, I've been waiting for just the right person to live in it."

He winked at Francis before continuing. "I talked with Bill Dyer," he said. "My attorney and good friend—a remarkable fellow all around. Do you know Bill, John?"

"I've met him. His good reputation is well-known in Portsmouth."

"Yes," said Will, "and he agrees that the property needs occupants. I know you may be curious as to what I have to offer, Francis, so I'll set it before you. You need not answer now, but you'll have time to decide before you return to Portsmouth.

"I'm asking forty-nine pounds, to be paid seven pounds a year, for seven years. You can move into the house immediately, and when the seven payments have been made, you will be issued a deed of purchase. I'm willing to set the first payment a year from now, which will make the last payment due in December 1650."

Francis was stunned. He had expected the price to be much higher, and he was quite emotional. He stood and walked to Will, who rose to meet him, not sure what Francis was doing. "Will, I have never been offered such a fine arrangement in my life and did not expect this today. I'm pleased to accept. Mary was entranced with the idea of living in such a beautifully designed house, as am I. She will be very happy. We're both very happy! I can't wait to tell her!"

They shook hands. "It's settled then! Tomorrow, Bill will have the contract ready for your signature. John Brightman has whatever else you may need, and your payments should be submitted to him rather than being sent here to Newport."

In the morning, the three friends enjoyed a good breakfast in the large dining room with a view of the ocean. They parted company soon after, saying goodbye to Will. Francis, not knowing how to express his gratitude, finally saw it was not necessary. Will seemed pleased to have it settled.

William Dyer was ready for them in his office on Thames Street. The harbor glistened in the sunlight, and the town was busy up and down the streets and on the wharves. Francis signed the contract, and Bill suggested they go to a good restaurant, but both John and Francis were eager to get back on the road and home to Portsmouth.

They thanked Bill, and John said, "We'll come again with Mary and Susanna, and have a good visit together." Bill accepted that proposition, and soon the travelers were out of sight, heading north.

They made better time going home. Mary and Susanna were overjoyed to hear the good news about the Brenton house, which Francis declared would be the "Brenton" house until the deed was in his hand.

"Then, Mary, it will become the Brayton home, filled to the rafters with children." They had a hearty laugh as they pictured the large rooms filled with their sons and daughters.

36 ~ 1643

The next morning at the Resident Inn, Mary was sleeping when Francis took his cloak and scarf and quietly left their room and went to the kitchen below. He needed to sort the issues that had kept him awake most of the night. His anxiety had penetrated his sleep and he came awake in a state of panic thinking about the two contracts he had just signed, committing him to seven years of government service without pay in one, and in the other to a payment of forty-nine pounds. He was feeling that he had jeopardized the promising future he and Mary had come to Portsmouth to pursue. He was doubting himself as another Brayton burdened by debt.

In the kitchen he began to pace, waiting for the sunrise to light the roadways so he could walk to clear his thinking. Events had come about too quickly for his usual consideration. He always took time to review circumstances, to ruminate, and then to decide a course of action. He did believe the contracts would result in a better future; he would own land, not just work on it. The William Brenton house, which was beyond his expectations and had been enthusiastically offered to him for an absurdly low price, was like a gift. Despite these advantages, he had worries—how could he afford to furnish the Brenton house if he had no income? And if anything should happen to him, what would Mary do? She trusted his judgment and believed in him, but had he extended himself too far?

Light was penetrating the morning fog, and now Francis put on his cloak, wound his scarf around his neck, and went into the chill morning air. He walked to East Main Road and turned south. People were stirring, cows mooing, chickens clucking, and sheep bleating, reassuring him and reminding him how he had worked his way out of difficulties in the past. His long legs took him up and down the undulating landscape, and when he had turned west on Pocasset Ferry Road he could see Narragansett Bay. At the top of a hill, he paused to look as the fog slowly lifted and the sunlight penetrated through, warming the air. He turned around and looked at the several homes that had been built by the founders of Portsmouth.

These pioneers had begun with nothing more than a natural landscape and they had faced a harsh climate with a short growing season, soil filled with rocks or soggy swampland, and no convenient way to get to a mainland. Still these stalwart men and women had made the most of good neighbors with whom they traded goods and services. Francis was thinking more clearly now. He and Mary were strong and healthy. They could manage as these hardy people had, and Francis knew his pride would prevent him from reneging on any commitment he had made.

He continued walking north, back to the Resident Inn and to his Mary. Ahead he saw a faint outline of the Troop of Horse Training Place, which, Francis knew, William Baulston had been asked to organize because of his military experience. He had done so and, he had also donated the land for it, enough land to build Town Hall and the Resident Inn. Portsmouth had not been organized around a village green dominated by a church unifying people by faith; nor were there plantation masters with fiefdoms of slaves working cotton and tobacco fields; nor were there thick woodlands with men living in isolation like hermits. Portsmouth had been organized as a community of people who gathered in a Town Hall to make decisions by majority vote, and they had a written document as their ultimate authority.

Francis had been working at Town Hall for only two weeks before he saw that this was a place for him to contribute. The town relied on records—petitions, deeds, minutes of meetings, committee reports, and fiduciary accounts. Events had been moving quickly for the Town Council, and the records were piling up, needing to be organized; Francis was experienced with bringing order to records in disarray. He could keep up with his service obligation and still find time to work his land. The walk had given him perspective, and he was reminded of the day his father died, and how he had looked out the small window at the village of Hounslow, seeing the village with a new perspective, with different eyes.

Mary was still in bed but woke when he entered the room. "Francis, you've been out. I can feel the cold coming off you. Where have you been?"

He removed his scarf and cloak, hanging them on the hook. "I've been walking around trying to decide what we needed to do to move into the Brenton house," he said.

Mary pulled herself up and propped against the headboard, fully awake. "Francis! Are you not satisfied with our plan to live in the kitchen space?"

He clapped his hands together to get them warmed. "I'm very satisfied with our plan," he answered, "but I was getting overwhelmed by all the practical considerations—like furnishings, utensils, tools. You know, Mary—household things."

"Oh Francis, every journey begins with a first step and continues with the next and so on. We'll get a bed and mattress, you'll chop firewood, and I'll cook using the wonderful swing pot in the fireplace. We can borrow a bucket for well water, and we'll sit on two small barrels and enjoy ourselves by the fire.

Francis felt his heart swell as he watched her eyes open wide and saw her demeanor of confidence. He went to her—as she had expected he would.

They had a plan, as was their way, and it would be done a step at a time. First, Francis, with the help of friends, would cut hardwood trees from their Middle Road allotment. They would cut oak, since the kitchen was to be oak and the other rooms walnut. These would be transported to the Lawton's saw mill with an ox and wagon leased from Porter's Stable and Livery. Fenton Walen, who was making their furniture, would give instructions to Thomas Lawton, and when ready, Fenton offered to transport the wood to his workshop.

Mary had decided which furniture was to be made now: a bed, two chairs, side tables, a large sideboard with cupboard, and an extra-long, twelve-foot table with benches for all sides. They would order a mattress from John Anthony's weavery, and they could use the spacious pantry for storage. They expected to be quite comfortable in this space for several years, if need be. Fenton had estimated it would take four months to make the first order of furniture, and April became the probable time for moving.

Fenton had listened to the list of furniture items the Braytons were requesting, and he scratched his head, looking down and up—obviously thinking. "Well now," he said "the table will be a challenge."

Mary interjected, "Oh please, Fenton, my heart is *set* on this table."

Fenton said, "Well then, it must be done!"

Francis was affirmed on what he had believed all along. Mary was a charming person who could charm.

George Brownell, Jack Slocum, and Adam Pearce offered to help Francis cut the oak trees. George had gone with him to lease the ox and a wagon, and they met the other two at the Brayton Middle Road tract. They selected the trees and decided which to cut first. Those were loaded and transported by wagon to the Lawton Mill. The last to be cut was the tallest tree in the woods, the tree for the table. John Anthony came to help, as well as the others, and still they had quite a time getting it loaded on the wagon. As they moved along West Road to the mill, they gathered a crowd.

People asked one another along the way, "What is Brayton going to do with that tall tree?"

Someone shouted, "Hey, Francis, that sure is a tall tree! I thought you already had a house."

Francis shouted back, "We have to keep Fenton Walen busy."

The tall tree had become part of Portsmouth legend, and it was inevitable that the table would be known as "Talltree."

Francis arrived at Town Hall by six each morning, and he read records during December and part of January. He read all the minutes of the Council meetings and committee reports, studied the financial history, read every grant petition, disciplinary action, license, and land transaction, and he had by then, no doubt, a more comprehensive knowledge of the Portsmouth community than any other resident.

Francis could not hold an office or vote on some issues until he was accepted as a freeman, which could not be done until he had satisfied all the requirements in his land-grant contract. This did not concern him because he was not aspiring to hold a political position, but he must provide for Mary and himself and pay Fenton Walen. He did what he was able to do—he cut down trees to split into firewood.

Firewood was in demand year-round, and he was able to trade and barter for items he and Mary needed. The winter months went quickly, especially for Francis, who worked from dark to dark every day. Only a few couples stayed at the Resident Inn, and they had been as busy as the Braytons. It was interesting to listen to their stories. The first, William and Eva Delle Gatchell, had already moved into their new house. Also, the four Gibbon brothers had arrived and were going to open two grist mills. They had come from New Hampshire, attracted by the swamplands, which they would dredge first and then construct their mills. Their wives were waiting in New Hampshire until their houses were built.

Before going to help Susanna, Mary went below and sitting at a table with quill and ink, she began a letter to her parents, writing:

January 12, 1644

To my dear Mother and Father,

I do pray you received notice of our safe arrival in Boston. Captain Isaac Headly took my letter to be mailed on the first sailing ship to London. That was just three months ago, and although the delivery of mail is very irregular, I do hope our correspondence is delivered to you and not inadvertently misdirected.

Events are unfolding so quickly I am hard-pressed to remember all of them. Our trip from Boston, through Providence Plantations to Portsmouth is a distant memory, but I do remember the Indians who were living in Roger Williams settlement. A few tried to talk with us but John Anthony said something in what I believe was in their language, and they went on their way. A few come to our island who are hired to work, mostly for our government, but none stay overnight. They have been no threat to our island, and I wanted you to know that, because I believe you have heard sensational accounts of the American Indians.

The most important event since our arrival was just finalized yesterday. I believe you are familiar with the Brenton family of Hammersmith—his son William is a friend of John Anthony, and they have included Francis when they meet occasionally, which began in England. William was the person who encouraged John to emigrate. I'm writing this because we have bought the house William had built for himself in Portsmouth, before he decided to move, with eight other men, to found a settlement named Newport. The house has sat vacant for five years, and while dining with William in Boston, he suggested that Francis buy the house for us. John was so animated, very excited about the offer, and now that we have examined it ourselves, we understand. It is a solidly built two-story house with many windows and six fireplaces. The woodwork is walnut in the front rooms and oak in the kitchen, with the same design up and down and same woodwork on the second level.

William was insistent that we should have the house and offered it for only a bit more than we would have paid for our voyage, had it not been waived since Francis served as a Liaison. We have engaged a skilled furniture craftsman to begin making our furniture. So, we will move in April into the large kitchen while the furniture for the rest of the house is being completed, a room at a time.

In the meantime, we are comfortable at the Resident Inn, which was built in 1640 for people like us, to live in temporarily while waiting for their houses to be built. It is not elaborate but so nice to be able to be on our own and not a burden to John and Susanna. Such lovely people they are, and I adore their two-year-old twin boys, Joseph and John, and pretty baby, Hannah Mary, born June twenty-first. Their house is a busy place as you can imagine.

Francis will serve half a day for the Portsmouth government in Town Hall, which is next to the Resident Inn. He is doing almost the same work as he did in the magistracy, so he is pleasing the men who are getting this new system of governing on its feet, so to speak. Once we are into a routine, I am sure I will feel the effects of living on a small island. The entire dimension of Aquidneck is three miles wide by fifteen miles long, and Portsmouth is in the upper third of the island. There are very few houses, and one family has a large tract of meadow with a large stable and livery for boarding or leasing horses. It works well, and the individual tracts of land are free for planting gardens, for chicken coops or even sheds for cows. Francis has a twelve-acre field to plant, granted to him by the government. He will work half-days for the next six years to pay for the land. Now we also have another twelve-acre tract, which came with the purchase of the Brenton House.

We are in awe of our situation. After just three months in New England, we own a grand house and twenty-four acres of land. I have a plan to start a small school in our large house. Papa, I have a request. If you would send me some books and slates and chalk, I would be so excited to be helping with something as important as teaching young children. They have plans for a school in Portsmouth, but it will be a while before it gets started with so many other projects having higher priority getting attention now.

I can say that if people were not so hard at work, they all would be fatter than the Biblical "fatted calf." We have good hearty food and most of it comes from the gardens and the woods. Venison is frequently served, as well as rabbit, wild hog, and other vile creatures that the Braytons refuse to eat. Fish is a staple as well, and I have a lot to learn about preserving food. The weather is glorious in the fall and lasts until late November, but I've heard the winds from Canada are fierce in the winter.

I miss you both, and Francis and I talk of you almost every day—I say almost, since some days we see very little of one another. I like this adventure so far. I'll write as often as I have ink and paper to use. We wish you good health and send our love to Mark and Henry.

From your loving daughter, Mary

And Francis says hello and sends many thanks for the heavy scarf that has been keeping him warm—reminding him of you dear ones in England.

Mary took the letter to Francis to mail and walked over to the Anthonys.

Mary enjoyed helping Susanna with the children, and as they did their duties, they became acquainted and before long true friends. Susanna accompanied Mary to the emporium, which was operated by the Adam Mott family, as she was keener on the necessities of housekeeping than Mary. They selected candles, a flint, two candle holders, a chamber pot, cups, plates, a bread box and food staples. They added flour, salt, barley, corn meal, and sugar. They giggled like two schoolgirls as the items were loaded into John's wagon, and the four of them delivered the lot to the Brenton house. Mary thought, "I hope we will switch from the Brenton house to the Brayton home soon."

Fenton Walen had completed the bed, two chairs, two small side tables, and the cupboard, which was beautiful, with decorative details on the doors. He had told them in March that he would have all but the large table finished and delivered by the fifteenth of April. They were ready, which wasn't surprising, since they had practically no possessions. Mary's trunk would finally find a permanent resting place in the Brenton house.

April the fifteenth was an exciting day. Fenton was proud to show them their new furniture and they were pleased. John and Susanna were also anticipating how pleased Mary and Francis would be with their gift to them, a cupboard full of linens that had been woven at John's shop. The Braytons were touched by such generosity. Francis made a fire, warming the kitchen with logs from the big wood box alongside of the fireplace. He was relieved that the tools had been left there by William Brenton. Also, they found two buckets in the mudroom at the back of the pantry, which was used as storage space for hanging dirty clothes and storing muddy boots. Every house in the settlement had a mudroom.

Mary and Francis had decided the gold coins would be kept aside for the seven yearly payments on the house. They had been tempted to pay off the contract, but that would have been risky, leaving them without any reserves. They could manage to make the monthly payments for the Walen furniture.

Francis had done better at the bartering than he expected, since several people had offered him trees from their land in exchange for his cutting and delivering a supply of firewood for them. Everyone knew that Francis Brayton was not a hunter, since he let it be known that he believed it ruined a good walk in the woods. They were more astounded that he didn't own a gun, so he was often given rabbits, pheasants, and woodchucks in exchange for his firewood.

The Anthonys had gifted them with a mattress for their rope bed and a woolen blanket. They delivered these items, with the children in tow, and Susanna also brought bread and preserves so they could have coffee together. The boys ran from room to room, which delighted Mary and Francis, both looking forward to having their own children doing the same one day.

Later, Francis and Mary lay spooned in their wonderful new bed, in their new home, but with the same old love, and in less than a month they were celebrating Mary's pregnancy.

Mary said, "Now, Francis, such a coincidence could not really be a coincidence. So much has come together for us, better than we could ever have expected. We must give thanks to God."

"I willingly admit that there's a providential hand in all of it. I have some old habits, old ways of thinking and believing, but I do doubt that mere coincidence could be so clever."

Mary had two reasons to write her parents. She sat at Talltree and wrote to Elizabeth and Stephen:

June 10, 1645

Dear Mama and Papa,

I have a wonderful announcement. I am expecting a baby in January. I have waited to be sure of it before writing to you. Francis and I are quite excited about beginning our family. I hope to have my very own children to teach, but for now I have twelve of the neighbors ready to begin school in our large home.

Papa, I appreciate how thoughtfully you selected the books and materials. You are dear to help me with something that I feel needs to be done, and that

I want so much to do. While we were sailing, I worked with the young children every morning and learned how to hold their interest with my songs and stories that I taught them. We had no space or materials, so it was a challenge.

Now I have both, thanks to you, Papa, and to William Brenton for our large home. Are you familiar with the Brenton family in Hammersmith? I think I already asked you that before, but William Brenton is worthy of praise. He made it possible for us to have the finest house in Portsmouth and we want to repay that gift in any manner we are able to do. We are living comfortably in the kitchen, and my large table will be a good place for the children to write on the slates you sent. I will work out assigning work for sharing the materials.

Francis is gone from early morning until six or seven in the evening. He comes home for the midday meal and a short rest. He is more involved than before in government business, as he has the experience they need in this unique government. In order for the people to be involved, they must understand the purpose for the decisions they make during the town meetings. The preparation for presenting the needs of the community is complicated work, but we have able men involved. There is a concerted effort to prove the democratic way can be practical and effective. Educating these youngsters is essential in that purpose.

We are working hard, but there is excitement among all of us in Portsmouth, and it seems to be a worthy cause. We have an amiable group of friends and we enjoy gatherings in our homes. We are doing well, and on the island, we are safe, in fact we don't need to think of our security.

We do miss all of you. Give our love to Mark and Henry, and continue to write us about the grandchildren, and we will soon be able to share with you our tidbits of a Brayton child.

With love and affection,

Your daughter, Mary

Talltree and the benches had been delivered the week before, as well as the two chairs that Caleb Arnold had upholstered. Francis and Mary decided to have a party, and they invited their friends who had helped them prepare the house. Many came with gifts. Jack and Nora Slocum brought a crystal nut dish with a sack of nuts. Luke and Anna Tripp brought a braided rug that went nicely by their bed and would feel better than the cold floor each morning. Thomas and Betty Brownell brought sconces that were gladly accepted for better lighting, and John and Catherine Tripp brought a beautiful maple cutting board for the sideboard. They gathered around Talltree and enjoyed a delicious stew from the swing pot. As they went to bed after the guests had left, Mary said, "Francis, it couldn't get any better than this."

"Mary, my love, I agree. I am as happy as I need to be."

They slept very well.

It did get even better when Francis Thomas Brayton was born on January 25, 1645, the same birth date of the twins. From the start they called him "Frankie." They doted on the child but eventually they allowed the baby to become a person in his own right—the child's first blessing in his new world. The Anthonys' children welcomed Frankie, and another baby, Elizabeth Martha Anthony, was welcomed March 21, 1645. Mary had made a small coverlet for sweet Elizabeth, and she and it were inseparable for many years.

The Braytons managed to plant a large garden behind the Brenton house, and the year went by with work and good companionship.

The next spring, they added a chicken coop, and Frankie enjoyed chasing the chickens, but Mary believed it kept the hens from laying so he was left outside the fenced area. They had decided to make a move from the kitchen. It was time.

Fenton Walen was making more furniture, beds, dressers, and washstands for the upstairs and more chairs and small tables for the parlor. He had made the extra-large cradle that Mary wanted, yet Frankie crawled out of it every morning and into their bed. Mary was pregnant and due to deliver her baby in April 1647. It had been three years since they moved in, and she had hoped they would be sleeping in the upper level before the baby arrived. Fenton aimed to please, and he did finish the furniture.

Also, Fenton's son, Richard, was a carpenter who built a back staircase at the end of the kitchen where Mary and Francis had been sleeping. It was a wise addition for the convenience of the family.

Once the stairway was completed, as well as the furnishings for the bedrooms, Fenton sent another son, Samuel, with a message.

"Papa would like you to come to the shop Sunday afternoon at three o'clock," he said.

They assured Sam that they would be there. They expected it to be about the next payment on their bill. He had been abundantly patient with them so far.

They walked up the pathway to Fenton's shop, and above the door was a sign that read "The Brayton Furniture Workshop." They stopped in their tracks and laughed heartily.

Fenton came out smiling and said, "I'm relieved you're laughing. We appreciate your orders you know. It's helped to put my business on the Portsmouth map."

He went over and took the sign down and handed it to them. "Well, Francis, when and if you can get the walnut for your dining room table and chairs, I'll be ready to begin on them."

They hung the sign in the kitchen and treasured it. It made them feel that they had contributed to Portsmouth's prosperity in a small way.

Part Four

THIS AND THAT

Chapter 10: Freeman

Things that are equal to the same thing are equal to each other. —
Euclid

37 ~ 1655

Mornings began the same in the Brayton home, varying only by the dictates of the harsh New England climate. On this June morning as the sun streamed into the parents' bedroom, Mary, already awake with baby Sarah at her breast, listened as the birds outside woke one another. Mary was savoring the time with the warm sun and the chirping birds, forgetting in that moment the press of her usual morning duties. Francis had not stirred, and she found it appealing that whatever her husband did, he did it thoroughly.

Mary glanced at Sarah, who looked up and smiled, the milk drooling from her mouth as she kicked her feet in the way an infant expresses the joy of life. When the baby had her fill, Mary got up, leaving her happily waving her arms and legs. Mary pulled on her day-frock, then lifted Sarah into her arms and walked into the nursery where the other five children were sleeping. Frankie, the oldest, would be the first to be wakened and he was asleep in the alcove, the space beside the back staircase. This space had been where the live-in nurse had slept during Mary's six confinements, but there would be no more because of complications during the birth of Sarah.

Frankie at ten years was pleased to be separated from the others, and Mary believed he had earned this privilege, since he worked from dawn to dusk. Ten seemed a cruel age for children to work, but it was the custom in this new frontier, which was forging its way through the wilderness. Portsmouth was far from a wilderness, but also a long way from the civility of England.

"Wake up, Frankie, it's time to get up." His eyes flew open and he looked as if he had been caught neglecting his duties.

"Yes, Mama, I'm awake."

Mary checked on the other children. Stephen, five, was sleeping in a bed by the fireplace, and he looked just like his papa and he slept as he did also. He insisted on being called Stephen, but Martha was Marta, Mary was Molly, Elizabeth was Beth, and Sarah was Sarah. Across from him were two beds in front of the back-facing windows. Marta, at eight, slept lightly like a mother who is alert to her children's safety. She was also a conscientious child, who had begun helping with babies several years ago. She was a mix of Mary and Francis, less sober than Francis, but not as lively as Mary. In the bed next to Marta's was Beth, almost three now—determinedly independent—and beside her was Molly, who at seven seemed to be "somewhere else" most of the time.

"Good morning, Marta. Are you ready to start your day? Up-up-up, my chickadees, and down for breakfast."

Mary walked down the stairs as the five children, in all their individual ways, began their day. From this moment on, the goal of every member was to prepare for the family breakfast.

Mary put Sarah in the cradle and then stoked the fire, adding more logs for a good blaze. Then she stirred some oats and milk for porridge. Once she got the right consistency, she put it in the swing pot positioned by the heat but not directly over the flames. Mary put the kettle filled with water on the iron grate closer to the flames, and while she worked, she talked to Sarah.

"What a good baby you are," and "Are you trying to climb out of your cradle? Oh no-no-no-no!"

Frankie came down the stairway and passed through the pantry to go outside for wood and water from the spring. Soon the other four children came down the staircase and began the tasks each did every morning. At the same time as Stephen got the spoons and mugs on the table, Marta stirred the porridge and waited until it was ready to put in the seven bowls. Molly placed the toppings for the porridge on the table while Mary sliced the crusty bread and put it on a trencher, along with the jam and butter. Beth struggled to get on the bench and then scooted to her own space at the table. Once the bowls of porridge and bread were on the table and everyone had been seated, Francis came down and, with some decorum, sat at the head of the table.

"Good morning, children," he said.

"Good morning, Papa!" they said in chorus.

Francis and Mary smiled at each other, and all bowed their heads and said grace.

"We humbly thank you, Lord, for the bounty of your blessings that nourish our bodies and our souls, amen."

Conversations at mealtime were encouraged, but all were governed by Papa, who was the arbiter for any disagreements, and his word was final. Once the meal was finished, the children cleared the table while Francis washed his face at the washstand. Then, he and Mary walked arm in arm to the front door where they embraced, more from inclination than habit. Mary relished the feeling of Francis' strong arms around her, and he coveted the feel of Mary in his arms. They reluctantly pulled apart to pursue their daily activity.

Brayton mealtime rituals had not come about willy-nilly. Instead they had been designed and executed by Mary much like a commander with raw troops, except Mary dearly loved each of her children and wanted them to be prepared for their future life in Portsmouth. Mary was not a typical housewife. She was a teacher who was skilled at nourishing young minds, and she adapted to each of their personalities, accepting them as they were, not as she thought they ought to be. These past eleven years had been challenging, but she had some advantages: She had an education, and she had been a mature woman of twenty-five-years when she married and twenty-seven when she gave birth to Frankie.

Mary had other attributes that gave the children an agreeable atmosphere, namely energy, creativity, and a calm and reasonable approach to problems. Mary had observed how young wives had become bitter from the hard, never-ending work they faced each day, and she decided early on she would not let her role as wife and mother become burdensome. When she was overwhelmed by circumstances, she had her abiding faith that kept her humble and patient, traits she relied on God to supply.

Francis enjoyed his work at Town Hall, which had similarities to what he had done in the Ellington magistracy. The small staff and the political notables in Portsmouth's government appreciated the contributions of Francis Brayton as they had been from the beginning in 1643. Besides bringing order to the record-keeping of the town, he had made it possible, with written protocols and guidelines, for anyone to step in and manage the paperwork so essential for orderly operations. Francis had fulfilled his obligation to Portsmouth for the land grants he received. On May twenty-second at the General Assembly, he had been admitted to full citizenship. Now he was eligible to serve in any official capacity and in all matters of government. He was a freeman.

Francis had seen how the democratic processes were working as intended, with the minority giving sway to the majority and the majority respecting the minority. Such a fragile system of government required people to be civil with one another and to produce and promote people of good character. It was, after all, a dynamic process that required constant attention to keep things in balance.

Francis had more interest in the processes than in the people involved with them. He also had practical concerns. Earlier he had been approached by William Baulston about an appointment as one of the town's commissioners. He had thanked him but said he had to increase his income to ensure a legacy for his children when they reached adulthood—land for his sons and dowries for his daughters. It wasn't long after this conversation that Baulston approached him again, this time with a proposal much to his satisfaction.

"Would you consider continuing to work the same hours for a quarterly stipend of twelve shillings, New England silver?"

"Yes, I would," was his immediate response.

Francis was pleased to be offered remuneration on a quarterly basis, for the one hundred hours he worked per month, and it would be paid with New England silver coins. These coins were of good value and were minted in Boston.

New England silver was a new enterprise that had come about in 1652. Before that time, it had been the prerogative of the king to issue currency, but England was currently without a king and was being ruled by a Commonwealth, with Oliver Cromwell its Protectorate. The fledgling government, needing much attention by the leaders in Parliament, had been neglecting affairs in New England.

John Hull and Robert Sanford had established a business of minting silver coins. At first, they modified Spanish and European silver coins by stamping marks to identify the value (weight of silver) and the place of issue (NE for New England) and a symbol (willow tree) on the reverse side. The coins were being circulated without government sanction, and soon the Massachusetts legislators passed the Massachusetts Bay Mint Act of May 26, 1652, allowing Hull and Sanford to issue coins of twelve pence (worth one shilling), six pence, and three pence coins. In return, the "mint master" was allowed, as payment, one shilling out of every twenty shillings minted.

People were urged to trade items of silver for New England silver coins. These minted coins became desirable for the growing business climate in New England. Francis and Mary had no silver items; therefore, the Council's offer of NE silver coins for his work in Town Hall was meaningful and desirable.

He had paid his debt to William Brenton in 1650. Five years later he was admitted as a Freeman in the Portsmouth Community as a full citizen, and he had fulfilled his obligation for the land grants. And now he had been offered a salaried position in the Portsmouth government. He would certainly add to these accomplishments, having already, despite his humble beginnings, married an exceptional woman. He had come to understand his reliance on Mary's strengths where he was vulnerable, as in social situations.

Mary had believed she had the strength, the flexibility, and wisdom to flourish in a subservient role, and she had proven to be right. She was competent and assertive, and she was a natural leader, but she had not become arrogant or strident. She was humbled by her abiding faith, and that strong belief was deeply embedded in her soul.

The relationship with the Anthonys had become uncomplicated and familial. The children came and went from one home to the other, knowing they were welcome. Susanna and Mary were enjoying a relationship that Mary, for one, had never enjoyed, not having sisters. As for Susanna, she had a large family, but no one as close as Mary.

Both Francis and John were away from home most of every week day, but the four of them somehow found time to be together.

Mary and Francis were amazed by John's commitment to the community and Susanna and John were delighted to see how easily the Braytons had integrated into Portsmouth activity.

One much-appreciated service that John had advocated for was a postal service in Portsmouth, having made arrangements with Richard Fairbanks in Boston, who already had post to London for Massachusetts residents, and he agreed to include Portsmouth. John asked Gavin Mills, who was eager to earn a stipend, to become the first mail courier in Portsmouth. John had influenced the General Assembly to provide the money.

John had business dealings all over New England. He learned in Boston about new developments and also about new items on the market. He even learned to play a card game that had caught on in Boston called Ruff. It was played in partnerships with two couples competing against each other by bidding on the cards they each held, against what they guessed to be in the other three hands. It was challenging, and soon there were six couples playing the game regularly. They became known as the Ruff Club. Thomas and Ann Brownell were one of the couples and Thomas loved games and competition. Jack and Nora Slocum, Luke and Anna Tripp, and Silas and Catherine Townsend rounded out the group, meeting once a month in each other's homes.

Groups of people with special interests were forming clubs in Portsmouth. The music club held recitals that were so well-attended that they had to move their performances to Town Hall. Soon dances were sponsored by the musicians. There were poetry readings by the book club and chess tournaments, too. One evening, the Ruff Club had a conversation about why Portsmouth had so many clubs:

"Up in Massachusetts, the focus is on purity," said Thomas Brownell, "and they consider laughter, card playing, and dancing as sinful. I'm glad we have a different perspective here!"

Catherine Townsend offered, "Maybe it's because we live on an island, and a small one at that, and we've been dependent on one another. We have a better understanding of our needs or what matters to us."

Anna Tripp added, "And we enjoy our time together."

"The people who helped found Portsmouth, like John Clarke, Roger Williams, and Anne Hutchinson were quite religious," said Jack Slocum, "but they insisted that civil government and religion be separated, and remember, the founders built a town hall but no church."

Mary added, "Without a church, we formed small groups instead."

"That's true," said John Anthony, "but we have plenty of sharing and caring, charity, fellowship, respect, diligence, and hope for the future."

Ann Brownell piped up with, "And we have lots of babysitters available!"

Everyone laughed at the practical truth of Ann's quip.

38 ~ 1656

Early morning of the sixth of June, Francis was in the records room reviewing the most recent town transactions. He paused to glance out the window and became mesmerized by the undulating leaves outlined against the deep blue sky. He felt a sense of contentment and, on a whim, he picked up his journal of cryptic jottings of events, and he began reading at random some of the entries.

June 15, 1646, Portsmouth School dedicated. Built by volunteers on land donated by John Porter, funded by subscriptions.

May 19, 1647, Roger Williams returned with a Charter of Incorporation in Narragansett Bay, New England.

November 5, 1647, John Coggeshall died suddenly at his desk in Newport. We are grieving for this patriot of our island. He was only forty-seven years old.

July 1, 1648, Founders Day Celebration at the Puddingstone. Speeches, good food, and a large gathering. Ten years. Much accomplished.

January 1, 1649, Beginning of mandatory militia training for all male residents 17 to 40 at the Training Center. Four hours a month is required.

December 14, 1650, A beautiful healthy son born into the Brayton family at 7:55 AM named Stephen Michael.

November 12, 1651, Remodeling of Resident Inn completed this date. Lower level now the Safe Harbor Inn, and rooms for let on upper level.

May 10, 1653, Elizabeth Holden Smith died at age sixty-four. Mary and I are in sorrow for this beloved mother.

May 26, 1655, A freeman at last!

Reluctantly he put aside the journal and turned to the stack of papers that needed attention, and soon he was fully focused on his work. Once he had the work completed, he left for home and the midday meal. The children were eager to tell of their morning adventures, and Mary listened attentively while Francis smiled, enjoying the exuberance of the children. After the meal, when Sarah was napping and Francis resting before leaving for his work in the fields, Mary said, "Francis, I sense you are mulling over something. Are you concerned over a problem at Town Hall?"

"No, nothing is amiss there, or anywhere else for that matter. We're finally out of debt, and I'm now being paid for my work at Town Hall—unexpected. However, I'll be forty-three soon, and I'm thinking of our assets. Will there be enough for our children? I'm trying to think what more I can do to increase our income."

"Give it some time," Mary said. "These large families, including our own, will have the same concerns.

Portsmouth is like a flower bed that's been planted and nurtured. Now the flowers are about to bloom, all at the same time. Each phase has been attended to, and Portsmouth's garden is surviving—flourishing, in fact!"

Francis nodded. "Yes, I have great faith in the extraordinary men who have invested heavily. For a time, there was more money than laborers. The land grant was a great advantage … all of that has been good." He shifted in his seat before continuing. "I've been seeking a way of my own all along, and when I had nothing, I used my muscles to work my way out of Fulham's leasehold agreement. I was fortunate, and fate led me to the magistracy and a position I was qualified to perform. My determination to succeed in Ellington helped too. But here in Portsmouth the situation is difficult for me to understand. It's almost as if I were being pursued rather than me doing the pursuing. That makes me wary. I'm not comfortable among the politicians, the statesmen, and the religious leaders here on Aquidneck Island."

Mary looked at him with concern and sympathy.

"On the other hand," he went on, "I don't want to carry on forever in a custodial position either. That's not how I want to be seen. I was, I admit, offered a higher position as a commissioner, but I can't work without being paid."

Mary leaned toward Francis and said in earnest, "You know that I don't believe in fate. There is a divine hand in your life and also in the formation of this democratic government. I believe God knows when men are ready to be inspired and encouraged. That is when He intervenes. I see God in your life, Francis, and I wonder why you don't see that yourself."

Francis very seriously replied, "I do wonder that myself, Mary."

The Anthonys were preparing for Joseph to sail for England. He was fifteen years old and ready to pursue his life's ambition to study medicine and become a licensed physician. This advent was stirring the hearts of the members in both families. All wondered how Johnny, his twin brother, would get on without Joey, but no one had been privy to the countless conversations between the twins during the past five years. Joey had talked about his future studies in England, and Johnny about working with their father in the weaving business. They prepared themselves for the inevitable separation.

Susanna was distraught. It seemed to her that the time had come too soon to be sending her children "out into the world," especially across the Atlantic, and for such a long separation. John had made plans to help Susanna and himself, to see Joseph board a ship for London. He had arranged for Martha and William Brenton to meet them for dinner at the Golden Plate restaurant in Boston. John then asked the Braytons to accompany them and to spend three days in Boston. Mary was excited, and Francis liked the idea, and their hearts were lifted as they prepared for Joey's farewell party. It would be held at the Brayton home, which could accommodate the large gathering.

The day before the Saturday party, Mary and Susanna were working on the food preparation, and John and Francis were behind the house sitting on benches at the edge of Mary's garden. It was warm, and the usual bugs were buzzing around the flowers as the two men settled down for a rare chance to talk.

"I received a remarkable letter from Father," John began. "It seems he has been given new life at seventy with Joseph coming to Foxgrove. I had not expected such enthusiasm. He's so proud to think there would be a physician once more in the Anthony family. Charles' son is an attorney."

John sat quietly for a minute then relayed to Francis the details of the plan for Joseph.

"My father has contacted Weedon Academy. Joseph will begin classes there in September. He'll room at the academy until he qualifies for medical school at Pembroke College. Father has offered to pay all his fees, and he also has set up trust funds for Johnny, William, and Abraham, to be distributed on their twenty-first birthdays."

Francis was astonished. "Well, I say. That's very generous of Sir John."

"I'm relieved," John added, "that it's been put in trust. I don't think Charles would have allowed the will to go uncontested. I'm so pleased that Father has honored my family. I wish he and Susanna could have become acquainted. I believe they would be great friends. My father was devoted to my mother, but it was a strained relationship."

Francis thought back about his own father and his devotion to Martha, with very little return. John Anthony had always given Francis praise for staying in Hounslow to care for his parents. And now these two good fathers sat quietly in the garden, thinking and speaking of the past until they were called inside for a light meal.

The party for Joe on the tenth was successful as everyone expected it to be. Mary and Susanna had a rhythm when they entertained together, and the guests were dined and fussed over, enjoying every minute. The children were in the kitchen playing games at Talltree, while the adults were in the parlor and dining room. One of the Potter girls was watching the Brayton and Anthony babies in the nursery above. Later in Boston, Mary and Susanna planned to share with Martha and William Brenton how this house had been enjoyed by so many Portsmouth families.

The next Friday, the sixteenth, they were all on their merry way to Boston. The trip was as good as traveling could be on such a rough roadway in an uncomfortable coach. Nothing could dampen Mary's spirit, but Susanna was sad as she kept her eyes on her handsome son, Joseph. She managed a slight smile when Joseph, understanding his Mother, quipped, "Mama, don't forget you have another one just like me back at home." The others laughed.

They spent Friday night at the Wayfarers Hotel and the next morning they all accompanied Joseph to the docks. Joseph left in a flood of tears, but the lad could not conceal his excitement as he waved from the tender on its way to the barque, *Venture*.

The four turned away, once Joseph was on board, to while away the afternoon in the city. They ate a light lunch, visited some shops, and bought a few gifts, then returned to the Wayfarer to dress for dinner.

The table for six at the Golden Plate was resplendent with fine china and crystal. The candelabrum reflected light over the table, and the six guests who had just finished eating a fine dinner enjoyed lively conversations.

The men—John, William, and Francis—had been bantering rather than discussing serious business. They had a history that went back to the turn of the century and to Hammersmith, England. The women were wives of busy men, and Susanna, Martha, and Mary had twenty-three children, so it was impossible to cover that topic, but they did note that there had been three sons born within three weeks of one another. This was news mainly because William Brenton II was the first surviving son of Martha and William. Abraham Anthony and Stephen Brayton came along soon after.

The dinner guests on this evening of July 18, 1655, were at ease and joyous. Mary privately thought, "If we had stayed in England, this would not have come about with the six of us."

The trip back to Portsmouth was uneventful, but there was tragic news for Mary and Francis in a letter from her brother Samuel. Stephen had died after a short illness on March ninth. "Oh Francis, he was the best of fathers," Mary sobbed.

"Yes," Francis sadly replied. "I loved him too, as you know. He changed my life for no other reason than that he was a good, caring person. All those hours he spent tutoring me without recompense. Do you think he forgave me for taking you so far from him?"

"Francis," she said with a tone of annoyance, "don't think of yourself! He is lost to the world that gave him so little in return."

"Yes, but he was respected by all who knew him, even those who knew only of his reputation. Not once did I mention his name in Ellington that I did not hear what a fine, honorable man he was."

"That is true. I heard it myself."

Francis looked at Mary with his steady intensity. "Mary, you are everything I hold valuable. I still don't feel I deserve you, but you seem happy with our life here in the wilderness. You work all day, leaving no time for yourself."

She looked at him soberly and said something she had never expressed to him before. "Francis, you always bring out the best in me. I shudder to think how pointless my life would have been had you not come along."

He rose from his chair and clasped her knees as he knelt in front of her, resting his head in her lap. She put her hands on his back and laid her head against his. They sat still, happy together.

39 ~ 1657

Francis had become intent on finding a way to increase the Brayton assets, mainly by the purchase of land. He was ever on the alert to the sale of a piece of property, since most sales came about from word of mouth. The Town

Council members could be heard in conversations among themselves on various matters as they stood talking of this and that, especially after their meetings in Town Hall.

In early January, Francis overheard a conversation that began a series of events that were, over time, to change the conduct of his life. The instance was generated by Samuel Wilbur and Gideon Freeborn, standing near the door to the records room. Gideon said, "Samuel, I think we need to explore the prospect of Hog Island again. I'm convinced it could be of value, with the demand for land these days."

"I've thought of it too," Samuel said, "and I remember when it was presented to the Council before, and it was discussed and put aside because of the problems involved in developing the island. Transportation to and from is the main obstacle. Getting implements, equipment, and animals there as well. There are no roads. The soil is rocky and not ready for planting. It seemed too risky a business to offer the men of Portsmouth, despite the possible hundreds of acres of land."

"But still," Gideon added, "since the land belongs to Portsmouth, and there's a need for more fields to plant, it could be seen as a fault if we don't pursue the idea."

The men moved out of Francis' hearing, and he sat thinking of what he had overheard. He continued to contemplate the land on Hog Island until he was provoked into investigating the problems Samuel had mentioned: the transportation, the lack of roads, the rocky soil. He spoke with John Anthony about the prospects of the island. John had the means of transportation, so Francis asked him if he would take him to the island on any day the weather permitted.

"Francis! I am surprised," John said. "Where is your hesitant, cautious self? It seems unlike you to be interested in such an enterprise. It could be a very risky investment, my friend."

"Yes, but so were all the settlements in New England. I'm ready to at least explore the possibility. First, I need to see for myself, and your advice will be valuable. Maybe it could be profitable for you too. I could plant flax."

John laughed, and said, "Let's go to Hog Island!"

Using one of John's canoes, they made the trip to the island on January 10, 1657, a memorable day despite the harsh wind. It was a bleak, winter day, but they managed to avoid the shoals and were able to get ashore and pull the canoe to land. They decided to walk the perimeter, and soon were exploring coves. Once around the island, they followed a ridge, not very high but distinct—a sort of dividing line of the island, and broad enough to become a roadway. The slope to the west was gentle, and from the center they could see the possibility for tillable acreage.

The trees were toward the eastern slope, and they were weather beaten and not tall enough for use as lumber. There were shrubs and wood enough for camp fires, and much of the land was grassy. It was almost perfect for animals, but who would tend them, and what about the long cold season? The growing season, once seeds were planted, would support the planting of only one crop, but that was true of all New England. They decided that there could be close to two hundred acres, once the soil had been readied. The two men made further assessments.

The rock would need to be removed and the grass cut (but it could be sold if transported to Portsmouth.) John suggested that a small flock of sheep might be used in a fenced area of the meadow to clear vegetation while the rocks were being removed. They could build a shed for implements and a shelter from the storms.

"It would require a flat-board ferry to transport materials and men for the first two seasons," John suggested. "Not much could be accomplished from December to March—maybe even longer in some winters. The sheep idea may be more bother than it's worth."

"Well," said Francis, "I have enough information to write a proposal to the Town Council. They seem to take time deliberating everything except our tax rate for the year. It'll take an effort finding laborers needed the first two years."

"Maybe not as difficult to find them as you expect. We have many large families and more young lads than work to keep them busy. It seems you have decided on taking the risk, Francis."

"Yes, but I'll have to sell some land, and I have twenty acres in mind, acreage I could not get planted with this project. It seems wise to sell before this year's planting, and that will allow me a couple of months to get the word out."

The "couple of months" took only five days. William Foster heard of the land Brayton planned to sell and was on his doorstep that evening. It was then that Francis embarked on the riskiest venture of his life—certainly since he had sold good land even before he made his proposal to the Town Council.

In February, he was prepared and attended the Council meeting held Thursday, February the eighth. His proposal was astounding even for these eight worldly-wise men.

He told them that he would undertake to develop Hog Island into a source of income for himself and the town of Portsmouth. "As the Council is aware, there are challenges and expenses involved in its development—and I would bear the expense—which I estimate to take no less than two years, but the island should be ready for some planting by the third spring. During the first two years, I shall build a road from the shore, inland to a place from which I can manage the work of the land."

He paused looking at his attentive audience. "In return for the development," he went on, "I should like a grant of seven years. Beyond that time, the town could either sell or lease tracts of land or find another use for the island. I estimate it will take a few years before I see a return on my investment, since I will need to employ lads to work the land. I take on this risk for my own benefit but believe it will eventually become a benefit and means of income for the town as well."

The Council had a lengthy discussion on the Brayton petition but had to admit that they were risking very little by accepting this proposal. They decided to award a seven-year grant to Brayton for having accepted the jeopardy of his own investment if any of it should fail. And so, Francis had only to wait until it was approved in the General Assembly meeting in May. He was thwarted when the discussion at the May meeting became heated and a vote was unlikely to pass, so it was agreed to table the proposal until the November meeting. Within their authority, they allowed Francis to proceed with the initial work on Hog Island. He was chagrined but decided that since he had already sold twenty acres of good land, he would go for the "whole hog!"

The Braytons and Anthonys received uplifting news in March from Joe in England. He was enjoying Weedon Academy, loving his relationship with Sir John, and even, getting on famously with Charles and his sons. His studies required most of his time because he was behind most of the students, which he had expected, but he was advancing and would soon be on an "even keel" with the class. Joe added a surprising tribute.

"I do want to thank Aunt Mary. I could not have made it in Weedon Academy if it hadn't been for her four years of teaching. She would, I believe without a doubt, be able to hold her own among these instructors. Thank her for me and express my gratitude."

This was the reward teachers hope to hear and seldom do. Education in Portsmouth had been a trial for parents. They could hardly afford the subscriptions charged for teachers who were, at that, far from qualified. The town could find more qualified teachers, at a higher cost, and even those would be hard pressed to accept the offer since planters' children were so unruly. The children were not disciplined for the formal classroom, and their antics continually disrupted the teaching.

Mary had enjoyed teaching early on when they first moved into the Brenton house, inviting neighbor children of school age. Eventually, she could keep on teaching only the Brayton and Anthony twelve. Also, there was a need for more formal education. Families had been very concerned about education, and now that they were no longer struggling for survival, the future of their children seemed in greater peril over lack of knowledge and mathematical skills. The whole town was relieved when the new schoolhouse was completed. The situation improved, and the children began to appreciate and enjoy the process of learning, which was a good thing—a very good thing.

Francis was given an assignment in May, after the General Assembly meeting, to do a survey of all roadways in Portsmouth. He was to prepare a written assessment of their condition and usefulness and also to make recommendations for improvements for streets and roadways within the town proper. This report would be presented at the November thirtieth General Assembly. This had been accomplished, and the Assembly approved a highway commission to be formed and given the authority to make a formal plan for the improvement of town streets and roads.

Francis was fully occupied all summer and fall. The Walen family had expanded into a complex wood business, and Francis was able to hire two Walen workers to build a storage shed on the island. It was a lark for the men to go to the island—an energizing change from ordinary work. By September, Francis, with the Portsmouth lads, had managed to build a roadway good enough to handle wheelbarrow hauling to the fields. It would take more time to do a proper roadway. Stacks of rocks came out of the soil, which would be used for many purposes. They cut grass as well, to be bound and transported to Portsmouth for animal care.

Francis bought two canoes from the Gatchells, and John had provided a flat-board raft for ferrying equipment. There was a convenient area on the Portsmouth side that John Porter leased to Francis to be used as a mooring. The distance from there to the island was about two and a half miles.

People became curious about this Hog Island enterprise, and tongues were wagging. Enough so that at the November 30, 1657, General Assembly meeting, the seven-year grant for Hog Island was passed without opposition.

Enough work had been accomplished on Hog Island in the first year that Francis was satisfied. It had cost more than he estimated but not more than he could pay, so he was encouraged to continue. Four regular workers would continue again in March of 1658—Josiah Arnold, Thomas Borden, William Brown, and Zeke Hall. The Braytons had gone into a different occupation, a different routine, and at this point they were encouraged.

Chapter 11: Commissioner

Excellence is never an accident. It is always the result of high intention, sincere effort and intelligent execution; it represents the wise choice of alternatives. Choice not chance determines your destiny. — Aristotle

40 ~ 1659

By the summer of 1659, the Hog Island project had not been progressing as Francis had planned. There were no lads working for him, since they disliked the isolation of the undeveloped island. They had lost their sense of adventure. Also, Francis was uncomfortable requesting help of John Anthony to transport men and equipment; it had been more of a burden on John's business than either had expected. Nevertheless, Francis was reluctant to abandon his investment after only eighteen months, though he had never intended to do the job on his own.

He needed reliable workers and transportation, and he needed a solution for these problems soon. He identified large families that had several sons, and Adam Lawton's was the most likely candidate, since it was known that he was struggling to find work for his nine lads. He spoke to Adam about his island project and his need for labor.

Adam seemed hesitant. "Well, Francis," he responded, "I'd like to say I could help you. I do have sons available, but it seems to me you can't pay enough for the length of time it would take for them to work and to come and to go to the island."

"It's true, I can't afford higher wages than I've paid before. The whole venture will fail if I can't get the land ready to plant. There's more land than I can use, I see that now. Would you be interested if I were to lease you some of the land in exchange for your sons working my fields?"

Adam's expression changed as the idea sank in, thinking about growing grain and having an income, plus getting his sons to work. "Well, yes, I'd consider that, Francis, if you find a way for us to get over and back."

"You know, I've heard that John Tripp is thinking of getting a fishing business started, along with a ferry service. It would be worth a try to see if he'd be interested in providing transportation, maybe even taking a parcel of land. I'll talk to him."

"Do that, Francis, and let me know."

Francis added, "I'm afraid I I'll need a commitment through 1664, Adam."

"That's no problem for me. I'm not going anywhere."

After several discussions and a trip to Hog Island, John Tripp had been convinced Hog Island would be good for his fishing enterprise. They each reached agreement on which parcel of land would meet their plans—John Tripp opting for the beach area, Adam Lawton the land nearest the mooring, and Francis Brayton the land he had already worked. The agreements were put in writing, and all signed it on August 1, 1660. They also agreed that if any problems arose, they would be discussed and resolved with all three taking part.

Most of the children of Portsmouth were following in their parents' footsteps—planters, tradesmen, and homemakers. So far, Joseph Anthony had been the only son from Portsmouth to be sent to England for an education. The children were marrying into families they knew quite well, and even though dowries were no longer obligatory, the wedding gift from the bride's family had become a substitute. There were linens and needlework lovingly offered by brides, and occasionally money or land by the father. The bridegroom was expected to provide protection and a home for the bride.

The assets of families were judged very much as they had been in the Old World, perhaps given new names and different ceremonies, but still the old customs were lying beneath the new world veneer. All children were loved and protected, but still valued differently by sex. Sons had to have property and the means to support a family, and Francis Brayton had an eye out for his sons' future in his planning, which had begun in 1645. Land was an essential asset, but of course there were other considerations that he valued such as education, contributing to the community, and honorable citizenship. Mary had provided educational opportunities, and during her father's lifetime he had sent many books for the children.

Francis was aware that his sons would go in different directions. Frankie and Stephen were very different, Frankie resembling Thomas Brayton in appearance and personality and Stephen favoring his father, Francis. Frankie was obedient but preferred to be given directions. Stephen did not wait for doors to be opened; he had already begun to push doors open himself. Francis had heard that Stephen was visiting the Gibbon Brothers' Mills, Earl's Tanning Yard, Wilcox's iron monger works, and possibly other tradesmen's places.

"I like to see things processed and made," Stephen said when asked about it, "especially in the mills. It's very interesting, and I think I'd like to be a miller."

This pleased Francis. He could see some of himself in his son. He and Mary often spoke of the differences they were noting in the children, and Francis listened to Mary's comments, which seemed insightful to him.

On June 4, 1662, Hannah Mary and Enoch Biggs wed and moved to the house the Biggs family had built for them. It was nearby the Anthonys, which was good for Hannah Mary when baby Susanna (to be called Suzy) was born on July 30, 1663. The next generation had been launched, and twenty-two-year John Anthony followed his sister by marrying Abigail Tripp on December 2, 1663. It was such a gay time for everyone and a bit hectic as the Anthonys vied for bedrooms now that three children had left the parents' nest.

In March, sad news arrived: the announcement of Sir John's death on January 10, 1663, at age seventy-five. The one consolation was the joy of having Joseph doing so well in his study of medicine. Francis had thought that Sir John would be supremely proud of his son John if he could see his contributions to the community of Portsmouth.

Sir John's death was another broken tie to England for the Anthonys and the Braytons. However, the political ties had been maintained, not broken, since Portsmouth, Newport, Warwick, and Providence Plantations had been awarded a charter in 1644. It had not satisfied the leaders of Portsmouth and the rest of the Rhode Island settlements, since they wanted colonial status and more definitive guides for governing.

In 1654 this was accomplished when both Williams and Clarke returned to England. Williams did not stay long, but Clarke remained in England, at considerable personal expense, to maintain a presence on behalf of Rhode Island. Clarke's statesmanship and friendships with John Milton, Sir Henry Vane, and Lord Clarendon were useful when Charles II was restored to the throne. All previous acts of Parliament that had been passed during the Commonwealth (it was known as the Long Parliament) were annulled. Clarke put pressure on his friends to influence the Crown, and on July 8, 1663, he obtained King Charles' seal of approval. The Colony received the name of "Governor and Company of the English Colony of Rhode Island and Providence Plantations in New England, in America."

Clarke and Captain George Baxter returned November 24, 1663, with the charter in hand. They were received by the Rhode Island Court of Commissioners, and George Baxter was given the honor of reading the document to the large crowd that had assembled for the solemn occasion. Baxter began with the opening of Clarke's petition to the king, which stated:

"They have freely declared that it is much on their hearts (if they may be permitted) to hold forth a lively experiment, that a most flourishing civil state may stand, and best be maintained, and that among our English Subjects, with a full liberty in religious concernments; and that true piety, rightly grounded upon gospel principles, will give the best and greatest security to sovereignty and will lay in the hearts of men the strongest obligations to true loyalty."

Francis thought as he heard this, "No wonder he obtained the favorable attention of King Charles! Who would not want such a colony of men protecting your realm thousands of miles to the west?"

After the lengthy reading, the charter was placed in the sturdy box that had safe-guarded it across the Atlantic, to remain in safekeeping for years to come. It then became the duty of the Court of Commissioners to execute the guidelines so meticulously presented in the charter. The basic structure of government would comprise a governor (Benedict Arnold), a deputy governor (William Brenton), ten assistants chosen annually, and the House of Deputies appointed from the colony: six from Newport, two from Portsmouth, two from Warwick, two from Providence, and two from smaller towns within the colony. These bodies were to meet as a General Assembly twice a year; the first Wednesday in May and the last Wednesday of October. For now, the place of meeting would alternate between Newport and Portsmouth.

This written document, the governmental authority, provided the leaders the freedom to elect their governor and deputy governor, to appoint their own representatives, and to write their own laws. Further it declared that "no person to be molested, punished, disquieted or called into question for any difference in opinion of religion." It allowed that the majority would prevail in matters under consideration.

The citizens (men) of Rhode Island were energized to put such a system, such a firmly endorsed declaration, into practice. They, as a committee, took pause to give thanks to John Clarke, a superior statesman, and Roger Williams, a caring honorable man. Francis thought about those two men of different demeanor but united in purpose. He mentally described Roger Williams as making waves as he promoted and defended his ideas, and then John Clarke rode those waves into the shore, where they merged into the landscape and benefited the people.

These leaders encouraged other citizens to support their communities by continuing to serve on juries and committees to ensure that the people of the Colony of Rhode Island and Providence Plantations would be justly and honorably served.

The business of Portsmouth continued in commerce, in homes, in the General Assembly, and all the other places important to the life of residents. The wives and mothers of the colony had little to do at the celebration that November 1663, receiving no recognition at all, and yet they knew they were deserving. The reward came from the children who were on the cusp of civic responsibility, and in the weddings, christenings, and burials of individuals sanctioned, connected, and solemnized among loved ones.

The United Christian Church had been built by faithful people before they had a pastor. There were smatterings of members of the Society of Friends, the newly named "Baptist" followers, Jews, Anglicans, separatists, and others, but now there was a church, and just recently a pastor, Ephriam Adams, who had been willing to try ministering to those who desired a place where the focus would be on soul. Mary Brayton had been involved in the genesis of this church.

Mary said to Francis after a day with Susanna, "I'm worried about Susanna's health. She has a terrible swelling in her legs. I try to help her with her laundry, but more than anything, to sit with her and let the willing daughters do the work. It isn't easy for her, Francis. She pops up to take over because it's hard for her to be off her feet."

"What's causing the swelling? I don't see Susanna indulging herself, except maybe with work."

"I think it may be edema, which gets very serious in time. It's a symptom of kidney disease." Mary was unconsciously wringing her hands, and Francis knew she was afraid for her friend.

A tragedy occurred on September 25, 1664, bringing grief far and wide in Portsmouth. The story went around the community and finally to Francis, who heard of it before the Anthonys. It concerned Thomas Brownell.

Francis told Mary and the Anthonys about it at his first opportunity. "Tom had gone to his field south of the Lawton place, just this past Thursday, the twenty-fifth, and he was riding Fleet, his favorite horse. On the way back, he met Adam Lawton's son, Daniel, who invited him to stop by the house on his way by, and Tom said, 'I'll do that.' Then Dan challenged Tom to a race and Tom said, 'You're on,' loving to give rein to his high-spirited horse.

"Tom took the lead, but soon Dan passed him by. You know how hilly it is in the area, not a good place to be racing. They both passed William Wodell's property, over the halfway mark for the racers. Then Dan noticed he could not hear Tom approaching behind him, so he turned to look back and saw Fleet heading riderless in the direction of the swamp. Dan didn't hesitate—he galloped after Fleet and caught a flapping rein. That was a sign, Dan told me, that something was seriously wrong.

"He found Thomas lying under a large tree, in a pool of blood. He was dead, and there was blood coming from his head. A piece of rein was lying next to him and Dan guessed the horse had something to do with Tom's death. He rode to his house, not far from the scene."

Forestalling his listeners' questions, Francis went on. "The coroner, Samuel Wilbur, investigated, with the help of William Baulston and John Sanford, and they found hair and blood embedded in the tree, at a spot that indicated that Tom was probably propelled into the tree. The ruling given from the investigation was accidental death."

During that week's end, people came to give solace to Ann, who was now alone and responsible for their nine children. George, the oldest at twenty, had the legal charge for the family. Many people came to the funeral, and the burial was on the Brownell land, which was customary. Tables were fashioned from planks supported with logs, where food was served on them in abundance. This was also the custom in Portsmouth. Ann confided in Mary that she felt very angry with Thomas for being so reckless, racing over hills with young Daniel, but she added, "I got through my anger, Mary. Thomas lived life without fear or ever hesitating, and it was part of who he was. I loved him."

"We all enjoyed being around Tom," Mary said. "Life is filled with perils, is it not? Most of us must say we are blessed to be spared."

All male residents of Portsmouth were fulfilling their required four hours a month at the Baulston Training Place. Francis Brayton had become a competent horseman, even though it had taken over twenty years to accomplish. The militia training had seemed a precaution in the founding years, as there had been some minor incidents, but now there was a threat of an Indian alliance among the tribes in New England. Residents of Aquidneck were protected by the difficulty of transporting groups of people to the island. However, it was not unheard of for Indians to canoe in the dark to attack by surprise. Francis was relieved he had been taking the training. It was prudent.

41 ~ 1665

Large families living in close proximity in Portsmouth had inevitably led to intermarriage among neighbors. This first generation, as they married, were getting settled on land provided by parents, and in houses built and supplied by local tradesmen and artisans. The Portsmouth families had invested heavily in their unique experiment and it was working, and work was the guiding principle of the community. Laziness was a scourge, and there was no place for it in a developing society.

Mary and Francis Brayton did not resort to the strap to discipline their children because obedience was not the goal. To them, teaching the six children to become independent adults was the essential thing. Nurturing good habits and discouraging bad was not so easy when natural inclinations came to bear. Frankie was inclined to depend on his parents to direct and guide him. Mary had an awakening to this one morning when she listened to a conversation between Francis and Frankie.

"Now, Frankie, today I'd like you to finish the planting on the Pudding Lane field," said Francis. "The frosts are behind us, but there are many fields waiting for seed, so get it done as quickly as possible. Did you get the seed like I told you?"

"Yes, Father, I got enough for that field."

"What about the West Main Road field?"

"No, I only thought about Pudding Lane."

"Well, go get the field planted and get back to the seed store. Think about all the fields and get enough seed. It gets hard to buy seed later in the spring. You need to think of these things, son."

"I will. I'll remember next time."

Mary thought about this and realized something she had not taken seriously before—Frankie expected Francis to tell him each task. Frankie was already twenty years old and should be thinking for himself. She would talk to Francis about it and urge him to get Frankie on track.

"Why hadn't I noticed this before?" she asked herself.

Stephen was not yet fifteen, and he had started working on his own the year before. One day he came into the parlor where Mary and Francis were sitting.

"I don't want to be a planter," he said. "I know this for certain, and I think I need to start trying other jobs, like the mills. I know you need help, Papa, so I'll try to do both. I'll get up earlier now that the sun comes up sooner, and I'll work later in the evening. It's what I want to do."

Mary and Francis were stunned, but both held their composure. "Let us think about this," Francis said. "I promise we'll give you an answer soon, Stephen."

The parents watched their lanky son walk from the parlor, and they both knew they had an important decision to make.

Francis spoke first. "He's going to go his own way. The worse thing for him is to not pursue his idea and become resentful. I could get field help—we can afford that, dear. Maybe he'll see how difficult and dirty millwork is and give it up. Or, just maybe, he'll soon be on his own!"

The officers in Town Hall had as much work for Francis as he had the time to work. He was still leasing land on Hog Island, as were Adam Lawton and John Tripp. His grant had expired November 20, 1664, and the three had asked the Town Council (who had been given the authority to manage Hog Island) if each could have separate leases. The proposal was discussed, and the Council offered yearly leases for a fee of fourteen shillings per person. The high fee demonstrated to the men how valuable their labor on Hog Island had been.

John Tripp had yielded a higher income from his fishing business, and he surprised Adam and Francis one day, saying, "I use your roadway and boat mooring, and I'll pay each of you four shillings a year for their use."

It was a good faith offer that neither Adam or Francis ever forgot. They continued their arrangement for two more years.

In August 1665, Joseph Anthony had returned from England. Such joy to see all his family, including the Braytons, lined up to greet him as he emerged from the coach. His elation at seeing his dear mother brought tears to his eyes. Somehow he was able to hide his shock at her altered appearance, so bent over and, frankly, old. His father looked unaltered to Joseph when he met him at the dock in Boston, but he had not been prepared for what nine years had done to his mother's health.

He greeted Hannah Mary, who was holding two-year-old Suzy in her arms, with husband Enoch by her side. The others rushed around to embrace Joseph, who looked familiar and yet more mature. John, had hung back, watching his twin brother, waiting for time alone with him. But Joseph yelled out, "Where's John? Where is my brother John?" There was nothing to do but go and hug his best friend. Joseph, the quick wit and the younger one by five minutes, said, "You look just like I do! How did that happen?"

The laughter was the nervous kind, a release of pent up emotion, giving the group time to move on, with Joseph in tow, to the house where a feast had been prepared for the "prodigal son," as John called him. John then turned to Abigail so she could meet Joseph. It was strange for her, seeing another person with the same appearance as her husband, but it didn't take long for her to see Joseph as Joseph and John as John.

The next day Joseph and his father went to Town Hall to look at the town map, which had the names of the tracts of land and the names of the owners. John was helping Joseph find the best location for his medical practice. He would need a house large enough for his practice as well as for himself and family. He would need a horse and enclosed carriage for making calls in all sorts of weather, some no doubt in the middle of the night. John owned several tracts, and they agreed on the best location. After assessing the five-acre lot, John asked John Brightman to prepare a deed for Joseph. While in the office, they met John Brightman's son, William, who had graduated from Harvard and was now studying law under an attorney in Boston. He would join his father when he qualified as a licensed attorney.

"Well, Joseph, you'll soon have another man of the professions to confer with, eh?"

Joseph just nodded and smiled.

The months passed until Christmas, which had not changed through the years except to include more of everything. For one thing there were two churches and a small meeting house for the Society of Friends. The United Christian Church and the Baptist Church were small churches that, despite differing doctrines, practiced the same Christian ceremonies, most especially Christmas. Gradually, there were more candles, more ribbons, more gifts, and more music. The Christmas of 1665 was festive because Joseph was back with the family and would soon be hanging his board on his home office front door.

Francis decided he would not lease Hog Island in 1667, since he had a surprise visit from William Baulston in August 1666.

"Francis, we need something done about our roads and streets in Portsmouth," he said. "The current roads need to be charted in all the northern area of Aquidneck Island. You'll need a committee of about four men to help you. What we need to know is, which roads are serving the public adequately and do we need more streets or roadways? If you and your committee would make an assessment and charts and draw up a proposal, we'd consider it a great service to our community."

Francis had listened carefully, then said, "I remember about ten years ago we did a survey of roads, and I imagine it's time for another look."

"You better than anyone in our town."

Francis was pleased. "I would not refuse such an honor, and I only desire to complete the assignment to the satisfaction of the Council."

Francis began the work in October, once he had a committee of four together, but they would not complete the commission for another two years.

Thomas Wait, an early settler in Portsmouth, a planter, and an expert hunter, had supplied many families with animals he trapped and hunted. He spent hours tramping the woods beyond the planters' fields and rode his horse there several times a month. On one such venture, he injured his ankle chasing a deer. He managed to hobble to his horse and get to "Doc" Anthony's office. Joseph wrapped the sprained ankle, and told Thomas to return in one week, which he did with his daughter, Jane, to help him into the office.

Jane was the youngest of the Wait children, and she was caring for her parents, Thomas and Letitia. She returned for the final visit and invited Joseph to dinner (not his first invitation to the homes of eligible daughters). He accepted the invitation because he was attracted by the deep dimples in Jane's cheeks. After the lovely meal with the Waits, Joseph had seen Jane's competence in household matters as well as her steady demeanor. He thought, "She would hold up in a medical office."

He courted Jane through the December festivities, and soon his love equaled his estimate of her competence. Once he had his house organized for a new wife, he proposed, and they were married June 10,1667. Jane proved to be a perfect helper as a doctor's wife, and even though it was not an easy life for her, she had friends and a family to fill in the many times when Joseph was with patients. Abigail and Jane soon became fast friends.

The Town Council hired a young man, Joseph Davol, to do necessary surveying jobs, including Hog Island. Francis met him and had a long conversation with him in the records office, where Joseph had been given a table to do his surveying figures. Joe mentioned that he had a two-year old-son who was currently living with his parents in Dartmouth, near Bristol. Francis asked if he got to see him very often and Joe told him his story.

"No, I don't get to see Matthew very often, but I need to work. My wife, Helen, died giving birth to Matthew, and I was grieved and could not pull myself together. My parents were so helpful, and Helen's parents live in New Hampshire, too far away to be of help. I had a job up there.

In fact, I worked for William Brenton. I met Helen and we married three years ago. When Helen was near her confinement—that was two years ago, my mother, a midwife, convinced me to bring her down to Dartmouth so she could deliver her grandchild. Since it was close to Christmas, it all worked out for us.

"After she died, I did nothing until I heard of the job here in Portsmouth, not far from Dartmouth. I've moved into Sarah Reape's boarding house off Sprague Street. I hope to get my own home so Matty can be with me. Say, Francis, if you hear of anyone who wants to sell their house, would you let me know?"

"Of course."

The Braytons had a party for Joseph Davol, and he enjoyed himself. It helped him recover from his loss. He and Francis worked closely together on the highway commission, and Francis was helpful with Joe's Hog Island assignment.

Francis was relieved that his highway commission assignment had ended successfully. The work had been, at times, frustrating, and he had to find two replacements for his committee. The weather was often a hindrance, but the proposal had been accepted in November 1668, and construction of new roads would begin in the spring. He had been away from home more frequently than usual through that year and into the next.

While Francis was concentrating on highways, Mary had been planning the wedding of Marta Brayton to Richard Pearce. By August, all was in order and the beautiful bride and handsome groom joined the ranks of the married.

Richard was working with the Porter family, adding a dairy to their horse and ox business. He hoped to eventually have his own dairy. He and Marta lived off West Main Road, not far from his work or Brenton House.

Everyone referred to the Brayton home by the name of *Brenton* House. Francis and Mary had decided soon after they had settled in that if they continued using the Brenton name, it would be a way of paying homage to William for his generosity to them. It was not difficult, since they had used the name from the beginning.

On October 16, 1669, John Sanford informed Francis that the Council was appointing him deputy to the General Assembly representing Portsmouth. The Assembly met in Newport twice a year, and the appointment was for ten years. Francis told Sanford that he was honored to be selected and would serve to the best of his ability. Mary was proud of him, and Susanna baked his favorite cake, while John heaped praise on Francis while thumping his back.

The year ended with drama. Molly Brayton and Joseph Davol left together on December 24, 1669, taking a coach to Bristol, where they were married by a magistrate. They had entrusted Marta to inform Francis and Mary, since the couple would be gone for three days in Boston on their honeymoon.

Later Molly said they had planned it that way because Joseph did not want to have a large gathering and celebration. Molly was already attached to little Matthew, and she thought Joseph Davol was the "best of men" (a phrase she had probably read somewhere). Francis was able to find them a house in Portsmouth. Joe continued to work on Aquidneck, getting odd jobs in Newport because of his connection with William Brenton.

At the Christmas dinner table, Marta announced she was expecting a child—another reason for the family to celebrate.

42 ~ 1670

The Brayton family was gathered for the celebration of Elizabeth Anthony's wedding, which would occur the next day. She was marrying James Greene, who worked for her father, John. The Braytons had not been together in five months, almost to the day, since it was then that Molly and Joseph Davol had eloped. Molly had just announced to her family that she would have a baby around the new year.

"Joe and I are delighted and Matty too, even though I doubt that he comprehends what it means, as a three-year-old."

"He'll survive," quipped Frankie, who did not have children and did not, in fact, have a wife yet.

Marta was expecting her first child in late July, and since it was now late May, she was a bit uncomfortable sitting on the hard benches at Talltree for long periods of eating and chatting with family and friends. However, husband Richard was starting to feel at ease, having experienced the close relationship between the Braytons and Anthonys.

Stephen asked, "Father, how was your meeting in Newport? It was a new experience, I imagine."

"That it was. I sat with other deputies of the General Assembly—quite an impressive group from all over the colony. Benedict Arnold presided, and the proceedings were more elaborate and ritualistic than I'm used to. And after many words, most of which went over my head, I could see that the issues were pretty much the usual concerns. After a few days, my opinion was—it takes too long to do too little. Yet, I shall serve as best I can."

The family made it clear that they believed in him by offering their hearty approval and support. They were proud of their father.

The next day, May 29, 1670, the large congregation witnessed the union of Elizabeth Anthony and James Greene, then all came together at the Resident Inn for the reception. After the joyous occasion, the newlyweds settled into a house built and prepared for them in Portsmouth. James had no close relatives of his own, and John Anthony had been like a father to him. He was struggling in Boston, and James had done some work for John there, who, seeing potential in the young man, offered him work in Portsmouth. He was willing and had readily learned the processing of flax, and he was now working with the two sons, John and Abraham. It was a family affair—so like the story of Portsmouth.

Frankie had learned to work independently these past five years, and when he set his eyes on Thomas and Mary Fish's daughter, Charlotte, he was beguiled. He courted her, but with some resistance from her parents. Mary Fish was of the Soule family, whose ancestor had been one of the signers of the Mayflower Compact. Mary had metaphorically remained on the Mayflower, and it was her "duty" to check the lineage of prospective in-laws. The decision was to deny approval until "Lottie" was nineteen, a bit more than a year's postponement.

Mary and Francis suspected the attitude of Mary Fish was about Frankie's lineage and not Lottie's age. She had often played the grande dame in Portsmouth, but she was ignored. Frankie was patient, and the couple did a lot of planning together while they awaited Lottie's nineteenth birthday on March 21, 1671. With that goal in mind, Francis and Mary secretly made plans to build a new home of their own, leaving Brenton House to Frankie.

Stephen had a location identified for his mill, and with a bit more land he wanted to build his own home. Mary and Francis were not surprised, but they could not help but be amazed that his ideas were so far-reaching at the age of twenty. Francis examined the location Stephen had in mind and also listened to his explicit plan of developing his business. Francis offered to buy the land as a gift, and then give Stephen a substantial amount of silver as a "first investor."

It was like Stephen to say, "I'm grateful, Father, and I will make certain you're repaid handsomely for your faith in me."

"I have no doubts, son."

Marta had an easy delivery, and Francis Pearce was a strong and healthy baby. Mary was with Marta as was Hannah Mary, who had been her midwife. Mary stayed with

Marta until she was on her feet and ready to care for the baby. She would have no difficulties, since, after all, she had been a second mother to her brothers and sisters from her eighth year on.

Molly, who lacked the focus and skills of Marta, was nonetheless competent with little Matty. Mary believed she would cope very well with a second child. Her parents offered to have Molly to come to Brenton House to deliver the baby. Their reasoning was that Hannah Mary was nearby, and there would be many offers for the care of Matty. The other consideration was the Christmas holidays, which Molly and Davol (which became his name for the sake of clarity) could enjoy if staying at Brenton House. Travel for Molly, so heavy with child, would not be wise.

The newest member of the Brayton and Anthony families was the infant, Francis Pearce. He was such fun for everyone. "See how his eyes go wide when he looks at the decorated tree!" said his Auntie Sarah.

"Yes, and with his drooling too," laughed Auntie Beth.

The Davols were still at Brenton House on New Year's Day, and Molly was terribly uncomfortable. Everyone had left, including Sarah and Beth, who were staying with other family members until after Molly had delivered her baby. All was in order, and almost on schedule Molly began her labor. Hannah Mary was sent for and came at midnight. Francis and Davol were in the kitchen and could hear the movements of Hannah Mary above them in the nursery. Molly was having difficulties, and there were indications that it would not be an easy delivery. Mary went below and asked Francis to fetch Doc Anthony. This alarmed Davol, of course, and he offered to go, since he could do so more easily. In less than an hour, the two Josephs had returned.

Mary came down, leaving the two experienced ones to attend to Molly. The three below drank too much tea and tried to remain calm, which was not going well with Davol. Francis and Mary, seated in their comfortable high-back chairs by a warm fire, were napping now and then. At six o'clock in the morning, the sounds of Molly struggling with the birthing increased, and then everyone heard the muffled sound of an infant. Davol went quickly up the stairway. Mary and Francis were alert to the expectation that soon they would be holding a new grandchild. Then Davol wailed, his cries resounding through the house.

It was not, after all, going to be all right.

Mary and Francis took to the stairs and entered a scene they would never forget. Hannah Mary was holding the infant. Davol was pacing the room, and Joseph, the attending physician, the almost-brother of Molly, was in a chair by the bed, bent over with his head in his hands, weeping. Mary hurried to the bed, saw that Molly was dead, and her knees gave way. Francis caught her, and they cried in each other's arms.

Davol continued to pace, saying, "No, no, not again, not again!"

Francis whispered to Mary, "I'll take Davol, you help Joseph." She nodded.

Francis led Davol down the stairs and into the kitchen, talking calmly and urging him to think of Matthew and how he would be needing him. Francis hoped to get the grieving husband to concentrate on something he could be doing.

Back upstairs, Hannah came over to Mary, who stood looking down at Molly.

"Aunt Mary," she said, "would you take the baby down below and tell Francis to stay with Davol? We'll take care of Molly, and then Joseph can go to bring the coroner."

Mary took the child, and Hannah Mary said, "She's a beautiful little girl."

Down below, Mary decided to wait before presenting the baby to Davol. Francis came over and peered at the infant. "We have a granddaughter, Francis," Mary said.

"She's a bitty thing, isn't she?"

"Yes, she is. She is bitty."

That would be her family name, even though Davol insisted on naming her Mary, for his darling Molly.

Hannah came down and took Bitty so she could nurse her. Hannah had been nursing her fourth child and said she would be able to nurse the baby if she could stay with her or be brought to her.

Mary thanked her. "That's very helpful, sweetheart. We'll manage it together somehow. It is providential that we live so close together."

"Yes, Aunt Mary. Life has a way."

"Or God," said Mary, and turned away.

The burial was terribly sad for everyone. But events moved quickly, and the outcome was life-changing for Mary and Francis. After several discussions and negotiations, it was agreed the baby, Mary Frances Davol, would be adopted by the Brayton grandparents. William Brightman, attorney, witnessed the agreement and signatures. Joseph

Davol and his son, Matthew, would move to Newport, where he had been working in recent months.

Mary said, "You know you can visit us any time, Joe, you and Matty. We welcome you to remain in the baby's life, to be sure."

"Thank you both," he said, "and I'll always remember your kindness to me when I arrived in Portsmouth." He fought back tears. It was time to start his life over again.

The date, March twenty-first, had arrived for Frankie and Lottie's wedding, which was her nineteenth birthday. Mary had stepped back and let Mary Soule Fish have her way with all arrangements. Lottie was balking at the idea of moving into Brenton House with the Braytons, therefore Mary and Francis decided to pursue the move to a new house as quickly as possible. The Fishes invited the newlyweds to move into their home until the Braytons had left Brenton House.

Francis found just the location they wanted and was able to negotiate a four-acre lot from Stephen Burton. The deed was handed to Francis on July 20, 1671. He and Mary had worked up the design of the house to be a small version of Brenton House. There would be space in the back for a nice garden and a cow shed. It seemed logical to have a steady supply of milk available for Bitty. In December, with a series of serious ice storms, it was obvious that the house would not be completed until March or April of 1672.

Mary was delighted with her granddaughter, and the cow had been installed behind Brenton House. The day the cow was delivered, Mary and Francis went to the shed to examine the newest member of the family.

Mary patted the cow and rubbed her smooth hide. "Isn't she lovely, Francis?" she asked.

"Very handsome indeed."

"Handsome! Females aren't handsome, and besides she's a cow."

"Well then, she could be cowsome." And "Cowsome" became the name given to the Braytons' first cow.

By April, the Braytons, including Cowsome, had completely settled into their new home, on Brayton Lane (so named by the members of the current Town Council, to honor Francis).

It was perfect. They had their chairs by the fireplace, newly upholstered, and a smaller table, replacing Talltree, which remained at Brenton House. There were smaller fireplaces and smaller rooms all around, but it was comfortable and quiet, except for Bitty, who giggled a lot more than she cried.

On September fourteenth of that year, Beth married Jared Bourne. The Bournes were "Newporters" and a lovely family. Jared had leased land from William Brenton, and his plan was to have a large area planted with fields of corn and wheat. The home would be near the fields. Beth had Mary's energy and spirit and there was reason for optimism in this ambitious endeavor.

Abraham Anthony married Alice Wodell on December twelfth—the largest gathering of all the weddings to date. Abraham was the image of his father and had his personality as well. His responsibilities in John's weaving business befitted his personality. Abraham made alliances with the mills, other proprietors in neighboring towns as far as

Newport to the south and Boston to the north. He was on the road frequently, making deals, and Alice very capably took care of matters at home. This was providential indeed, since she would give birth to thirteen children, among them three sets of twins.

Sarah Brayton married Ralph Gatchell on August 30, 1673. Ralph was the son of William and Eva Delle Gatchell and was in business with his father. It was good for Mary to have Sarah so close to their new home. In Portsmouth, everything was convenient. The only concern was having land for the members of these large and expanding families. Sarah and Ralph had a lovely spot for their home with views of Sanford Cove, stretching all the way around the Aquidneck neck.

There were grandbabies, including Bitty, of course, but no more weddings on the horizon for either the Braytons or Anthonys.

Susanna Anthony was not well. She had serious retention of water that was interfering with her breathing and general strength. It was heartbreaking to see the woman who comforted everyone in her life needing it for herself. John was distraught and was keeping closer to home—possible now that Abraham was traveling for him. Susanna and John had always enjoyed one another's company, accepting each other without judgment, and that was the best recipe for any marriage.

Mary sat by Susanna's side for long hours, giving Mary some time from the care of Bitty, who had plenty of aunties to take her into their homes. Mary and Susanna reminisced about their years together, often chuckling. One day Mary said, "Susanna, you promised me the recipe for your biscuits, how you make them fluff up, but you haven't delivered it. Will you tell me now?"

"It would do no good, you know that. You insist on your shortcuts, and we both know you only bake out of shame."

They laughed until Susanna began to wheeze from the water in her lungs. Sometimes John and Francis were with them and it turned into a shameful bragging contest—about how wonderfully well the children were doing and how good the community of Portsmouth had continued to be, and once John had even broached a subject that had not been mentioned.

"How has it happened that none of our children became life partners?"

"Well, John, that was because it would have been like marrying a brother or sister!" Mary answered.

"Yes, yes!" they all agreed. (In fact, it would be five generations before a Brayton man would marry an Anthony woman.)

Susanna died on September 27, 1674. She had been ready to leave the body that had stopped her normal life. John grieved profoundly, and while everyone was trying to distract him from the pain of his loss, only time would give him respite.

The Anthony sons stepped in to do all the duties John had been performing, and he might have become the gentleman he had been born into, except that he no longer had any part in the genteel life. Instead John Anthony went about Portsmouth like an inspector, checking on this and that, talking to proprietors, planters, councilmen, and children. He listened to them and passed on worthwhile information to the appropriate persons.

Francis was able to convince John that they should have a visit with William Brenton. He agreed, and Francis sent a message to Hammersmith Farm. The reply was shocking, informing the two that their friend William Brenton had died just the week before. The news spread and people shared their stories of his generosity to them. He was a great person, and at the November Assembly he was eulogized and honored. It was said, by someone who knew, that the number of pages in his will could suffice to cover all the streets in Newport. He was a very wealthy man who lived easily among those who were not.

On May 2, 1675, John collapsed, with Abraham at his side, as they were about to take the ferry to Boston. He clutched his chest and fell to the ground. Abraham was frightened.

"Father! What's wrong?"

He could not answer because the life of John Anthony was gone forever.

As Mary and Francis were dressing for the burial of their friend, Francis sat on the chair in their bedroom.

"Mary, I'm feeling all wrong. I'm resenting the people mourning John. I want to shout at them that they did not know him as I knew him. I'm thinking that they're crowding me out, that I alone should be mourning him."

Mary bent over his forlorn body. "You're angry, my love, but you're misdirecting it at the innocent ones who genuinely feel a loss. No one, except yourself, can know the depth of your pain, to have lost someone so dear to you. You must see their pain as well as endure your own."

Francis looked up at Mary and felt something deep inside shift—not comprehending it, just feeling it. He stood and continued preparing for the burial of his dearest friend.

The event of John's death was not unlike his life because it affected people as he had in their presence—somehow putting them in touch with the possibility of what living has in store for everyone, and how important it is to embrace life on its terms but doing so honestly.

John's body was laid to rest in a grave next to his Susanna, a place for people to pay homage.

William Anthony was deeded the Anthony home, and in February 1676 he married Nancy Wilcox, who helped him adapt the family home as their own. Nancy reminded Francis and Mary of meeting her parents on the *Courser* as they sailed together to a new land and a new way of living.

Of the twelve children, Stephen was the only unmarried child. He had been fortunate to have chosen to build his mill on the other side of Hope Bay—away from Metacomet's "seat." Metacomet was dubbed King Philip by the English because of his audacious demeanor. In 1675, he brought together four tribes of Indians into an alliance to permanently drive the English from their hunting grounds. The resulting battles were horrific, but after many deaths and atrocities all over new England, and after the assassination of Metacomet, Canonchet, the next sachem of the alliance, asked the English for a treaty to end the fighting.

Francis at age sixty-three was selected by the General Assembly of Rhode Island and Providence Plantations to accompany the other representatives of the five governments at the peace treaty signing to be held at Casco Bay, Maine. He had to be persuaded to accept, and then could not be dissuaded by Mary, who was fearful of his going so far from home. He did make the trip to Maine and had stories to tell when he returned. The one etched in the minds of all members of the family was his description of the few remaining Indians of Metacomet's alliance being forced into canoes, which would take them as slaves to the salt mines in Bermuda. Francis could never think of Captain Isaac Headly's idyllic retirement home without picturing the slaving Indians in the mines. There was no written record of the meeting, and it would be confused with a later meeting called by the New York government, hoping to find a solution for the Indians in the region. It had not been any more successful than the other treaties with the Indians. There would be no relinquishing of the right of sale and ownership of land among the English.

Stephen ended the string of weddings by his own marriage to Ann Tallman. He insisted on having the wedding at his "Brayton Homestead" in Swansea. The weather was beautiful on June 15, 1677, and it was held outdoors to accommodate the large crowd of people who attended the bride and groom's day of celebration.

The close of the decade was a series of burials of notable men who were instrumental in the founding of Rhode Island. John Clarke, Samuel Wilbur, and William Brenton died one after the other. Many mourners gathered for these stalwart men, some of whom would become heroic in the years to come. The one remaining founding father was Roger Williams, the one who led the way, out of the Puritan persecution and into the beginnings of democracy, which would not have survived without the "wall" separating church from state and the governing principle of religious freedom.

Chapter 12: Progenitor

If the needle doesn't pass, the thread doesn't follow. — an African proverb

43 ~ 1685

Mary woke knowing something was amiss. Her first thought was of Bitty, but she was in Swansea visiting Stephen and Ann. Mary's mind took a detour, thinking of her fourteen-year-old granddaughter. "She wants to be around younger people—who can fault her?"

Mary turned to look at Francis, surprised to find him looking at her. "You're awake—that's unlike you at this hour of the morning. Is something worrying you?"

"Nothing's worrying me. I am mulling, that is all."

"Well, mulling means it is important to you, so do share it with me."

Francis rolled onto his side and faced her. "In a few months I will be seventy-five, and I'm carrying on my work in Town Hall with men the ages of my sons. I have outlived all of those who founded Portsmouth, and I'm still healthy and have good strength. I wonder, should I be doing something more purposeful?"

"Francis, you know what I am going to say," she told him. "God already knows what will be. You're mulling because you don't believe that. Maybe God is nudging you. He's waiting for you to acknowledge His presence in your life. As you know, I do practically no mulling, worrying, or wondering. I do what needs to be done, knowing that God will guide and guard me. I'm not waiting for a bolt of lightning. You have usually done work without hesitating—what's different now?"

"I am not responsible for doing the work I've been commissioned to accomplish. I'm responsible for seeing that others get it done. That's very different."

"Francis, how are the younger men going to learn to do things properly if people like you are not helping them? That is the job of the commissioners and committee chairmen."

"As always, dear, you put a good light on things to get me thinking realistically."

"If you can't trust God to guide and guard you, then you need to trust yourself. As I see it, the two of us are like two oxen yoked together ready to plant a field. It's time for us to get yoked this morning."

Mary swung her legs around and got up and was ready to start the day.

"How spry you are, Mary."

"Up, up, up, my chickadee!"

Francis watched his wife until she had left the bedroom.

Later that morning, John Anthony made one of his frequent visits with Francis at Town Hall. John and Frankie had become special friends. John was now forty-five, and he and Abigail were grandparents. The weaving business was doing well, and John and Abraham worked together, each having a part of their father's good traits. Abraham enjoyed people, and he had sales contacts all over Rhode Island; John managed the production end. Abraham and Alice raised nine children, but still grieved for the two sets of twins they lost soon after they were born. However, the last set of twins were thriving.

John and Francis were talking one day of many things when John commented on the increasing interest among the people in the fiftieth-year celebration coming in 1688. It was already known as *the celebration*.

"I'm proud of our town," he said, "and that our democratic processes are still functioning. We even managed a few years ago to switch to a representative system without disrupting services."

"It's remarkable," Francis said in agreement. "I think we may have influenced England too, instead of the other way around. I can't prove that, but still, they have left us alone to rule ourselves, and that's quite something!"

"We have a new challenge now though," added John. "We're running out of space. Our third generation is getting squeezed."

"Some are leaving for the coast or across Narragansett Bay. I heard that the Council is looking at a section southeast of town. They're thinking of much smaller lots laid out like you see in some cities. Fewer people are planting these days, so it's a good thing the fishing business is increasing."

"It seems Portsmouth is continuing to be forward-thinking, which is good for all of us," John said. "Well, I must be moving on now. I always enjoy our conversations, Uncle Francis."

They looked fondly at one another as they said their goodbyes.

Mary always had some project she was attending, and the current one was getting a library established in the town. She talked about it wherever she was and always asked for books. It had progressed to the point that she was now asking for donations to purchase books. She wrote a proposal to the Town Council asking for their support for a library, one that would be free for everyone to use. Mary knew it would require something extraordinary to get the idea accepted. She wasn't surprised when she got a negative response from the Council. She decided to start her own library at home. She used the end of their dining room and had the Weylans make a long bookcase to fit under the window. She easily filled it with a variety of reading material. She got an accounting book to keep track of who had which books. The children in the neighborhood spread the word, and soon adults came to browse.

Francis did not try to dissuade her. In fact, he was very much in favor of the idea. Had he not longed for reading material as a child? Therefore, when more shelves were needed, they rearranged their house to make space for the books they were buying with the money people donated. Francis told his wife, "After all, it's been common practice here in Portsmouth to have rooms set aside for 'entertainment'—that is, to sell alcoholic beverages to the public, a substitute for taverns. Why not for a library?"

In November of 1686, Benjamin Sherman, President of the Town Council, came to Francis' desk at Town Hall, and after offering an assessment of the weather gave his reason for visiting.

"I have a special request to make on behalf of the Town Council, and therefore the town of Portsmouth, to offer you another appointment, another commission. As you know, the fiftieth commemoration of the founding of Portsmouth is coming up in two years. We of the Council would be very appreciative if you would accept the role of Commissioner of the Fifty-year Celebration of the Founding of Portsmouth. The dates are Saturday the tenth and Sunday the eleventh of July 1688. That would allow you twenty months' time to organize committees to plan the celebration."

Francis was quiet, feeling conflicted about what he was hearing. Benjamin seemed not to notice and went on. "The Council has given me the authority to set aside funds for the commission, but I cannot give you a specific amount since our currency is, once again, being challenged in London."

Francis didn't smile. He was anxious and instinctively felt he needed to give this serious consideration.

Benjamin did not want to fail in his mission and carried on impulsively. "Francis, you're the most knowledgeable person in our town about the period of our founding. You knew the people, and you're known for meticulous planning and execution of anything you undertake. We need you and would be so grateful if you could see your way to accepting this commission."

"If I could have a few days to think about it, I promise to give you my answer soon."

"Very well," Benjamin said. "I thank you, Francis."

Francis told Mary, who did not hesitate to say, "Of course you must accept. Who but you could take on such a task among our Portsmouth residents?"

"Oh, Mary, I had counted on using you as the reason I had to refuse."

Mary laughed and laughed. "Too late for that," she said. "No one would believe you had you tried."

The formal appointment letter came on November 30, 1686, and the most complicated undertaking of his adult life was launched.

It was difficult for him to represent the founders of Portsmouth. He often felt like a charlatan. But he knew that there was no one else who had experienced those early years of settling the community. His intent was to be fair and to stay as close to the truth of the early circumstances as possible. He began by gathering as much information as possible. Even with a mere fifty years, a drop in the bucket of man's history, he encountered discrepancies in dates and the details of events. Not even the two most revered personages, Roger Williams and John Clarke, had been consistent in their records, and neither of them had written of Portsmouth's founding. Both were in their graves now. All the historical literature was focused on the intent and purpose of the settlement.

As he thought about the celebration, he pondered what the hopes for the community had been in 1638 compared to the current operation of and daily living in the Portsmouth in the late 1680s. Had the purpose and intent been realized? He went to John Brightman, even though he was not about because of bad health. Nevertheless he always welcomed Francis whenever he came for clarification and suggestions for the July festivities. His son, William, was also helpful, keeping Francis informed with the perspective of the younger generation.

There were no records of the twenty-fifth celebration because it had been a festival celebrating the 1663 Royal Charter. It did occur to Francis that much of the literature surrounding that event fortified the idea that the original intention and purpose of Portsmouth was, indeed, still relevant. This understanding gave him new life in the planning, and enthusiasm for the incredible feat that had been wrought by the founders of establishing a government ruled by the people and empowering the ordinary man to greater achievement. He could see that he himself was one of these ordinary men.

Francis conferred with all the sons of the founders, relying especially on John and Joseph Anthony, two young men he loved because they were loyal reminders of his friendship with their father. Somehow Francis was able to design a commemoration, assign committees with leaders to carry out the various functions of preparation, and to fine-tune the execution of the grand affair.

As the months passed and July tenth was only a few weeks away, there was no one more relieved than Mary Brayton. She had been understanding of the considerable responsibility of Francis' mission and also his frequent anxieties. Mary was worried about his age. He was seventy-five and hardly rested during the day.

July tenth arrived, and everyone and everything was in place in the common area behind Town Hall and near Resident Inn. Saturday, there was ample food, decorations, competitions, and award ceremonies, with music and dancing in the evening. Sunday, after church services were over, there was more food, a few competitions, and a final solemn ceremony recognizing the glorious "experiment in democracie"—Portsmouth, Rhode Island. Peleg Sanford was guest speaker, and other speakers preceded his oration.

After these speeches concluded, Francis believed the program was finished, but not so.

John Anthony came to the stage. "It is my honor to present a tribute, on behalf of the people of Portsmouth, to Francis Brayton." Everyone applauded, and Francis blushed, looking at Mary and knowing that she knew what was coming. "Francis has been serving this community since September 1643, for forty-five years. He has become almost a permanent fixture at Town Hall. He has been selfless in his service and tenacious in his commitment to each and every one of his assignments. He has been judicious, understanding, and thoughtful. His efforts to bring this celebration to a cheerful conclusion has been accomplished. So, personally, I say, well done Uncle Francis!"

There were shouts and cheers all around, and Francis stood by Mary, weak in his knees. It was as if the people of Portsmouth had been with him when he first arrived and was chopping firewood for his neighbors.

Joseph also said something praiseworthy about Mary "Mary Brayton has been keeping herself occupied with helping others as well. She taught school in her kitchen all through our childhood, to many of you here today, and she organized a midwife program. The program trained women and then made sure midwives were available for expectant women all over Portsmouth. Mary is now working to establish a library. This is for you, Mary, from a grateful community."

Joseph started the clapping, which was equally robust.

On October 29, 1689, the wedding of Mary ("Bitty") Davol to James Tallman, a doctor, took place at the Swansea homestead of Stephen and Ann Brayton. Bitty was gleaming. She looked stunning, reminding Mary and Francis of their beautiful Molly. Her father, Joseph Davol, had come from Newport with Matthew, now a young man who was learning surveying from his father. Joseph had not remarried and was doing well in the Newport society.

James had fallen in love with Bitty when he met her at a visit to his Aunt Ann and Uncle Stephen, soon after he had graduated from medical school and just before he joined Joseph Anthony's practice. Francis and Mary enjoyed the reception. There had been many guests, and they did not have a chance to talk with many of them. Nevertheless, they had started home before it got too dark. Stephen had arranged a carriage to transport them to Brayton Lane.

Being alone would be a change for Mary and Francis, and somehow they felt it as they lay in bed in their usual spooning fashion.

"Francis, we're living alone for the first time since, well, since we moved into Brenton House."

"Yes, and that didn't last very long then. Now there are no children under our roof, but I'm sure we will soon have a string of grandchildren coming and going."

44 ~ 1690

It was October 17, 1690, and Francis and Mary were meeting with William Brightman to prepare his will. He had written out, with Mary's help, what he wanted each member to receive. There were certain decisions that he felt needed to have her opinion. It was not a pleasant task, and they had delayed until William convinced Francis that it would a serious problem for the family without a will to guide them.

So there they were, prepared to go through his list, and William would then write it up with the customary words. William asked, once it was stated that Mary would be the executrix, "Who would you like to designate as the overseers? There are usually three persons named."

"Well, William, I'd like three young men who have become my friends since their fathers died over a decade ago. John Anthony, George Brownell, and John Borden." William wrote the names on his worksheet.

Then they spoke of the real estate, and William said, "It should be stated in the will whether any land had been given in advance of Francis' death. Now, let's begin with Mary."

Francis looked at Mary and said, "I want Mary to remain in our house on Brayton Lane, on the land we bought from Stephen Burton, with everything that is in the house or on the grounds of the lot. Oh yes—I also want it stipulated that she could dispose of anything if she desires to do so."

"And who should inherit the property at the death of Mary?"

"Mary and I are thinking Frankie because Stephen is further away and has adequate property of his own, some of which I have given him."

"It's customary to indicate that the bequeathed will pay the legacy fees, and in this case it will be Frankie."

"Right," Francis acknowledged.

"We will confirm the land already given to Stephen?"

Francis nodded. "I'd like to give him five shillings," he said, "because he paid that to cover the costs for the transfer of the deeds to his name."

"Yes, all right. Now, about your daughters?"

Francis gave a list and William read it aloud to be sure:

Eldest daughter, Martha Pearce, five shillings
Daughter Elizabeth Bourne, two pounds
Daughter Sarah Gatchell, two pounds
Grandson Francis, son of Francis, two pounds
Grandson Preserved, son of Stephen, two pounds
Grandson Francis Pearce, two pounds
Granddaughter Mary, wife of James Tallman, two pounds

"Very well, Francis," he continued. "I will make a declaration such as, 'at the death of my wife, Mary, all movables to be divided to children and grandchildren.' Their names will be listed."

"William," Francis said with a note of regret, "I have excluded one grandson, Thomas, age nine, son of Francis, since he will inherit from his father the property I now own.

Also, we have been told that he is to be given a large piece of property from the Fish family." William nodded.

"Oh yes, we usually include the wearing apparel. Should I include that?"

"Yes, of course."

"So, we are set, Francis and Mary. Once I have prepared the document, we'll meet for a final review and signatures. We'll keep it on file in the office. On the date of your death, it will be probated and a copy given to Mary after the reading, which will include all members listed who are able to attend. If you have any questions, or want to modify the will, please notify me. It is my responsibility to notify the men you have requested as overseers."

Mary and Francis felt sad during the process, but both were surprised by the sense of relief they felt once they left William Brightman's office.

With just the two of them in their Brayton Lane home, life became a comforting and enjoyable routine, with few demands on their time throughout the rest of 1690, and through 1691 and most of 1692. They had no serious health problems, and Mary was the one who drew attention for her good health. Most women of seventy-two were creaking about or confined to bed with one ailment or another. Francis was still standing straight, except for a slight bend to his shoulders, but he tended the fireplaces and the garden, such as it was. He had been tempted to befriend a stray dog, but it seemed foolhardy on second thought.

Mary began planning a party for Francis' eightieth birthday and was trying to keep it as a surprise, but soon gave up on that idea. There would be mostly family attending, and it would be a reception with tea, the beverage now favored over coffee. Portsmouth had the Hawkins Bakery Shop, and Mary would order baked goods as well. Marta and Sarah would help set up and make punch and tea.

Francis was mumbling about the fuss, but Mary knew he would be pleased.

The day, September 5, 1692, was glorious. The air was warm, and it was early enough that the leaves hadn't begun to fall. People started coming at one o'clock, and as usual at Portsmouth parties, there was a lot of easy chattering. People knew one another and were delighted to meet the newest offspring and compare them to this or that relative. It was so nice seeing Stephen and his family, and Bitty, of course, with her James. Beth and Jared Bourne came from Newport as well. Frankie gave a short speech about his father and Lottie beamed with obvious pride in her husband.

Francis was hugged and kissed all afternoon, and even Mary got a few for herself. They had been energized by the crowd, the laughter, and the easy conversations, so that they did not realize how tired they were until people had said their goodbyes and the girls had put everything back in order. Marta wanted to stay the night, worrying how they would get upstairs to their bed.

"Now, Marta," Mary said, "we'll rest here by this good fire and we shall manage the steps as we do every night."

Francis had said before she left, "You're a good daughter, Marta." It gave Marta such a warm feeling inside to hear her father's praise. She thought, "I'll never forget how he said that to me."

Once alone, sated from all the food, liquid refreshment, and conversation, they sat in their comfortable tall-back chairs, and both napped as the sun was setting throwing its final rays in through their west-facing windows. They were warmed by the fire as they slept, but Mary woke feeling chilled and she got a lap robe and put it around Francis.

He looked up and smiled and said, "I was dreaming of Chester Holmes. I was sitting at his kneading table, and Tinker kept coming in and bothering us. That's strange because I never once saw Tinker go inside the bakery. Dreams are strange. Do you think of your home in Ellington, Mary?"

"Of course, I remember my mother and father often. Such good parents, good people, were they not?"

Francis said, "I'm not feeling right, Mary."

"Oh, you ate too many pastries," but she looked at him and went to him, putting her hand to his cheek as she did every single day.

He looked at her and smiled, then laid his head back against the chair, and he died.

Mary knew he was gone. "Oh, don't leave me, Francis. Oh no, take me with you!" She wept until she had no more tears, and then she stood looking down on her beloved husband. He looked peaceful, like he was sleeping. His lean body slumped only slightly in the chair, and his legs relaxed to the side.

Mary did not want to do anything, as if she could delay his leaving her, even though she knew he was already gone. She sat in her chair and she prayed, "Dear God, welcome the soul of my dear Francis. He is deserving of your forgiveness, and I ask you, on his behalf, to take him into your Kingdom. Please God, hear my fervent prayer." She did not say amen—that was too final.

Somehow, she got to the Clarks', next to their house, and they informed Joseph Anthony. When Joe arrived with his brother, John, they all cried together for Francis Brayton. They had contacted the coroner, Baulston Coggeshall, who came with two men who helped take Francis from the house, as Mary requested. She could not bear to have his lifeless body to remind her how achingly she wished he had not left her.

The burial had been stately and appropriate. The Braytons and Anthonys gathered together for several days, and all attended Mary lovingly. Mary could not get a grasp on her new identity—"Who am I without Francis?" She thought back, remembering the emptiness she had felt in 1640 when she had agreed to stay away from him, to not come to her father's bookshop. That had been difficult, but this grief was deeper, wider, and more penetrating by far. She survived then, and she would now. Mary was expected to be strong because she always had been; she had held up those who were crumbling. She could do that for herself, she would be strong.

And she did regain her strength and composure. She was visited every day by one or another of her family, and finally, by the end of September, she announced that she needed more time to herself. They were happy to see their mother her usual self again.

On October 7, 1692, Mary learned that Stephen had fallen while climbing to investigate a malfunction at one of the mills. This was something someone else should have done, but Stephen had never waited to do what needed doing. When he slipped from a height of twenty feet, landing on a sharp object that penetrated his chest, he died instantly.

The first thought Mary had when she learned of this tragedy was, "I'm relieved Francis did not have to endure this terrible loss." Stephen was only forty-two years old and in very good health. There were six children for Ann to care for, ranging in age from four to thirteen years.

Stephen had many assets, and people admired and respected him in the area of Swansea. Ann was near her Tallman family, including her nephew James and wife Mary, (Bitty) Brayton. Mary was able to attend the burial service, since Francis and Lottie offered to take her in their carriage. It was a difficult day. Mary could not reconcile or associate her energetic, full-of-life son, Stephen, with death. He was so like Francis. Now they were both gone from her. Back at Brayton Lane, she had lost her energetic spirit, and she sat most of the time in her chair.

She watched the sunrise and the sunset every day until December 3, 1692, when she entered the Kingdom of God for her own eternal rest.

It would be said that while life brings us painful endings beyond our understanding, surely it also brings wonderful new beginnings!

AFTERWORD

1.

What matters is the countless deeds of unknown people who lay the basis for significant events that enter history. They are the ones who did things in the past and they are the ones who will have to do them again in the future. — Howard Zinn (1922-2010)

Somewhere Else, Something Different is *biographical fiction* and the Wikipedia definition of this genre describes my work: "It is a type of historical fiction that takes a historical individual and recreates elements of his or her life, while telling a fictional narrative, usually as a novel."

I admit it wasn't wise to choose this topic and genre for a first novel. I had some expert help, and I have learned some essential writing techniques, such as, It is wiser to make an outline of your story before you begin writing. Yogi Berra's wisdom hits home here: "If you don't know where you're going, you might end up somewhere else."

Francis Brayton had two lives, the first, from 1612 to 1643, which has no records available, personal or public. The date given for his birth of 1612 was derived from a January 30, 1674, deposition in which Francis swears that he is called sixty-two years of age. There is no clue for the reason this deposition was needed, and it does not give definitive evidence of his date of birth. Despite ample public records of Francis' forty-nine years in Portsmouth, the thirty-one years prior to these are a mystery. We have no record of his country of origin, his birthplace, parentage, education, religious preference, marriage, or emigration. There is however evidence that he reached the highest levels of government service in Portsmouth, Rhode Island, and he had several real estate transactions as well.

I chose to invent his first thirty-one years by looking for plausible evidence in existing records, especially his probated will of September 5, 1692, which provides clues of his family and friendships. I surmised that Francis was not of the proprietary class or a titled family, since there would have been records. I found nothing and created his heritage as of the peasant class. There had to be an explanation for his ability to do the tasks he performed in Portsmouth, especially the ones requiring a high level of discernment, such as settling disputes, constable, tax collector, and Deputy in the House of Deputies in the General Assembly of the Colony of Rhode Island and Providence Plantations (its official title). His employment at the magistracy and studies with Stephen Smith provided Francis with experiences and skill development that would bode well in Portsmouth's unique government.

Mary (Smith) Brayton, like all women of the seventeenth century, had no legal rights or public records except if connected with a man's record. The Smith family is fictional, as is the Holmes family, as well as all of the characters in the first chapter, "French Emigrant." Thomas, Martha and all the Brayton children except Francis are fictional characters. However, John Anthony's family and the Potter family existed, as did William Brenton and his family.

I touch on historical events of the seventeenth century but only as background information. My focus is not on the manners, speech, or vicissitudes of life of that period; rather my story is about ordinary people who are diligent, show good will toward neighbors, and promote civility through law and order. Portsmouth plays an important part because it was the most successful experiment in democracy in early America. Diligence and opportunity go hand in hand in the harsh climate of New England.

Location helped the Portsmouth community, since being isolated on an island gave the residents protection from marauders and from Indian tribes avenging their misguided faith in the white settlers. Portsmouth became a tight-knit community that adhered to Roger Williams' tenet of separation of church and state, and during town meetings they conducted business and resolved issues by majority rule. In Portsmouth, each man had to be accepted and given a resident status commensurate with certain requirements, for example *inhabitant.* Nelson Wilbur gave a succinct summary of the Portsmouth Compact: "Laws pertaining to the allotment of land, the assessment of taxes, the conduct of community affairs, the protection of life and property, the punishment of criminals and other matters pertaining to orderly government were adopted, and provisions made for their enforcement."

I used the letters that John Anthony wrote to Francis during the nine years prior to his "coming to America" to give the history of Portsmouth, including the names of the good leaders involved in its founding. Also included was the family of Anne Hutchinson, who decided to move to New Amsterdam, to a place now known as the Bronx.

2.

First comes thought, then organization of that thought into ideas and plans; the transformation of these plans into reality. The beginning, as you will observe, is in your imagination. — Napoleon Hill (1883-1970)

I began writing about Elijah Brayton (1787-1866), and after a year with starts and rewrites, I decided to begin at the beginning and write the Francis Brayton story. What emerged from hours of research was how often the American people have had to reinvent their idea of the American Dream. There seems to be a strong thread that holds together the mysterious components that keep people in charge of their own destiny. I wonder if the breakdown periods are brought on whenever the people relinquish their own responsibility in supporting that destiny.

Opportunity is an interesting concept. What one person may decide is an opportunity another will declare is a *right.* I have pondered over the concept and decided opportunity isn't sitting on a shelf waiting to be plucked by someone eager to get on with his/her life. Civil opportunities happen when they are freely made available to everyone, and everyone may individually choose to contribute to sustaining the general welfare.

My ponderings will continue as I return to the 1800s and Elijah Brayton's story. He had a very interesting life, and I connect to it in a strange way. Elijah's daughter, Lucy, married William Davis, who was a migrant from Virginia who came, like Elijah, to buy public land in Ohio. He and Lucy built a homeplace in Wyandot County before it was a county and while the Wyandot Indian Tribe was still residing in Ohio (their reservation became Wyandot County once they were removed to Kansas in 1844).

That homeplace still stands, no longer owned by the Davis family, but I spent several nights there in my childhood. My childhood friend, Rose Marie Davis Cole, is a descendant of Lucy and William Davis, just as I am. Lucy Brayton Davis' two oldest children were Anna and Alfred. Anna was my great-great grandmother, and Alfred was Rose Marie's great grandfather. There was a generation gap because Anna Davis Hurd's son, Forrest (my great grandfather), was born fifty years before Alfred's son Brayton Davis (Rose Marie's grandfather). You see? We all connect if we pay attention to the details!

For anyone who might be interested in how history can make its way to your doorstep, I am including a brief ancestral run-through.

3.

When it all boils down, it's about embracing each other's stories, and maybe even finding the synergy to collaborate the common good. — Dhani Jones (1978-)

After Francis Brayton the Progenitor:

• *Francis II* lived very much as his father in Portsmouth, R.I.

• *Thomas* was born in Portsmouth, migrated across the Narragansett Bay to East Greenwich R.I., added to his inheritance and died at age forty-two, a wealthy man.

• *Gideon* sold his inherited farm, bought a vast estate in Vermont, and moved there with two sons until after the War of Independence. He had remained a Loyalist and sold his land before the court could confiscate it. He returned to Rhode Island, where he died in 1792.

• *Matthew* broke with his father Gideon and joined the New York State Troops in 1775 and served through the War of Independence. He likely received a land grant for his service. He remained in the Hudson Valley region and fathered nine children.

• *Elijah* left Vermont in 1814 with wife Anna and a son William to migrate to Ohio for cheap public land. Public land was sold to supply money to operate the government in Ohio. Elijah built a grist mill on his new land adjacent to the Wyandot Indian Reservation—land that was awarded to the tribe for fighting in the War of 1812. Elijah and Anna lost a seven-year-old son, thought to have been abducted by the Indians. (Not the Wyandots.)

• *Lucy Brayton*, daughter of Elijah and Anna, married William Davis, who came from Virginia with his family to buy Ohio public land. He and Lucy established their homeplace. Lucy's mother died in 1842 at age fifty-one. Elijah, homesick for family in Vermont and New York, walked there and back to visit them. Lucy and William had five children—one girl died at age 5. Lucy of a Vermont family and William from Virginia had children who served on the Union side in the Civil War.

• *Anna Davis* married William Hurd who migrated from New York and joined the Davis homestead. He left for Civil War in 1864, was captured, and died in a confederate prison in Danville, VA. Anna procured all letters exchanged between them, and I have copies of these letters—the originals are in the archives of the Carey Ohio Library.

• *Forrest Hurd,* son of Anna Davis Hurd, my adored great grandfather, was over 6'2" and had light blue eyes. He lived to be ninety-five and died in 1956, the year I married Dick Jewett.

• *Helen Hortense Hurd* was the only child of Forrest a. Laura and married Murray Pipes. His grandparent. migrated from Wales with the entire congregation of their Baptist church. They settled in Chesterville, Ohio. Many Lloyd, Jenkins, Pipes, and Douglas family members are buried in a church cemetery at the edge of the village.

• *Anna Margaret Pipes Dible* is my mother, who married Joseph Dible just six weeks before the banks failed on October 29, 1929. From December 1930 to January 1936, they had five children and managed to survive the Great Depression.

• *Ann Margaret Dible Jewett* married Lieutenant Richard Jewett on December 30, 1956, and they have lived in nine states and in Germany for six years. After Dick's retirement in 1984, they continued to move until locating in the state of Delaware, where they now live. They continue to enjoy their family and feel privileged to have lived a life of freedom and comfort.

ABOUT THE AUTHOR

Ann Jewett, having moved twenty-six times, has experienced many different cultures. She comes from a family who treasures their heritage and who safeguarded letters, deeds, and other documents that were recently donated to the Carey, Ohio, Public Library. Before retiring, she taught school and was Manager of Employee Relations at the George Washington University. Currently she is writing about Elijah Brayton, a nineteenth century pioneer in Ohio. She resides in Middletown, Delaware, with her husband Dick and daughter, Anna.

Cover and interior design by Kevin Brennan.

Special title fonts are used via Creative Commons licenses, and images on front and back covers are in the public domain. The back-cover painting, "Landscape with Rainbow," by Robert S. Duncanson (1859), Smithsonian American Art Museum, Gift of Leonard and Paula Granoff.

Made in the USA
Lexington, KY
20 February 2019